Science
Fiction
Salmo. J

THE DISFAVORED HERO
Book One of the Tomoe Gozen Saga

Jessica Amanda Salmonson

Illustrated by
Wendy Adrian Wees

Pacific Warriors, Inc.
P.O. Box 1410
Boulder Creek, CA 95006
www.pacificwarriors.com

ISBN: 1-890065-05-6 (limited edition)
ISBN: 1-890065-06-4 (paper back)

First Pacific Warriors printing: January 1999

Printed in the United States of America

LIST OF ILLUSTRATIONS
by Wendy Adrian Wees

in memoriam,
to Lumchuan "Lek" Salmonson
my Buddhist mother

I am coming to you, Lek,
on the river of many colors

PROLOGUE:
The Magic Nation

On that island empire, as it is perceived in our own universe and which the West calls Japan and the East calls Nippon, millennia passed during which the pious honored a multitude of gods, despite that no one had ever seen a godling walk the Earth. Those same people believed in magnificent monsters; yet never had there been so much as a tibia of proof for this outlandish bestiary. These folk were also convinced of magic, although every miracle resolved into a trick or natural thing. And if a curse were delivered to a foe, it would be so devoutly believed that the cursed individual might curl up and die of painful imaginings; or the cursed one's family might make ready a grave in advance and grievously encourage the curse to work true, though all the while the fact was that no objective interference had occurred.

There would come a time, in Japan, when these discrepancies were noticed, and people would ask, "If there are gods and demons and gigantic beasts, where do they hide?" For the physics of the known universe left no hole in which might be encompassed the unknown. Godless people scoffed the vilest and most damning of curses, and were not surprised to pass unhindered, for words could never injure.

In those days, the edge of the sword had become the muzzle of a gun. Life which had once been bright like steel, and fearful, was no less fearful, but had become dull and small and leaden. Death, then, had no meaning; and if war was not more cruel, it was at least less holy.

In Japan, as in all the world of that terrible latter age, it would come to pass that wonder died.

But in a dimension next to ours, there is a world very much like Earth. On this world is an island empire called Naipon, which bears striking resemblance to old Japan; for Japan is a magic nation, existing in all human ages upon every Earth beneath Amaterasu the Shining Goddess. In that other world's Japan called Naipon, gods scored the cities with their rakes when they were angered, and if they were pleased, pissed *saké* in the wells and rivers and excreted gold in the farmers' furrows. On Naipon, beasts slew mighty samurai with claws and horns, or else their grim heads decorated the pikes of samurai who were mightier. Occult happenings were the meat of everyday life, and fell sorceries sprang from the fingertips of wicked villains. And most assuredly, you can well believe, a curse was never lightly spoken; for the fulfillment was not *merely* certain, but also rich with irony so that the curser, as well as the cursed, could meet unseemly ends.

On Naipon, it would never be, that wonder died.

Thus it is found out that things once believed by the people of Japan by rote of faith alone, they of Naipon witnessed absolutely. Even Amaterasu the Shining Goddess was unsure how this came to be— whether in Naipon the hopes and fears of Japan coalesced into a different and stranger reality, or if in Japan the glory and terror of Naipon echoed through the dreams of the Japanese.

PART I
The Way of the Warrior

In Naipon, as in the Japan of our own Earth, there lived a woman named Tomoe. She followed the bushido, or Way of the Warrior, and only once in her life did she stray from these tenets. This is the story of how sorcery caused Tomoe Gozen to break faith with her bushido, and what she did to regain honor.

Ushii pushed his kneeling friend off balance, causing Madoka to drop the shoulder armor he was attaching to himself. "You're not nice!" complained Madoka, then moved his foot quickly to unsettle Ushii in turn. Tomoe Gozen shook her head and passed a momentary smile to the room's fourth occupant, a severe and powerful man named Goro Maki. Goro's eyes glinted, even though he did not return the smile. "They are like little boys," said Tomoe. She suppressed laughter when Ushii slapped Madoka alongside the face in playful test of reflexes.

Goro Maki answered Tomoe in his resonant, intense voice: "They have been together since military school, since they were six or seven. I envy them their love."

They were childlike only when together, away from the eyes of servants or lords. Other times, Ushii Yakushiji and Madoka Kawayama were nearly as serious as Goro Maki.

These four samurai—three men and one woman—went through the grooming rituals and ritual of applying their own armor piece by piece. Goro and Tomoe, by not being rowdy, completed these processes first. They sat on their knees, with hands at rest on the upper part of their legs, watching Ushii and Madoka behave whimsically. The hilt of a shortsword protruded from the center of Goro's *obi* belt, and his longsword lay at his side on the floor. Two similarly paired long and shortswords waited on their horizontal racks near a wall. Tomoe's two swords were of an uncommon design, both of equal length, and sheathed one at each hip rather than through her obi. Goro's head turned until his gaze settled on these swords. Tomoe noticed his lack of appreciation.

"You still think these will cause me trouble, my friend?"

Goro looked mountainous on his knees. He visibly shrank in upon himself over Tomoe's minor challenge. Then he replied in a harsh, measured tone, "You have killed warriors as strong as me for doubting the metal of swords forged on foreign ground. It is not for Goro Maki to say Tomoe Gozen has changed since returning from the Celestial Kingdoms of Ho."

"You are too formal," said Tomoe, her mood still pleasant. "Please be more blunt. If you doubt I should wear foreign blades when we take new oaths of vassalage to our warlord, do not hesitate to criticize."

"Your swords are very good," said Goro, but his growling intonation suggested otherwise. "Do not tease me as Ushii does Madoka; I am too proud—too proud to die by a sword not made in Naipon."

Tomoe was stung. No one had ever dared to say they would be ashamed to die by her swords, although as Goro stated, she had killed those who thought her style and weapons inferior. She did not press the matter further with Goro. He was a stickler about warrior codes; he would never fully approve of her alien steel, even if it were true that the swordsmith in Ho had been Naiponese born.

They were butterfly-longswords, wrought by a smith outcast from Naipon. Tomoe had traveled to Ho two years previous and assassinated the Naiponese traitor who served foreign strengths, who made for others swords with edge and temper intended by the gods for samurai alone. It had been a special mission performed under guidance of a messenger of the Mikado. She had been directed to find and destroy every bastard sword of Naipon craft and foreign design. She warred against the nefarious mainlanders with effective haste and completed her mission; but they had left their mark upon her by route of their variant and seductive philosophy. For the samurai's sword is the samurai's soul; and the second sword was always a short one which could never violate the longsword as true soul. The shortsword was considered "guardian of the soul." Contrary to this norm, Tomoe's blades were mirror images of one another, defying any to guess which bore her soul.

People of Ho had taught her of the dual nature of the human soul and of the universe at large; and it did not seem to Tomoe that the concept would be an affront to Amaterasu the Shining Goddess. Indeed, on careful reflection, it seemed to Tomoe that she had always had two souls, and that if she accepted them both they would no longer be in conflict. When wrecking the swords of the traitorous smith she had saved aside two, and had not yet regretted it. The alien swords accommodated her new feelings, while in no way hindering her faith with the bushido.

These swords quickly became her trademark. On returning to her own land, they had made her seem, even to other samurai, as awesome as she was skilled. Yet, she would never convince Goro Maki that her swords were proper. As she valued his friendship, she let the issue pass.

Ushii was still in his playful mood. He grinned sidelong at Tomoe, saying, "A good day, hey, Tomoe? We are Lord Shigeno's finest samurai! Our retainership might have expired tonight, but we have been asked to pledge ourselves afresh. With the sorcerer Huan exiled from his own country and living in this valley, there is need for strong defense. We are a good four! Together, none of us will ever die, even in the face of foreign magic. Apart, *hai!*, we would not be half so strong."

"Speak of your own strength," said Madoka Kawayama, interrupting his talkative friend. "Tomoe and Goro are stronger than you or me!"

"*Hai!*, but we have saved their lives as often as they have saved ours! Is it not true, Tomoe?"

"It's true, Ushii. Together, the four of us are invincible. We have proven it many times."

"Then—," Ushii had tied his last piece of armor in place and scooted on his knees toward Tomoe Gozen and Goro Maki. He looked less mischievous than a moment before. He said very seriously, "Then, let us swear fealty to one another. When we come before Shojiro Shigeno tonight, let us do so as a single samurai, not four!"

Tomoe looked pensive. This was not a matter for hasty decision. "It has been done before," she said.

By then, Madoka Kawayama had also finished attaching his armor and scooted near. He said, "Ushii and I swore ourselves to be brothers when we were children. Never since that time have either of us made similar vows to others. But the four of us are unique! I agree with Ushii. We should swear lifelong fealty to Lord Shigeno and always be together."

Goro Maki's face was long. His arms remained folded across his chest.

"You are silent, Goro," said Tomoe. "Would you disagree with our friends' proposition?"

For a long time he did not speak, which trait they had all grown accustomed to. Ushii was more anxious than usual, however, and lent encouragement, "Lord Shigeno would be glad to give permission, and bind us officially by his insignia. Even were the sorcerer Huan no threat to the clan, still would Shojiro Shigeno be glad to keep us. He is a great warlord, and we are great samurai."

Goro Maki placed both hands on the floor before himself and bowed until his forehead touched the *tatami* mat upon which he knelt. When he rose, he said in his deepest, most serious tone, "As you know, I am last of my family. If I die without heirs, there will be none to hold the tablets of my ancestors. Because I am an orphan, I have valued all of you as my only family, though you may think I seldom show it. Also, being last of my line, I appreciate the invulnerability we provide each other, so that I may live long enough to sire many brats, if some girl will ever have me."

Ushii began to bow before Goro many times, as might an excited peasant. Madoka took up this adamant occupation as well. Madoka said, "Never an orphan, Goro! You have us! We will honor your family's tablets as being our family too!"

"The word of the samurai!" promised Ushii.

Tomoe Gozen was moved by all this, although she felt a little bit apart from it. As her swords were different from theirs, so was her way of thinking. She recognized something excessively sentimental in the nature of her friends' exchanges; yet she knew these men to be entirely sincere, and she loved them.

Goro Maki, never one to register much emotion, was for once profoundly affected. He could not speak easily. His eyes glistening with moisture, he managed to say,

"Thank you! Thank you very much! I will happily swear myself to Lord Shojiro Shigeno, not for a standard term of retainership, but for as long as I live, and in the same breath bind my life to yours!"

The three men flung themselves into each others' embraces and wailed a happy lament. Ushii opened the circle of arms to invite Tomoe Gozen:

"Will you, too, Tomoe? Will you be our only sister?"

Their mutual love drew her like a magnet. Tomoe started to scoot toward her friends, but a paper door slid aside and a servant interrupted. It was a maid. She came into the room on her knees, carrying a folded letter. Shyly, she set it on the floor and pushed it toward Tomoe Gozen. "From my mistress, the warlord's daughter," the girl said quietly, then slipped backward from the room, gone as fast as she had come.

When Tomoe took up the folded letter, Ushii, mischievous again, dared to say, "She likes you, Tomoe! Lady Toshima likes you very much!" But Tomoe Gozen looked disturbed and Ushii shut his mouth.

Madoka Kawayama leaned forward to say to Tomoe, "You live your life unexpectedly for a woman. A girl's crush is a natural thing. You should always expect it."

Tomoe Gozen bowed as quickly and curtly as she could and, touching the letter to her forehead, she stood to go in haste. Ushii and Madoka were grinning more boyishly than ever, but Goro Maki spoiled the mood. He had regained his greatest severity of expression as he said in a low, guttural voice, "She did not say she would be our sister. She did not say so."

His two friends were instantly drained of gaiety, knowing Goro Maki so well that they could see beyond his scowlings to the sorrow underneath.

Tomoe's white stallion Raski had been groomed and armored as fully as the samurai. Because of the horse's fighting spirit, he too would be sworn a vassal. Tomoe walked to a small, narrow exercise yard. It was yet more than an hour before darkness or the oaths made to the warlord. Tomoe hoped to take Raski once more through his movements before that time. Or, perhaps, she only wanted an excuse for leave-taking prepared in advance, should the meeting with Toshima be uncomfortable.

An array of weapons hung from the steed's saddle and three sharp horns had been fitted to his forehead. For all that, he seemed gentle. Tomoe patted his muzzle and whispered kindnesses to him. To hear him snuffle and see him dote on the woman who had raised him from a colt, it was difficult to comprehend how he had acquired the nickname "man-eater." In battle, he was a different animal, ferocious as a tiger from the Celestial Kingdoms.

Raski bolted away from Tomoe for a moment, circled a corner of the exercise yard, then came back with his eyes peeled back in a strange way. "Are you nervous, brave boy?" asked Tomoe, finding her stout animal's behavior out of the ordinary. "Are you, too, anxious to see our Lord?"

The animal stiffened. Thunder rolled over the valley, down from the clear sky.

"This is unlike you!" Tomoe exclaimed. "Thunder is your element!"

The ominous rumbling died away. Raski lowered his head, as though ashamed of his inexplicable fright. Because she knew her alert beast too well to believe he had quaked without reason, Tomoe was unsettled, but could detect nothing untoward about the yard.

"There is something to which I must tend," said Tomoe. "I'll return for you soon." She left the stallion and strode along a path's flat stones toward the warlord's garden. She put Raski's momentary discomfort from her mind. Entering the tea gardens, she absorbed the illusion of peace and breathed the flowery fragrances.

An ornate, highly arched footbridge crossed a pebble-bedded brook. Tomoe lingered on this bridge to peer across the valley. In the distance a misty waterfall could be seen, its crashing roar barely audible. Beyond the cultivated fields and over the hills, a storm was gathering swiftly. But on the warlord's tea gardens, Amaterasu continued to smile.

The woman warrior stood in harsh contrast to the genteel grounds. Each segment of her armor was made from strips of bamboo laced together with twine and hardened with many layers of dark brown lacquer. The segments were joined with red cord and held closed around her torso by a cloth belt. A metal *kabuto* or war helmet fanned down behind her head and bore a sickle moon on the top. Her hair was straight and cut at shoulder length. Her curved butterfly-longswords swung back from each hip.

As she looked over the valley, it took a moment for Tomoe to realize what was disturbing about the otherwise familiar and appealing landscape: no one tilled or planted in the fields. The absence of *heimin* was disconcerting; but Tomoe was of another class, ignorant of their ways. Perhaps there was a peasant holiday of which she was unaware.

The warlord's mansion stretched like a lazy animal among the gardens—not a tall structure, but spread out, with many terraces and windows and carved frames. The columns bracing the porches were made of lengths of thick bamboo tortured into unusual shapes.

Against a rice-paper window Tomoe saw the regal silhouette of Toshima, daughter of Lord Shojiro Shigeno, moving about her rooms with ethereal grace. An unobtrusive handmaiden slid a door open, and there stood splendid Toshima, gazing into the early evening's sun. Her layers of flowing kimonos were colorful, rich, and tasteful, made of silk brocade. Her hands were perfectly tiny. The beauty's languid eyes scanned the cool, moist gardens as she took each short step along a mossy path. Her gaze came to rest on Tomoe standing on the bridge, and Lady Toshima smiled narrowly, reminding Tomoe of peach blossoms about to open in sunlight. She beckoned Tomoe with her fan, and watched with sideways glance as the warrior approached.

"You are dressed for war, samurai?"

"No, Lady. Today my comrades and I renew oaths of loyalty to your father. Otherwise, our services would expire on tonight's moon. I am clad for the ritual."

"Then it is true you are staying?"

"How could I not, Lady Toshima? A Lord exiled from his own nation has been treatied to reside on Naiponese land, and bears strange magic from the Celestial Kingdoms. The Mikado is all-wise, I know, but this treaty does threaten native prosperity, and your father needs vigilant hands."

"Richer warlords than Shigeno have as great a need."

"Your father is the most worthy master," said Tomoe, a little puzzled.

"But you are a famous samurai. Many look for you to seek greater conquests. You have esteemed yourself in past exploits and even the Mikado knows of your name. By right, you should be a warlord yourself."

"A samurai's destiny is to serve," said Tomoe.

"You could serve all of Naipon if you achieved high position within the shogunate."

"It has never happened, Lady, that a woman was made Lord."

"You are wrong, Tomoe Gozen. Women have served under the shogunate and in the powerful office of *shikken*. Not so long ago the widow Masa Hojo made herself virtual Shogun. Six times in our history, even the Mikado was a woman."

"Ah, you are clever," said Tomoe. Toshima's eyes slanted demurely, seeming innocent. Courtly women were the best educated and most literate personages of the land. Toshima herself was a novelist of much renown. Sometimes, also, she indulged in intrigue. Tomoe asked, "Do you try to convince me not to serve your father? Or is my loyalty so in question that you are brought forth to test me?"

"Tomoe Gozen! You injure me with accusation!" She gave a wounded look. "And I had thought to include you in one of my fictions."

"I humbly petition Lady Toshima's forgiveness." Tomoe bowed subserviently, wondering if the dexterous Lady were not already testing some scene.

"Given," she said, without hesitation, and her mood instantly bettered. She peered suggestively from behind her opened fan, a shoulder turned to Tomoe, and added: "I will tell you why I urge you to greater success. You are samurai, and I am kin to the Mikado himself, through my mother's blood. Our classes may not mingle openly…unless…unless Tomoe Gozen achieves high office. Then her station would be equal to mine, and if she deigned, could see me often."

"Lady, please." Tomoe was disconcerted. "I am in love with war." She considered the excuse already prepared with Raski, but something kept her near Toshima.

Toshima looked down, the epitome of elegant ladyhood, at once modest and supreme. Her expression revealed nothing of displeasure at mild rebuff, but her cool words held a little of sorrow: "You have two souls, samurai. It makes you unique. Surely one of your souls has room to care for me."

"Both of them serve you always, Lady!" said Tomoe, anxious to soothe wounded pride. "Whoever else I serve in my life—your father or another—remember that Tomoe Gozen has promised to serve you also."

Toshima bowed graciously, as if Gozen were the greater lady; and it occurred to Tomoe that this very oath might be the only thing Lady Toshima had truly sought! If so, Tomoe did not regret the trap.

A bell rang from inside the mansion. Toshima said, "You must not be late to my father's court; but we have time to make an offering to the *kami* of this valley."

Toshima took a flat object from between the folds of her obi. It was a small raft made from dry, yellow reeds. "Come with me to the stream, samurai."

Tomoe followed Toshima to the bank of the winding brook. They knelt together before the water. Toshima set the raft near the brook's edge, then took flat pieces of colored paper from her sleeve's pocket.

"What will you make the kami?" Toshima asked, handing the samurai a square sheet of paper.

"What will you?" asked Tomoe, accepting the sheet and beginning immediately to fold it.

Toshima did not reply. Her quick fingers folded a red paper into an *origami* fox. When it was complete, she said, "I will give this valley my cleverness." She stood the fox on the raft. Tomoe had folded a blue crane and stuck its one leg in between the reeds of the little raft so that the bird would stand. She said,

"I will give the kami my courage."

"You are generous," the Lady stated, bowing to Tomoe. Then she placed a square, multi-colored sail on the miniscule raft. A breeze carried it down the stream. The two women bowed to the water as their offerings went away. The fox and crane stood face to face, and vanished where the water turned.

The sun was unexpectedly blocked on the horizon. Tomoe lifted her head to view the sudden clouds. The breeze became a gale.

A black raindrop fell on Toshima's pale hand. A similar foul drop struck Tomoe's armor.

"What happens?" asked Toshima, trying not to betray fear. There ought to have been another hour of light, but blackening storm clouds were coming off the hillsides with unnatural speed. Tomoe heard Raski's whinnying outside the gardens. He sounded anxious as he always was before a battle.

"Tomoe!" cried a man's voice. She and Toshima stood from the stream's bank. "Tomoe!" It was Ushii Yakushiji. He ran to the top of the arched bridge and cried out, "Listen, Tomoe! Listen!"

Until directed, she had not noticed the vague sound of the distant waterfall growing louder. Now that she listened carefully, she realized it was not falling water she heard, but raised voices.

"An uprising, Tomoe! Peasants riot on the north lands!"

This seemed impossible. Lord Shigeno was not like many overlords. He defended the heimin and did not take so much of their crops that they went hungry. But she could not doubt Ushii's veracity. Without hesitation, Tomoe begged leave of Toshima and ran to the top of the bridge to join the other samurai. She turned around once only, and saw Toshima vanish into the interior of the mansion.

The day had grown prematurely dark.

Storm clouds churned in the sky. Thunder rolled over the battlefield, commingling with the clang of metal, clatter of pole, and cries of the fallen and the mad. At intervals, strobes of lightning cast a platinum glow across the scene of carnage; then all was dark once more.

The peasants had swarmed into the valley estate of the warlord Shojiro Shigeno, their overlord. It was senseless.

They had been met by Shigeno's foot soldiers, who were skillful, but for the moment overwhelmed by the multitude. This was no simple peasant uprising, Tomoe was certain, for Shigeno was a good protector. The eyes of the farmers were black like those of dogs. When a foot soldier recognized one peasant and called his name, no reply was forthcoming. The peasants were not in control of their minds.

Into this bloody mass rode Tomoe on her white steed Raski. From her hand stretched a steel whip—chain links of double-edged razored knives—drawing a circle all about her and Raski. It was another weapon she had borrowed from the Celestial Kingdoms; and she had learned to use it well.

The spinning whip whirred angrily, slashing at arms and faces, clearing the way for a samurai approach. Behind her came three men: Madoka Kawayama, Goro Maki and Ushii Yakushiji, all on foot, their swords gleaming in the preternatural darkness. Shigeno's army was heartened by the arrival of the aristocratic warriors, and fought the more valiantly. The samurai would insure victory for the Lord.

A thousand foe surrounded the three swordsmen, for they had plowed into the melee on the path made by the horsewoman. Unlike the other soldiers, these samurai could not be overwhelmed: none could breach the woman's chain or the men's swift swords. Only a dozen heimin could approach the three men at any given time.

Forming a triangle with their backs, Madoka, Goro and Ushii slowly enlarged their formation, leaving no route for peasants to enter. The peasants, armed with sticks, hoes, and heirloom weaponry whose use they little understood, could not oppress these fighting elite, not even by the weight of numbers.

Sacrificing himself, a peasant ran into the path of Tomoe's chain of knives. It wrapped itself around his body, slicing him a hundred mortal scores. He fell, losing fingers by gripping the heinous steel whip to insure the samurai's inability to restore the weapon's intention. A horde of snarling, black-eyed peasants closed around her. The steed leapt upward, all four legs kicking at once, crushing peasant bones. He tore at their throats and heads with powerful jaws.

Tomoe clung to the saddle with strong legs. With butterfly-longswords in her hands, she drew deadly arcs of fine, mirror-polished steel—opening windpipes and removing heads on each side of Raski. Blood mixed with rain in the torrential darkness.

Had they been in control of their own bodies, the peasants would never have continued to advance on this butcher's field—but they came on and on, maniacal in manner. Night might already have fallen beyond the clouds; Tomoe could not tell. She was uncertain how long the fight endured. The shiny eyes of heimin were like stars around her. Their howling challenged the gales. A suicidal attempt was made by a mad-eyed old woman wishing to sever Raski's tendons. The horse trampled her, as well as a ferocious young peasant who was hardly more than a child.

Tomoe's mind seemed to disengage from the battle, her body's skill acting alone. Her thoughts rose above the slaughter to look down through the beating torrent, and she spoke to herself: These people are innocent! *These people are innocent!* But she was sworn to protect her Lord's lands; and even if the peasants were the innocent tools of the sorcerer of Ho, yet they would die. Four top samurai, even without the warlord's army, could have defeated these untrained thousand. The martial skills of the samurai were ancient, and well-honed. A thousand farmers could no more slay samurai than could a thousand samurai raise fine rice. There was no valor in it, but she was sworn by her honor to Shojiro Shigeno. For the sake of her Lord, these would die.

In the midst of the thunder that followed every blinding flash, the pound of rain, the clash of weaponry and hoe, the curses of the struggling soldiers and the demonic wails of a possessed foe, there came a new and more terrible sound:

War drums.

Atop the hill, a better army was appearing and descending into the valley. These were the soldiers of Lord Huan, the treated exile and sorcerer of the Celestial Kingdoms. The mercenary captains were also of that terrible land, where Tomoe had once fought. Many of the soldiers themselves were foreigners, though many others were from the lower echelons of the samurai class.

They marched with swordsmen to the rear, archers in the middle, and for the front rank: *dragonmasters!* The dragonmasters were fire-breathing warriors from the Celestial Kingdoms, brown-faced and head-shaven, frightening as the dragon whose fighting style they mimicked. The sight of them made Tomoe prickle with hatred.

But the dragonmasters were not joining the present carnage. They circumvented the battleground, leading the new army on another errand.

Tomoe took one glance and no more. Her eyes must watch her own field. Ushii, Madoka and Goro were impenetrable if they stayed together as a unit, so she must not allow them to divide simply because she might need aid. It would weaken their offensive, and the battle would go on longer.

Raski reeled, turning a full circle in air, legs kicking. His flat, yellow teeth tore off the face of a peasant. Tomoe's swords dashed around and around, but no longer did she feel only confidence with her sorrow. The peasants would die, certainly, but the ones descending from the hill were another matter. They were true fighters, worthy adversaries. But the sorcerer Huan had sent a thousand innocents to busy the samurai, while the enemy's true soldiers marched on the palatial mansion where only a small private retinue would be found standing between death and the Lord Shigeno's family.

Tomoe began the arduous task of carving through the sea of flesh into which the steel whip and Raski had brought her. She must escape this horde and go after the real enemy. A fourth of the peasants had already been hewn down, and her three comrades could destroy the rest with the help of the small army. Tomoe alone was mounted, and so she alone had any hope of stalling the enemy army and the dragonmasters who approached Shojiro Shigeno's mansion. Her own thought caused her chill: "stalling" the approach. Could even a samurai, alone, hope to halt the progress of an army aided by dragonmasters?

The enemy soldiers marched by the carnage unmolested. Tomoe could have reached them with a stone, yet her horse could not pull through the hemming peasants. Moreover, Raski's legs were beginning to bog down in the mud. The storm had worsened, though that hardly seemed possible a moment before. Tomoe watched the soldiers pass and vanish into darkness and thick sheets of rain, headed toward the mansion. She cried out in anger and frustration.

Raski reared and screamed an animal's war-lust. Tomoe raised both swords into the evil sky.

And lightning struck her!

A forked bolt hurtled itself at her two blades, attracted to the high-held metal. She felt it in her body, a murderous force that bowed to none. She felt Raski collapse and die beneath her, and she lamented the loss of the steed more greatly than the loss of her own life.

Yet, somehow she was alive. She was *more* than alive. By some heightened sense, she could tell in advance which peasants would have to fall long before she carved them down with rapid, exquisite grace. She carved a path toward the edge of the maddened horde. In her was a supernatural strength, as though all the power in Raski's limbs and muscles had transferred to the rider in the moment of the horse's death.

Her swords shone with the magic and power of the electrical force. She could not blink. She could not close her mouth. Her face was paralyzed in a hideous devil-mask. Teeth showed white in the darkness of her face and seemed, somehow, sharpened and long. She was transformed. No longer Tomoe, she had become a demon-woman, born of the mating of sky and ground. In the lightning crack of orgasm, a monstrous warrior was born of the elements.

She slew. Before she could recount herself, she was beyond the ring of battle. Incredible speed brought her to the back of the soldiers. They turned their entire formation at her coming, as though sensing in advance that it would take them all to defeat her.

The dragonmasters came first. Even in the torrent, their torches burned furiously. They took great mouthfuls of some highly flammable substance and spat it with archers' skill through the flame of their torches. A wall of fire leapt up before Tomoe, but she would not halt.

The flames licked her lacquered, wooden armor; and she might have been set aflame herself but that she moved too fast and was too covered with mud, rain, and the life's blood of the peasants.

The dragonmasters were unarmed but for their fire. They turned and ran away when they saw the devil-woman leap through the defense they believed impenetrable. Like a monster out of hell she came at them from hell-fires of their own making, and only her hair was set ablaze. The dragonmasters fled, scattered, and the archers behind them were given long pause. Tomoe cut them down to either side, her magically glowing swords moving faster than could be followed—like lightning itself, her swords moved—or like strange, swift, luminous moths, set to dancing unceasingly, dealing a visually attractive death.

The enemy soldiers, even in their shock, regrouped around their dead and falling. A barrage of arrows flew to one spot—but even arrows could not penetrate the shield of her twirling swords!

She did not turn to see who came at her from behind. The mysterious sight was still upon her, and she knew every move before it happened. Her swords' arcs reached behind, as murderous at her back as to her sides and front.

Senses magnified, she heard every muddy step and knew the position of every soldier, even those beyond her vision. She heard their every breath and moan, and would know them forever by their voices—could they have lived forever to use them.

Soon she was walled in by flesh dead and dying, and leapt this wall incredibly, to stand again, firmly, as the soldiers of the treated exile surrounded her. They attacked uselessly, and died one upon the other. She attempted to cry a samurai oath, but the paralysis of her face allowed only a horrid, monstrous sound to emit from her throat, more Raski's than her own, eerie and amplified—and it seemed to the soldiers that she had demanded god-like: "Yield!"

They could not resist the half-imagined command. They dropped their swords and other weapons, and fell upon their knees weeping for mercy and a better life in the next, as Tomoe walked among them, beheading them two by two.

The storm was dying with the enemy. A natural sky reappeared, bright with stars, as clouds dissolved. A sharp moon frowned in the valley. Tomoe returned to her comrades, trudging slowly, no longer able to lift her arms, her face grown lax and ashen. The glow was going out of her swords, and warmth out of her body.

Madoka had carved the last peasant in half, from the center of skull to crotch. The two halves fell away as he turned to see what Goro and Ushii had already seen: the spent Tomoe standing before them like neither a demon nor a samurai, but like a corpse. She was pale, her eyes all white, her flesh drawn taut beneath the mud and splattered gore. She was burnt in places, though she had not believed it in her earlier frenzy—burnt badly: her hands from bearing the lightning-licked swords, her body from the dragonmasters' breaths of flame.

She said, "My friends. I am dead," and she toppled forward without a bend in her body. Ushii was at her side in an instant, turning her over lest she drown in the mud. But she seemed not to be breathing. She was cold as ice, her body stiff all over; and anyone would suspect she had been dead a long while. Madoka Kawayama fell to his knees and wailed amidst the thousand slain. The surviving foot soldiers moved away into the night, too respectful to overhear this sad moment. Goro Maki stood with his face turned to the moon and hid his tears completely. Ushii Yakushiji lifted the seeming corpse and began to walk toward the further hill, away from Shojiro Shigeno's mansion.

"Where do you go with her, Ushii?" Goro demanded.

Ushii turned around to look at his two friends. With Tomoe in his arms he said, "I am a free agent now, Goro. As you have seen, the attack came before I was indentured anew. With the high moon, I am free to seek new employment."

"Our master is good!" cried Madoka, not wanting to lose two friends at once. "We have always been together, Ushii!"

"Our comrade is ill," said Ushii.

Goro Maki took one step forward and corrected Ushii, his tone not hinting at his own sense of loss. "She is dead."

"Have you seen the dead go rigid so soon? Or cold? No, Goro, she is not dead. But soon she may be, without magic to restore her."

Madoka lowered his head, knowing Ushii's plan. But Goro would not believe it. He said angrily, "There is no magic in this valley, but from the lair of Shojiro Shigeno's wickedest foe!"

"That is true," said Ushii as he began to walk away.

"Ushii!" cried Madoka on his knees.

Ushii walked on.

"Ushii!" Madoka pounded fists into the soft, bloody mire. He shouted in desperation, "Do not go there, Ushii! Tomoe would rather die than be restored by black arts!"

Ushii's voice trailed back to them, saying, "We will be beside one another soon. Too soon, I fear. On the field of honor."

Madoka buried his face in his arms. Goro Maki put a supportive hand on his friend's quivering shoulders.

"Goodbye, my friends!" Ushii said, and was swallowed by the darkness.

ⓢ ⓢ ⓢ

Tomoe Gozen awoke on a snow covered ground halfway down a mountain. She wore no clothing, but clutched in each hand were her souls. Slowly, she stirred, at first crouching and looking all around, then standing straight up with both swords pointing forward from her sides. The snow did not chill her naked body.

Death permeated this place. Tomoe was apprehensive.

Although it was not the proper season, light flurries were falling. Snow clung to her singed hair, rolled off her shoulders. The mountain road was cluttered with rocks of all sizes, against which the snows eddied. Nowhere did trees or grasses grow.

A monster stepped out from behind a boulder, oozing slime from every pore, incongruously clad in an open blue jacket and nothing more. Its sudden appearance surprised Tomoe, but she faced it without reluctance. It greeted her with outstretched claws. Her swords moved once each, severing taloned hands before they could tear at her breasts. The monster howled and ran into the snowfall, dripping yellow blood from its arms.

"Goro!" Tomoe cried, thinking of the last people she could recall having seen. "Ushii! Madoka!" Her calling echoed off the mountain.

Tomoe could not fathom how she came to be where she had awakened. Confused, she began to climb the mountain. She was not certain why she chose the upward direction. The path would be easier were she to go downward; but it seemed imperative that she pursue the harder course.

When she began to trek toward an unseen peak, two squat toadlike beings immediately hopped off the face of the mountain to block her path. They reared on bowed, spindly legs and glowered balefully from protuberant eyes. Tomoe's swords slashed without hesitation, without thought, bursting through the skin of both bloated creatures. Air seeped out of their wounds, spurting green fluid. Their bulbous eyes registered surprise. Without any sound beyond the air escaping from their bodies, the toad-creatures leapt off the mountain side and into limbo.

A wind cleared the sky of snow for one moment, and for that instant Tomoe beheld an array of bizarre monstrosities waiting along her path. They were hungry things, half human and half animal, wretched in appearance and posing threateningly.

A group of five oddities walked down the path on stubby legs. These

bore knives mounted on poles. Their bodies were pockmarked and scabby. Tomoe parried their spears a while, but became annoyed and dispatched them one after the next. Their screeching death-cries churned her stomach. Cursing, she struggled on up the mountain road, wary of the next attack.

It was a difficult journey, but the struggles were not the fault of the creatures she slew with ease. For although the road was not steep, it affected her as though it were. Her breaths pulled hard. Her legs dragged heavily. Only her arms were unaffected, so her swords could take their toll.

She sweated in the cold atmosphere. Snowflakes melted against hot skin.

It was a day without moon or sun, giving Tomoe the eerie impression of having come to a land within a cosmos not intended for human habitation. She wondered if she were no longer living in the universe she had known before the battle on Shojiro Shigeno's north estate.

Monstrous semi-human things came at her without pause. With dizzying insistency, her swords carved the monsters up and down. Some fell upon the road, others over the side. A few climbed, wounded, straight up the mountain wall.

As they died beneath her whirling blades, many screamed hideously, in pain or in sorrow, with bestial hatred or with solicitous pleas of mercy. They merited no pity for their agony and it was dangerous to share their hatred; to respond negatively or positively was to lose to them her strength. Their varied cries assaulted her ears and emotions more fully than the reality of their existence assaulted her flesh or sanity. She was grateful to the ones who made no sound at all.

Most of them fought like beasts, reliant on fang and claw. A few were poorly armed with rusted swords and iron mallets. Now they came in vast numbers, as many as could crowd abreast without pushing one another off the road. Tomoe's butterfly-longswords carved amongst them with unceasing ferocity.

Her eyes tried to search the road beyond the untrained, ghoulish army. The snow was not heavy, but it was relentless, limiting visibility. She looked backwards only once. She was shocked to see no monsters nor their corpses, no snow, and no boulders cluttering the way. The path down was more inviting. If she faced the way of the monsters, she needn't struggle more. It was with extreme difficulty that she looked upward again; and she didn't look down thereafter.

One huge monster pushed itself to the front of the rest. It had arms long and gnarled like thick branches, with several joints and elbows. It champed and frothed and had so huge a manner of confidence that Tomoe was given pause, though she would not give up ground.

The monster's extraordinary arms held the others back, as if to say, "She's mine! I will kill her by myself!" She was startled to realize it had said precisely those words; and it said more: "None walk up this path who have fallen toward hell! The only safe route is down!"

Its arms reached toward her throat, spidery fingers writhing. Although Tomoe's swords were not so long as the monster's reach, its confidence was unwarranted. It was too gawky to be coordinated. She had no trouble ducking beneath its gangling arms and running forward to stick the monster's belly.

Multi-jointed arms wrapped around itself in feeble protection, but still it would not move from her path. She stabbed it again, withdrew, and stabbed with the left. It stood there launching no offense or defense while she dug out its intestines and spleen and liver and gizzard. Its heart fell into the hole she made and she dug that out too. The monster spoke once more:

"O, Tomoe Gozen, of all the monsters on the road to Hell, you are the grimmest of us all." Then it toppled to its side, falling into eternity.

With the knowledge that she was fighting her way out of hell, Tomoe decided she must pick up her pace. But the determination had a reverse effect. The more necessary she felt it was to reach the peak, the less accessible the peak became. The monsters lined up against the wall, allowing her to pass without interference. They laughed at her, wheezing and spitting and slapping their thighs. She could barely move.

"I cannot go on!" she cried, and cried tears.

The assemblage of beasts hooted and jumped up and down and performed antics like a cheering crowd. Tomoe felt like a clown entertaining the vilest of sentient beings—beings who might once have been human like herself.

"I will help you, Tomoe!"

It was a familiar voice. Above her on the road, Ushii stood in full regalia. His armor had turned to gold. The monsters hid their faces and covered their eyes and fell upon their knees, whining and sniffling. Ushii Yakushiji held his hand down to Tomoe.

"I cannot reach you!" she wailed.

Flurries of snow were pushed away by the light of Ushii. He yelled at her almost with anger, "You can!"

She raised one leaden foot and took one step. Ushii took a step of equal distance backward. She raised her other foot to approach but he stepped back again so that she was no closer.

"Wait for me, Ushii!"

She nearly fell forward on her face, but saved herself and stumbled three steps up the mountain. Ushii's feet did not appear to move, yet he was still no nearer. He floated backward like a wraith; and Tomoe saw that his feet were a hand's width above the ground.

For a long while she could not move. Ushii faded back into the snow, which had returned to its former thickness. Soon, he was invisible. Tomoe called for him to come back.

"Follow me, Tomoe. Follow me to the top."

"I cannot see you!" she cried desperately.

"Follow my voice."

"Ushii!"

"Come to me."

"Where are you!"

"You are more powerful than the road to hell, Tomoe."

"Ushii, I cannot hear your voice!"

"Yes, you can hear it, and you will come."

She stumbled another step onward. "No. You are wrong. I cannot hear. I cannot move."

It went thus, step by step. There were fewer monsters on the road and they no longer hindered her passage. She struggled upward, staggering through the snow. When she had come nearly within arm's reach of the top, the oppressive atmosphere closed on her more tightly. She fell and could go no further.

Ushii appeared again. He lay on his belly, reaching down from the top to where she had fallen. "Take my hand," he said. She reached up until their fingers almost met.

"You are too far away, Ushii."

He replied, "I am right behind you, pushing up."

She felt him then, behind her, pushing up; suddenly she could reach his hand, and he gripped her wrists. He pulled her onto the top and vanished. Tomoe Gozen curled into a ball of weariness and cried herself to sleep.

🌀 🌀 🌀

On regaining consciousness, Tomoe did not open her eyes, but tried to decode her whereabouts by her other senses. The first sensation was of a vast interior. Warmth surrounded her. Oddly, she was standing firmly on her feet, and felt the weight of full armor upon her. She felt bathed, rested, and at the peak of strength. A strange ennui alone kept her from opening her eyes.

A sweet but repulsive odor filled her nostrils, commanding relaxation. A muscle flexed spontaneously along her shoulders. Along her jaw there was a momentary spasm. She presumed there would be no problem moving about, but there did not seem to be any occasion to do so.

There were others in the room with her. A familiar voice asked with unfamiliar meekness, "Does she live? Is she well?" It was Ushii, sounding more cowed than she had ever known him to be. His presence should have heartened her, for they were closest of comrades; or his tenor should have alarmed her, for she had never known him to quail. But she could muster no sense of emotion or concern. Whatever may have broken Ushii's spirit, she felt no interest in the matter.

It was as though some part of herself had been left on the mountain road from hell, leaving her callous and unfeeling, devoid of solicitude. Yet she felt the necessary weights of her souls hanging from each hip, like equal portions on a balancing scale, and knew that she was whole. The dark, brooding presence of her swords was all the comfort she required.

A voice as honey-sweet and repugnant as the thick air replied to Ushii. "She does live, samurai, and is well." There was odd laughter, like that of an old crone. Then there was a command which Tomoe knew was meant for her: "Open your eyes."

It was not a master's command, for she had taken no oath. She was a masterless samurai, and felt no compulsion to reply. Yet politeness was one tenet of bushido, so she obeyed. Before her stood Ushii, not as the golden warrior who had helped her on that otherworld road, but a hunched and drained man with circles beneath his eyes, frightened as a small animal.

He gasped, stepped away from her, and cried out, "Her eyes! What have you done to her eyes!"

Beyond Ushii, at the far wall of the richly tapestried chamber, a skeletal man sat upon an ornate throne of gold and jade. The seat was too large, making the oldster look even more narrow. He might have been taller than either samurai when standing, but sitting his depleted thinness made him seem small and frail as a sparrow. His head wobbled slightly, too large to be supported by a body with so little muscle. He had a long, thin beard. His eyes were gleeful. His extended yellow teeth were homely and gay. In front of his oversized throne burned a brazier on three bronze legs molded in the shape of hawks' feet. From this the sweet odor exuded.

Once again the thin, grey man deigned to reply to Ushii: "Have you not seen eyes such as those before, samurai?" His voice was that of an old woman, teasing and urging Ushii toward a realization of Tomoe's fate.

"In last night's battle," said Ushii, "on the faces of murderous peasants."

The sorcerer looked more pleased.

Tears rolled down Ushii's face as Tomoe watched him, unmoved, empty of compassion.

"O, cruel master!" Ushii began. "You have tricked me! I bargained my service for her life, but what kind of life have you wrought?"

Streamers of smoke thin as the sorcerer's beard rose from the brazier. From behind this faint curtain he spoke in a lecturing tone: "I am told that a samurai without a master is little more than a samurai without honor. I am delighted to serve as master to Tomoe Gozen, thereby to insure her station." He liked his own jest, and grinned horridly.

"Woe!" cried Ushii, and scratched his own face until it bled. "It is too wicked to be true!"

"How so?" the stork-thin venerable snapped. He gestured toward Tomoe with a hand that looked like bones. The hand wavered like a snake. He said, "Hers will remain the life of a warrior, the only life she ever sought. I could have made her a sing-song girl. I could make her play lute or samisen, and recite lurid poetry for all who visit my court. But I value her for her prowess, and am pleased that you brought her to me. She is known even in the Celestial Kingdoms of Ho as a courageous fighter, having slain many of Ho's best soldiers to reach a swordsmith from Naipon and end his career. It will be rich irony when I return to my country to overthrow the old dynasty, with Tomoe Gozen as my general. Weep no more, Ushii Yakushiji, for Tomoe is alive and mighty, whereas you are merely alive."

Ushii fell into a crouch, wrapped arms around his knees. In obedience to his new master, he did not weep.

The sorcerer called aloud, "Tomoe Gozen."

Like a titanic stone warrior come to life, Tomoe slowly turned her head and looked precisely at the one who called.

"Tomoe Gozen, you have dishonored yourself. What must a samurai do?"

Although Tomoe could not recall what she had done to bring dishonor to herself, she felt vaguely that this was true. She removed a short knife from a sheath at her thigh and raised it to her throat. *Seppuku* among men involved inflicting disemboweling wounds upon oneself; among women, the ritual suicide consisted of *jigai,* the stabbing or cutting of the throat. Ushii shouted,

"It is not true! The honor of Tomoe is unreproachable!"

The sorcerer waved an unsteady hand and said, "I was mistaken, honorable Tomoe." His glee manifested itself in an ugly fashion when he peeled back his lips to reveal black, receding gums. Tomoe replaced the knife in its sheath, taking once again her rigid posture. Throughout the brief ordeal, her expression had not altered.

More delighted than ever with his puppet, the sorcerer started another game. "Tomoe!" he said. "An evil man reposes on this throne, thin as sticks and easily slain. What deed would a strong samurai perform?"

Butterfly-longswords slid out of their scabbards. Tomoe stalked forward. Ushii was caught between fear and delight. Tomoe's swords were held at her extreme sides. They were long enough to reach across the brazier. The skeletal sorcerer spoke calmly to Ushii,

"If I said for you to stop her, you would have to try." Again, he exposed his gums with a horrible grin. "Am I right?"

"I am sworn to your service," Ushii said simply.

"I would not think of that command!" exclaimed the sorcerer, toying cruelly with Ushii's emotions. To Tomoe he said, "Why do you hesitate?"

Her swords came together so quickly it was almost impossible to see the motion.

The sorcerer didn't flinch. The swords stopped a hair's width from either side of his neck. Even Tomoe could not guess what staid the double blow. For a moment she felt concern rise from inside her, from wherever feeling was hidden. The sorcerer must have seen the change in the woman's visage, for his homely smile dwindled and he said swiftly,

"Tomoe, you must forget that swords forged in the Celestial Kingdoms cannot harm me! Forget my game immediately and feel at peace with yourself."

The woman stepped away from the warmth and sweet repugnance of the brazier, her sense of smell deadened by the fumes. The fear that had almost awakened her was forgotten. She saw Ushii Yakushiji on his knees beside her, whining pitifully. Why he was so dispirited she did not know and could waste little effort considering.

"What have I brought upon you, Tomoe?" Ushii wailed. "What have I done?"

"Honored warrior," said the sorcerer, a bony finger leveled at Tomoe. "If you can speak, pledge service to me."

Ushii fell from crouch to knees and crawled toward the side of the sorcerer's throne, begging, "Lord Huan, do not command her oath! *My* service was the price of resurrection, not that of Tomoe Gozen."

He ignored the begging samurai and waited for Tomoe's response. Although her mouth opened, she could make no sound. It was as though her tongue were cleaved to her palate.

"As I suspected," said Lord Huan, mostly to himself. "No matter!" He affected a bored demeanor as he tossed particles of sorcerous incense into the pot before his throne. He continued, "She will obey me in any case, whether or not she is bound by her own word. But I am intrigued by this code of the samurai, this honor you value above your lives. It provides you a framework for pristine logic and action, but the ends are not always moral. That makes samurai valuable to one as myself, for I too value loyalty above morality."

He leaned forward in his large seat, clutching the arms of the throne as though he were so weak he might fall, and continued, "Like all samurai, you believe the Mikados have reigned since Naipon's beginnings strictly because they are divine children of your sun-goddess. But it is this unshakable loyalty among the samurai class that holds the power above you. In the three kingdoms which make up Ho, dynasties come and go, some lasting longer than others—while in Naipon, the same family rules on and on. Whether strong leaders, or decadent figureheads; with a tyrant's fist, or a gentle opened hand—the Mikados endure. Because of you. One day, I will rule over the nations of Ho. And to insure an everlasting dynasty, I would introduce the virtues of the samurai to the Celestial Kingdoms."

Ushii sat on his knees, staring at his hands in his lap. His faith did not allow room for the considerations of Lord Huan, Tomoe knew. Except for her presently discompassionate state, she might be as deaf as Ushii. For Ushii, the concept of samurai at once honorable and immoral was not to be assimilated. The notion that the power of the Mikado heralded elsewhere than from the Shinto pantheon was supreme blasphemy. Ushii knew he served a wicked master, however; and a servant need not comprehend *any* master's reasoning, and especially not Lord Huan's.

Tomoe, however, was affected, though in no way did it show.

Lord Huan leaned back, resting as though speech wearied him; but in a moment he gathered strength to continue: "I am fascinated that you could bear me such malice and yet serve with implicit loyalty. You call it, I believe, *giri:* fealty and duty to your master. It takes precedence above your own family. Without it, you have no honor. Without honor, the virtues of justice and benevolence mean nothing. I understand your kind, Ushii, or begin to. You grovel to me now, but you are no coward. I might be helpless as a babe against your sword, but it will never turn against me, because I have your word. Only through a master can the seven virtues of the samurai be meaningfully fulfilled. Only I may judge if you are polite, courageous, benevolent, veracious, just, loyal and honorable. Is this not so, samurai?"

Ushii nodded faintly, looked up, and whispered, "You do not consider my *ninjo,* Lord Huan. Through it, I may judge for myself what is benevolent and just, aside from my master's command. The ninjo is my conscience. If it tells me that through you I am without honor, then I must die."

The sorcerer clapped his hands joyously. "Ah, Ushii, you do not understand the wisdom of your nation's founders! Even dishonored, you must be loyal to your master. You would slay yourself to be free of me, whereas in the Celestial Kingdoms, an emperor despised must be ever on guard against treachery. Oh, glorious were the days when ancient rulers taught the Way of the Warrior to samurai! By emulation, I will rise to glory in the Seat of Heaven, the Throne of the Celestial Kingdoms whose splendor dwarfs my own small seat! Never will my dynasty fall!"

The sorcerer gazed at the ceiling, reverent of himself, whose idealized life was depicted in the relief above their heads. When he looked at Ushii again, he said,

"Who do you serve, samurai?"

Ushii stood and touched the hilt of his sword, saying, "I am pledged to the defense of Lord Huan!" Strength and pride crept back into his tone. If all the cosmos came undone, still would Ushii Yakushiji feel complete, for he had bushido to keep him whole. Or so he believed. Tomoe, though unable or unwilling to act, was yet able to reason. She knew that to survive, Ushii must sever his giri from his ninjo, maintaining honor with the first and despising himself with the second. This separation of self meant insanity, and unless it were resolved, Ushii would go mad.

The knowledge should have moved Tomoe deeply, but she felt nothing beyond simple comprehension.

The sorcerer was cackling loudly, then stopped short. "Tomoe!" he called. "Come stand to my right. Ushii, to my left." Ushii took up his station, squaring his shoulders and affecting his old self. Tomoe moved like a juggernaut to the right hand side of the exiled Huan. He said, "Yesterday, I spent vast stores of magic bringing forth the storm, manipulating a peasant population, and opening the door for Ushii Yakushiji to aid Tomoe Gozen. These demonstrations have left me weak. But I need not fear, for I have two fine *yojimbo:* samurai bodyguards. Shigeno was allowed the illusion of victory, yet he is ruined—for without peasants to till the fields and bring him tribute, he is lord of nothing.

"Soon, I must sleep to regain my powers. Before I awaken, Ushii, you will execute the dragonmasters for their cowardice in the battle. They alone survived yesterday's battle, because they ran away; and I shall replace them with a more effective army. Tomoe, you will carry me to my bedchamber, for I am presently too drained to walk. You will stand over me and see no danger befalls. I will sleep three days. On the fourth, I will return to my throne to accept tribute from all the warlords. They do not know my sorcery is for the moment spent, so they prepare even now to honor me lest the example of Shojiro Shigeno be made of them as well."

He looked at Tomoe and then at Ushii, and it seemed the evil man had a kind of awe for both of them. He finished, "I trust you both implicitly."

Then he laughed louder than Tomoe had heard before. It was the mirth of malice which cannot be defeated.

That night, Tomoe stood over the silk-upholstered couch of the dark sorcerer of Ho. Since she placed him amidst the covers, he had not moved. He lay curled fetally, a child as old as time; and evil was, after all, ancient, yet never wholly matured.

Tomoe's black eyes glistened in the faint light of a single, failing candle. Ushii lay on a bamboo mat on the floor. He watched his captivated friend and the sleeping Lord Huan, with a wild expression framed by the self-inflicted scratches on his face. He asked, "Why do you never sleep, Tomoe?"

She could not reply.

Ushii shuddered. "How terribly you have changed!"

Huan, in his revitalizing trance, would have been easy prey but for his intent guardian. Even were Ushii mad enough to attack his own master, Tomoe would stop him with the least necessary effort. She was not sure why she would bother, for the sorcerer merited none of her consideration. Perhaps she would stop Ushii so he could not dishonor himself, although that did not register with much importance either. Nor was she certain why she felt no inclination to kill Lord Huan herself, except that she no longer served Shojiro Shigeno and bore Shigeno's adversary no personal grudge. She hovered above the frail sorcerer without movement, barely with thought. Not even her moist eyes blinked.

Ushii said to her, "By the danger brought to the heimin and by keeping an army, Lord Huan has broken his treaty with the Mikado. It may be that the warlords prepare tribute as we are told, but if this is so, it is only for the moment—only until reinforcements can march from Kamakura or Kyoto. There will be many samurai, and perhaps *jono* priests and priestesses to fight the magic. It will be a remarkable war, Tomoe."

A remarkable war seemed unlikely to Tomoe, for she had slain Lord Huan's soldiers herself, and Ushii would soon execute the surviving dragonmasters for their cowardly flight when Tomoe broke through their fire. Or, more likely, they were to be gotten out of the way because they did not fit into the next phase of Lord Huan's scheme. Whatever Huan's plan, without an army of comparable force, the inevitable confrontation would be decidedly unremarkable. Yet the sorcerer rested easy on his rich couch. Who was to say what miracle he could perform on regaining the fullness of his power.

"When war comes," said Ushii, "I, for sake of honor, must serve the enemy; and you will serve him too. I would slay myself and be done with all this, but that my soul would never rise from hell to its next life, knowing I had left you in this state. A glamour is upon you, Tomoe, though you seem not to care; and it is the fault of my unthinking devotion. Goro and Madoka warned me, but I would not hear. Now I must wait until you are free before I can consider the mettle of my own honor."

When Ushii slept, Tomoe noted from the bottom of her unwavering vision that the sorcerer was smirking within his cloudy tufts of beard. Even entranced, he had listened.

Through three nights Tomoe stood without motion, taking no nourishment, accepting no drink, without apparent depletion. Ushii came and went as he pleased, handling the affairs of Lord Huan's palace. Servants obeyed him absolutely, having witnessed his swift method of dispensing with the dragonmasters, and fearing his darkening mood. On each of the three evenings, he returned to his mat like an obedient cur, and gazed earnestly upon the stone-still warrior until too tired to keep awake.

On the third morning, Huan rose as from a nap, refreshed and in good humor. He was able to walk on his own, albeit in a gawky, spidery fashion.
Servants hurried with fresh clothing, food, and drink. Huan ordered Ushii away, as one would shoo a dog, while he and Tomoe feasted. Already the messengers of the warlords were arriving with tribute of horses, grain, gold and chests of coins; but the sorcerer had them wait until he could see them at his leisure.

As they ate, Lord Huan watched Tomoe with an intensity matched only by that of Ushii on the nights previous. Tomoe sensed that Ushii had been reluctant to leave her alone in the presence of the wakened sorcerer. Perhaps he thought Lord Huan was senile enough to forget that Tomoe Gozen was a warrior. Indeed, it could not be denied that the sorcerer's respect for the samurai class was of an intellectual rather than literal nature. But all Huan did was gaze acutely, watching her as she ate and drank with slow, meticulous purpose. It was as though she were the prize of a conquest, his favorite province, an object like a jade temple or a golden city to possess but never touch. Yet Tomoe could not tell Ushii how little transpired whenever she and Huan were alone.

It became evident that Ushii was disturbed by grave imaginings about these meetings. This aggravation made Ushii edgy, and his edge made him dangerous.

One warlord made tribute of fifty Shirakian slaves, prizes from a mainland war on the upper coast. A much frustrated Ushii mistreated them badly, until Huan ordered them out from under foot. He gave them the seemingly pointless task of gathering stones around the estate; and Tomoe wondered abstractly what the stones were for. Surely the iniquitous Lord Huan did not send them on a foolish errand out of mere concern over their welfare or the manner of Ushii's management.

Ushii Yakushiji became a wicked man, his unjust deeds overwhelming his conscience. He hid his self-loathing beneath the blood of others. Those who came with tributes often as not left with scars. His quick temper cost the lives of half Lord Huan's own servants, and those who were spared sudden deaths consistently effaced themselves when Ushii walked the halls.

Within him, Ushii's giri and ninjo were locked in the throes of mortal combat, and Tomoe knew at last that Ushii Yakushiji was truly mad.

Even the realization of Ushii's madness awakened no pity in Tomoe Gozen. She watched all these things come to pass from her dispassionate posture, ever at Lord Huan's side, for he liked to keep her near. She felt that all was less real than an excessively stylized Noh play. She viewed the world through glazed, black eyes, and nothing quite touched her.

The prospect of war was all that piqued Tomoe's bored, unfeeling spirit. She knew that war must be imminent. Ushii had slain two messengers of the Shogun himself, and the result was that several warclans were rallying. The Mikado might remain heedless of broken treaties, but the Shogun was too proud. The very worms and crickets were Lord Huan's spies and he delighted at the news, welcoming the certainty of battle.

Tomoe wondered casually why the sorcerer had not sent to the mainland for his own reinforcements, unless his allies there were already expended. He had many servants, but only two warriors. Surely he did not believe that Tomoe and Ushii alone could win against the combined wrath of those clans most faithful to the Shogun. Lord Huan's delusion did not worry Tomoe, however. A samurai's concern was never with death, but with valor. She would fight with courage and skill. Every movement of a samurai reflected the perfection of the very gods.

Whether victorious or defeated, the Way of the Warrior was the Way of the Gods, and an end in itself. Tomoe Gozen was prepared for battle, careless of risk. Whether or not it were true, as Ushii claimed, that she was held by magic, in this thing she would always feel the same: war itself was holy.

For many days, the mystery of Lord Huan's court was that he kept the Shirakians busy gathering stones from every corner of the valley. Outside the palace, the rocks were piled higher and higher, making a loose, rough pyramid. Daily, Huan investigated the growing pile, and laughed, and danced like a clumsily animated skeleton before the stones. Then he'd return to his throne, once more to toss incense in his brass pot and accept tribute from all the warlords but Shigeno, who had nothing left to give.

The day came when the warlords brought no more tribute, no more wealth for the coffers of a sorcerer who dreamt smoky dreams of conquest. Instead, the warlords sent a declaration of war. Ushii beheaded the offensive messenger with one swipe of his sword, and took the scroll from the hand of the falling corpse. Lord Huan clapped and giggled and bounced in his throne. Ushii gritted his teeth in madness, handing the scroll to Huan. Tomoe stood at the right of the throne, no change upon her visage.

Lord Huan read the scroll, nodding and grinning, then rolled it tight and handed it to a furtive servant to take away and burn. "The attack will come at dawn," he said, long-nailed fingers toying with his wispy white beard. His mien was that of an emperor well pleased with himself, as certain as any peasant that those who rule are gods.

"Before me, Ushii!" he commanded quickly, as he dug deeply into his clothing like a miser searching for a hidden coin. Ushii fell onto his knees beside the large brazier, eyes down, awaiting his master's words. "O, obedient samurai, at dawn your might is tested. Although you do not yet know how, the odds will mark your favor. Yet once before I came this near, but was overcome and cast off the yellow earth of Ho. This time, I cannot fail. Take this vial."

Ushii stood and took the orange, crystalline container. Its cork was sealed over with brown wax. Through its translucent walls, an effervescing liquid churned.

"It holds your last resort, Ushii Yakushiji. I do not believe that it will be necessary that you drink it—but if the battle turns against you, this vial contains a formula which will give you strength far greater than that which possessed Tomoe Gozen when lightning struck her swords. It is fatal. But as I have learned, a samurai who is faithful to the bushido is ever prepared to die for a master."

Without comment regarding his own fate, Ushii tucked the vial inside his armor.

"And Tomoe?" Ushii asked with the faintest tone of calculation.

"She is indestructible," said Huan. "She could not be sacrificed even were that my wish."

Ushii bowed, pleased.

Then Huan rose from his throne, a tall, swift stick figure moving across thick carpets. He ordered the two samurai to follow him to the pile of stones outside the palace. There he bid Ushii slay the gathered Shirakians, which was a better reward than they might have guessed.

When the dead lay all around, Lord Huan indicated the rock pile with a flourish of his bony arm, proclaiming, "This is my armory!"

Ushii looked puzzled. "You would defend against the combined force of the warclans with stones, Lord Huan? If so, who will throw them? You have raised no army. How can we hope to stand?"

"You shall see!" the sorcerer said. He produced a glass ball from his sleeve as might a common street magician, tossing it up and down to imply its lack of weight. Tomoe and Ushii could see that it was hollow, fragile, and filled with vapor. Lord Huan tossed this object atop the pile of stones where it shattered, covering the mound with violet smoke.

Immediately, with ear-chilling grating noises, the rocks began to change into swords and flails and hammers and axes and knives and staves and hatchets. They were not the works of artisans, but were crude and ugly. They seemed to have been fashioned by and for deformed hands. The two samurai were soon gazing not upon rocks, but upon an array of tools for destruction which were caricatures of true weapons.

"An impressive trick," said Ushii, and was serious, "but such rough-hewn weapons have not been used since the Age of Stone. Yet I will assume the stone arms will indeed hold against steel, because a supreme sorcerer fashioned them. Even so, what army will bear these arms?"

Lord Huan performed his scrawny, apish dance, beside himself with excitement. He looked up at the fighting-man, and said, "You have seen my legions before, Ushii! On the mountain road out of hell! Imagine the terror of the clans! Imagine the horror of the Mikado himself when demons descend upon his city! A once-immortal dynasty will fall at

last, and I will drain the wealth of Naipon and make the Celestial Kingdoms kneel to my worthiness! Laugh, Ushii, laugh!"

Obediently, Ushii joined Lord Huan's laughter, but the tone rang
false and flat. Even in his madness, Ushii could not dredge up pleasure
in leading an army of ghouls. He had stood at the threshold of hell, and
it had helped break him to Lord Huan's will. Now he would take as
comrades the horrors he had seen.

As for Tomoe, she neither feared nor respected the monsters she
had slain before with ease. She did not tremble when the mountain of
stone weapons began to quake and the hand of the first monster reached
out from a cairn, bearing an ugly blade. It crawled out from the rocks,
and another appeared behind, clutching an axe. They would come, one
by one, throughout the night, until the last weapon was taken up; and
on the dawn Tomoe Gozen and Ushii Yakushiji would lead them all into
battle.

She stood by Ushii and the sorcerer, whose laughter filled her brain.
The muscles of her jaw twitched as they often did, and perhaps there
was a greater glisten in her dark, dark eyes. Ushii peered in abject dread
at the slobbering oozing beasts that crawled forth to feed on the slain
Shirakian slaves. But Tomoe Gozen appeared as unconcerned and as
discompassionate as on the day of her similar ascent from hell.

Dawn bloodied the sky. Warlords on armored horses and eight thousand samurai afoot came in orderly formation to the valley they sought
to reclaim for Shojiro Shigeno. Shigeno himself led the four united
clans. He was fierce to see, angry at his ruin and the slaughter of his
peasants, anxious to regain honor and have vengeance. Long hair flowed
from beneath his helmet. His armor was lacquered to a shining ebony.
He sat high on a stallion bred of the same stock as Tomoe's lamented
Raski.

To Shigeno's left and right were two magician-ninja. They were
jono and not to be confused with ordinary ninja, who were clever but
knew no magic. The mysterious jono were descendants of an elite offshoot of the ancient spy class, an offshoot which had evolved into a
less underhanded cult of supremely deadly priests and priestesses proficient in martial sorcery. Even the Shogun dared not challenge them.
Their presence indicated the Mikado's interest in this battle, for only
Amaterasu's godchild commanded jono.

One of these jono was a man, the other a woman. They were swaddled in grey robes so that even the major portion of their faces was hidden. They sat astride horses too slender for war, but the riders' prowess was not to be underestimated. The priest and priestess were Shinto warriors, favored by the hundred thousand myriad of Shinto deities. Neither samurai nor common ninja were any match for them.

What the several warlords, two jono, and numerous samurai confronted in the valley were two mounted samurai—a woman with unnatural eyes, and a man frothing with insanity—who captained an army of slobbering, disorderly monstrosities. The creatures stood awry, naked with rare exceptions, waving mallets, sickles, flails and swords all made of stone. They champed crooked teeth and howled like a haunted wind for blood.

The two incredible samurai rode forth in slow, stately procession, and the legions of ghouls waited for command to follow. With precise movement, Tomoe Gozen raised one arm, as might a dream-warrior, to signal. The howling beasts began to rush forward with unexpected speed. They came slouching, crawling, hopping, scrabbling, in ungainly strides with bloodlust upon their inhuman visages.

Ushii and the woman drew their swords, spurred their steeds.

Their foe were momentarily stunned by the vision, not having been told they would oppose demons.

The two varied armies clashed, and the red blood of samurai mixed with the green and yellow fluids of the ghouls. The beasts were awkward, but no easy adversaries. They could lose limbs and still come on; they could do battle even without heads, though they could not be sure who they struck blindly. Even their severed parts would fight: a bodiless arm beat the ground with a hammer; lost fingers inched their way up samurai armor. Only the magician-ninja could deal blows of anything like a lasting effect, and even the ghouls felled by those two would spring back to life if touch by another of their ranks.

The magician-ninja produced darts, apparently from out of nothingness but perhaps from their sleeves, tossing them into the chests and eyes of ghouls. The darts exploded on contact, tearing rib cages and opening skulls. The victims of the magician-ninja hooted furiously and beat on the ground and sometimes appeared to die—but no samurai in service of the warlords fared so well in hurting them.

At cost of many lives, Ushii was dragged from his mount. His horse fled the field of battle in terror, and Ushii stood alone, making wild sweeping gestures with his sword. They who surrounded him were careful with the placement of feet, balance of hip, field of vision, while the madman thrashed among them. In the hands of a fine warrior, a sword could fell a tree, or carve entirely through a human torso. The ground was therefore littered with halved and quartered men, the victims of Ushii.

Ghouls began to tear at the back of those samurai Ushii had failed to beat back or carve down on his own. He had lost his helm; his hair had come untied. He looked more like an Ainu wildman than samurai as he snarled and fought and killed.

Finally there was only one samurai standing before him, and Ushii took careful measure of this imposing opponent. Ushii knew every strength and weakness of Madoka Kawayama, with whom he had trained and shared love since boyhood, at whose side he had fought many times until the last night of service under Lord Shigeno. Madoka knew Ushii's fighting methods as well, so was able to avoid Ushii's first rushing attack.

"Stop, Ushii!" Madoka shouted. "This need not be!"

He guarded against Ushii's insistent blows, but launched no counter attack. He tried to reason with the madman, not believing his boyhood friend could kill him. "USHII!" he pleaded, but Ushii's face only twisted with greater rage. Madoka wept and knew what he must do; he raised his sword to deal Ushii a killing blow. He struck too slowly. Ushii's sword moved so fast none could have seen how he had delivered the slender wound. There was no blood until after Madoka fell. Only then did the thinnest red line appear along his throat.

Ushii had no remorse. He turned to fight another.

Tomoe had ridden near enough to see this brief drama, though it had not fully registered with importance. She had a vague image of Ushii not as the magnificent-though-maddened warrior, but as a hunched and drained monster, not much different than the ghouls he fought beside. She remembered that image also from the moment she opened her eyes after leaving hell's highway; then, an ugly, hunch-backed Ushii had jerked away from the sight of her darkened eyes.

There was no time to consider these impressions more fully, for she was kept busy cutting down samurai. Arrows took Tomoe's steed in the sides and chest, but she urged the poor animal on for a long while before it had lost so much blood that it staggered and was more burden than help. The horse blew in angry pain, and the rider leapt off before it

died. She spun her weapons through the encroaching mass of flesh. Samurai died as she walked slowly, deeper into the thickening quarrel.

She worked her way further from Ushii, who presently fought shoulder to shoulder with a fierce two-headed ghoul more skillful than the rest. One head had been severed halfway through, and hung limp and scowling. Then from the jostling and new blows the head fell away altogether. It went bumping down the hillside biting at shins and ankles as it rolled. The former bearer of that head fought on, unperturbed.

The samurai Tomoe confronted moved with grace, but could not equal her. They wielded the traditional, single *daito*; when they met Tomoe, they were dueling two fencers at once. She would let them, one by one, break the guard of her left sword, while her right moved to puncture the spleen. She had become an automaton, leaving a trail of dead.

A mounted warlord of profound beauty bore down on Tomoe. She whirled. Her right sword completely severed the head of the horse, its blood showering her armor. Her left sword took the life of the warlord. The beheaded stallion ran blindly by, then fell, spilling its load. Only when the warlord lay at her feet did she know she had killed Lord Shigeno. But she could not mourn; she could not feel. She could only slay; and so she trod upon the dead, and went about her task of raising the tally.

The magician-ninja had throughout the battle fought near Shigeno. Now they rode their ethereal mounts toward Tomoe Gozen. Their supply of exploding darts seemed unending and they dealt hideous random wounds to the ghouls around them. Tomoe's two blades traced a repeating double-arc through the air, averting a dart intended for her. Its explosion dazzled her vision momentarily. When the sparkles cleared from her dark eyes, she saw the two magician-ninja rear before her on their slender horses.

She advanced on them unhesitantly. But the jono priest raised a palm, and suddenly Tomoe could advance no further. Her swords moved like straws through syrup when she tried to carve in the direction of the priest and priestess. The jono priest's other hand moved, it seemed, to a fold in his robe. Tomoe saw the sliver of a dart between his fingers.

The jono priestess said, "No, my brother. Let this one go." Her voice was muffled by the wrappings which covered the top of her head and the lower half of her face; but Tomoe heard the words as clearly as though they'd been whispered directly into her ear. The priest bowed slightly, as though the priestess were the greater authority. Then their steeds spun around, and they vanished in the carnage.

All around, Tomoe witnessed horrors which drove other samurai mad with fear; but she was unimpressed. The portions of the ghouls which had been severed began to put themselves back together to make still weirder monstrosities. One ghoul's severed hand ran like a spider along the ground until it found a severed leg. The hand attached itself to the leg's ankle, then dragged the new burden toward a ghoul who fought from a sitting position, unable to stand on its one remaining leg. The ghoul acquired the new leg, which was too long, causing a posture of whimsical insult as it stood and battled. The hand which served as foot wielded a stone club, with which it pounded samurai toes. Elsewhere, a head walked on two hands, fighting with a hammer in its third. Most terrible of all were the ghouls who fought using parts of fallen samurai, striking terror into the warlords' forces, who might recognize a friend's armored hand on a hideously miscellaneous body.

The sky was brilliant blue. The sun had risen to her highest point for the season, and baked the scene without relent. The warclans were weakening, but the battle could last the entire day before a definitive outcome.

The enemy's morale was further ruined by the sight of ghouls lingering near the slain, to feast upon the hearts, testicles and brains of samurai. Disciplined samurai were unafraid of death—but this horrendous disfigurement and ill-use of those who had fallen was beyond comprehension. Proven, hardy warriors dropped their swords or fled. Others fought with concern for personal survival, not for victory or honor.

The magician-ninja had dwindled the ranks of the ghouls somewhat, and a few samurai had learned to hack the ghouls into pieces too small to find one another again; but in large part the ghouls appeared to be as strong and numerous as when the battle had begun.

Ushii might have become wearied, but madness kept him unfailing. Tomoe felt little or no effect from the long battle, for her emotional aloofness had let her use the energy she had with mechanical precision. Ushii wore himself out in a whirlwind of activity and slaying; Tomoe was more inexorable in her killing—like a plague, like famine, slower but no less effective and therefore more terrible.

Unexpectedly she came upon Goro and readied herself for a worthwhile opponent. But he backed away, pushing two rag-clad peasant women who had somehow been caught in this horror. He was trying to save them, though it oughtn't be his business. Tomoe increased her pace lest he slip away. She knew that he was last of his line, that he was loath to die by alien steel. Yet, as Ushii's miserable state did not touch her, Goro's fate was no concern. She intended to slash him along the back, but he spun and blocked her blow, though it was so powerful it unbalanced him and he fell sideways.

Her next blow would finish him unless, as was possible, he surprised her with some maneuver. But one of the peasant women intervened by shouting, "Tomoe! Desist!"

A peasant could not command a samurai, yet Tomoe turned slowly, her dark eyes settling on the younger of the two women in rags.

"Tomoe!" she said. "Who is your master!"

Throughout the past month, Tomoe had operated under the supposition that she was a masterless samurai, without allegiances. But the voice reminded her of a day in a garden, a day which now seemed lives ago, when she was glad to be tricked into making an oath. Tomoe replied, "Whoever else I serve, I also serve Toshima."

Toshima said, "Then go from this field now, Tomoe. Go into the hills and meditate on what you have done this day and for many days before this one."

Goro Maki regained his feet and, protecting Toshima and her mother, led the disguised women away from the battlefield. It was doubtlessly Lord Shigeno's last command to his vassals, that his family be removed from the valley if the battle went badly or threatened the mansion.

Tomoe blinked her eyes, and the blackness of them became a cloudy grey. She was somehow isolated on a knoll amidst the field of combat, able to see that five distinct encounters were spread across the center of the valley. From her vantage point, she could see the inevitable outcome far better than the combatants. She blinked her eyes again, and the whites reappeared around each iris.

Tomoe Gozen was shaken by what she beheld, and by what she remembered. She scanned the scene, looking for Ushii, but he was not presently where she could see him. Poor Ushii! For love of a comrade he had risked face and sanity, and lost both! And until this moment, she had not cared. What could this say of her own face? Of her own honor? She had behaved as a masterless samurai, an unrestrained *ronin,* without loyalties; she had slain Lord Shigeno as heartlessly as Ushii killed Madoka—yet, all the while, she *had* had a master and had forgotten.

She had broken faith with her bushido; and if she could not regain it in some other way, there was only the knife strapped to her thigh…

In the east burned Shojiro Shigeno's mansion. To the west, an edge in sight, was the unharmed palace of Huan, sorcerer of Ho. On three sides of her, battles raged without grace. North into the hills was the only direction by which a coward, or the disillusioned, might flee. There, a tall, narrow waterfall shone in the afternoon sun, its beauty inviting.

For the first time in her career, at the command of her master, Tomoe Gozen left a battle not yet done.

Behind the waterfall was a small cavern. In the darkness of this place Tomoe Gozen sat with legs crossed, meditating on her late behavior. The sheet of water plunged before her like a supernatural deluge, the roar of its descent drowning the sound of distant battle, lending to her sense of oblivion. The fall was a living, diamond window distorting her view of trees and smooth boulders, so that it seemed she looked out onto an alien landscape, looked out from a hellish dark place into a lit paradise.

She ached to leap through that window, which would part for her passage—to find herself truly in another world, a world where Tomoe Gozen had never lived, had never dishonored herself, had neither slain the great man Shojiro Shigeno, nor helped Ushii Yakushiji become a hunched and haggard spirit within a samurai's strong body.

Had she never lived, perhaps the sorcerer Huan would not have seen to the destruction of Naipon's mightiest warlords. Without Tomoe Gozen, a ghoulish army might not have been victorious and prepared to march further, as Huan had promised, unto the Imperial City itself.

Her mind's eye envisioned thousands of samurai in the valley, strewn about the land with heads and teeth and faces bashed in by crude stone weapons. The eerie victors feasted. They picked amidst the dead for clothing. They replaced their own severed parts with pieces from samurai. Perhaps Lord Shigeno's own head had been torn from the shoulders of his corpse, and now kept the company of the two-headed monster. Perhaps the beast had eventually lost both heads, and found not only the head of Shigeno to place upon its shoulders, but also the head of the warlord's horse.

Tomoe shook with horror, shook the vision from her brain. All that she had failed to experience this past month flooded over her in waves more torrential than the plunging falls, and she quaked beneath the weight of those memories.

The warrior rose from her seated, meditative position, then lowered herself ceremoniously to the floor of the little cavern on her knees. She seized the knife strapped to her thigh, removed the sheath and placed it behind herself, and used the strap to bind her legs lest her corpse be found in a compromised position. Carefully, expression firm, she placed the sharp point of the weapon to the vein in her neck.

She did not regret this act, only the acts that had led to this last. It was the prerogative of samurai to regain honor through suicide. Her spirit would be pure again, ready for another and possibly better life.

The rustle of heavy robes stayed her hand a moment. There was someone else in the darkness of the fall's cavern. Tomoe looked around, to find who invaded her sanctuary, who intruded upon the private ceremony of self-inflicted death.

In the shadow stood one of the magician-ninja, though Tomoe could not fathom how the jono priestess had come without a sound.

The eyes of the priestess glinted in the dark, burned Tomoe's agonized spirit. She moved from the shadow, making herself into a silhouette against the wall of glistening water. She spoke to Tomoe, and in spite of the roaring of the falls, her voice echoed through the chamber with clarity, sounding somehow as from another place in time:

"Jigai is not your destiny, Tomoe Gozen." The jono raised her hand; the blade flew from Tomoe's grip and broke against the inner wall of the cave although the steel was tempered. Another pass of the slender hand, and the strap around Tomoe's legs burst like ragged yarn. The magician-ninja said, "Do not think that your honor can be restored by fleeing from this life, your tasks left half undone. It may be the way of the samurai, but not of Tomoe Gozen."

The warrior remained on her knees, anger rushing to blooden her features. She said to this intruder, "Tomoe Gozen *is* samurai." She did not like jono any more than she did a common, skulking ninja. Priest or otherwise, they had the same origin—children of dainty, flying ogres some believed. The original cult had arisen centuries before, and was not originally comprised of sorcerers. It had begun as a formalized society of spies—wily, but having no genuinely magic powers. Their group gained status through extortion and terrorism. When their family of spies made occult discoveries and added actual magic to their trade, there was a revolution among all the ninja clans; although revolution among spies was not visible to the world at large. Afterward, the ordinary agents maintained their furtive ways, and the jono elite raised shrines to their ambiguous faith. The honor of jono was said to be as sacrosanct as that of samurai. Still, they were sly.

The magician-ninja's eyes glistened like the wall of water behind her. Tomoe imagined that the mysterious woman grimaced behind her wrappings, perhaps guessing Tomoe's hateful thoughts.

"You are samurai," the priestess said, as though it were a grave concession. "But jigai is not your prerogative. You cannot regain honor in this fashion, for no master has given you permission, and you have tests before you. I do not threaten, but warn: If you die for seeking honor, you will search in hell and never find it."

The arrogance of the magician-ninja roiled Tomoe's blood, for she knew the prerogatives of samurai far better than this descendant of spies who sniggered in darkness and spread the most terrible secrets of others while guarding their own like treasures. Tomoe sprung to her feet, swords drawn in an instant, and slashed twice at the jono priestess, the dark Shinto warrior. But the jono was intangible as smoke, as an eclipse. Tomoe's swords struck behind the magician-ninja, finding no flesh or bone.

The word of a magician-ninja had no meaning to Tomoe. She crossed both swords against the back of her neck, prepared to pull the blades with enough force to behead herself.

"Do not! I beg you. Set aside your resolve."

Arrogance was gone from the posture of the magician-ninja. She fell upon her knees, the grey robes flowing around her, her head bowed as if to honor or to yield. She said, "The only possessions of the ninja *or* the jono are our names and our faces."

She looked up at Tomoe, and fingered at the cloth covering her face, pulling it down. Tomoe gazed upon beauty unlike any she had ever seen, like the very face of Amaterasu, blinding in its bright perfection. Tomoe averted her eyes and gasped, and the magician-ninja said, "My name...my name...is Noyimo."

Then the bright lady cloaked in darkness was gone, leaving Tomoe seared and cleansed of guilt, empty of all but the memory of a face. She sheathed her swords, and walked into the light. The wall of water cooled her of the remembered fire of Noyimo.

🔱 🔱 🔱

In the valley, a few hundred persistent samurai fought without hope. The last of the united clans might not fall until the sun was nearly down, but Tomoe saw no reason to rejoin the battle. She felt helpless in the face of Huan's magic. It was hard to know what direction to turn. She did not want to think, to question, to look ahead in time. These were not a samurai's duties. A samurai was meant to serve; and Tomoe's master was Toshima. "I will find Toshima and beg instruction!" she told herself, and considered the route by which Goro Maki led Shigeno's wife and daughter to safety.

Tomoe's plan was predictable, and someone had foreseen it. An unexpected adversary strode the path from beyond the valley.

"I have come for you, Tomoe Gozen," he said. "I am sent to deliver the Mikado's justice."

The magnificent warrior's armor was studded with emeralds and rubies, his helm rimmed with diamonds. The wood of it was lacquered in rich colors, so that he seemed to be clad in enamel, shiny like a beetle's shell, strong like a turtle's carapace. The glitter of the warrior was dazzling and Tomoe wondered what famous, rich family this noble samurai represented.

"A grudge match?" Tomoe asked. "Who bears me animosity?"

"Not a grudge match, Tomoe Gozen. You will know me by my name: Ugo Mohri."

Tomoe started, and moved back. She said it aloud: "The Mikado's executioner."

He came at her. An honorable act would be to bow and accept the killing punishment; but the magician-ninja had said there would be *no* honor if Tomoe died with tasks undone. She fled up the path, toward the waterfall. Like a frightened animal she hopped away, seeking some hole in which to hide. She would have slunk to some distant sanctuary and stayed there, but she was quickly backed against the sheer cliff from which the waters poured.

Fear upon her face, Tomoe scrabbled up the stone wall, a surprising feat, and clung there, high enough that the executioner's blade could not reach her. In all her life, she had never met her match in swordplay; but Ugo Mohri was already a legendary figure, and even were he not, could any lower samurai think to defeat the Mikado's executioner?

She was not surprised that her execution day should come. The past weeks had found her in dubious occupations; and although a generous judge might find her behavior in accordance with the bushido in spite of Lord Huan's manipulation of her strength, deeper seeds had been sown for the harvesting of her head. Once, and not so long ago, a prince had come to Tomoe and entrusted her with an important mission. She was to travel to the Celestial Kingdoms and seek out a renegade swordsmith from Naipon. It had been a successful venture, and she had performed all but one part of the Mikado's will, as outlined by the prince. Against what she was bidden, she had saved two of the slain smith's finest swords, neglectful of the command to destroy them all.

The mission in Ho had changed her in many ways, she knew. She combined samurai training with mainland ki'ung fu. No school taught her unique style, and none would do so unless Tomoe herself became a master of a school, and even then it might prove difficult to acquire students. None emulated her, for there were those who whispered, "The style of Tomoe Gozen is an evil style." Yet Tomoe was perfectly committed to the seven virtues and all the tenets of bushido, so that none dared say she was renegade, for she was not. Even to insult her methods led inevitably to a fight to preserve face, a fight without quarter, and thereby death came to Tomoe's detractors. Those deaths upheld her honor, and the honor of her style, so that she continued to fight with two swords. All the same, Tomoe knew she would be forgiven less easily if she ever strayed from the Way, for not all samurai were devoid of jealousy, and some would declare her a malignancy if given the opportunity.

The last month had given detractors ample opportunity.

But Tomoe was not for a moment convinced that her enemies were motivated as much by truth as jealousy. She perceived how the things she had learned during her campaign in Ho had made her mightier. The ill words of her enemies reached the Mikado, that was clear, and although the Mikado was all-wise, she would not believe her style corrupt.

"I am guiltless!" cried Tomoe from her perch. Her hand clutched a slender root, so that she was in a most precarious state. Ugo's longsword wavered hypnotically, waiting for her to fall.

"There are those who say," Ugo Mohri began, "that Tomoe Gozen does indeed have two souls—her own, and that of Jingo the ancient amazon. Therefore fate necessitates that she wield two swords in order to bear the burden of her mightiness. A wonderful story!"

He laughed at her.

The root to which she clung tore a little ways from the cliff, and Tomoe raised her feet lest the executioner cut her tendons.

"You think you have doubled the might of your spirit, but you have only cut it in half." To punctuate the statement, he swung his gleaming blade. "You think the philosophy of Ho has strengthened you, but it has not."

"No one has bested me!" she said, the boast sounding silly given her position.

"Come down to me and duel."

As if by his command, the root broke in her grip. He stepped aside to let her land safely. Her swords flashed to her hands before she had struck the ground.

In a swift flurry of motion, she strove in a murderous fashion, but Ugo Mohri evaded her cuts, and laughed at her again. His sword moved only once, effectively slicing the armor of her shoulder so that it hung loose.

"Your soul is divided, not doubled," he said again. "You still have one soul, but it has become like the eyes of a bird. I can approach you through the middle. You cannot see me."

It was infuriating that he should lecture her, like her master of the samurai school. Another flurry of assaults met no result, and the woman shouted angrily, "No one defeats Tomoe Gozen!"

Ugo replied, "Ugo Mohri defeats Tomoe Gozen."

Proud of the synthesis of sword maneuvers she had devised and practiced, Tomoe could not believe hers was an evil style. The honor of her weapons was at stake, and she fought with intense ferocity, the while saying, "You too have two swords! I see one sheathed across your back!"

"I have never drawn that one," he said cryptically, and his one sword slipped toward her, cutting her waist-guard so that it flopped loose.

"You were soiled by your mission in the Celestial Kingdoms," said Ugo. "You went away with the balance of a samurai, strong like a tower. You returned with the balance of a scale. What becomes of the scale that loses one dish? It falls! It is not samurai."

"I am samurai!"

"In the name of honor, you have slain many to uphold that status. But could the sorcerer of Ho have contained a true samurai for the span of a month? You bear steel wrought on foreign land. It binds you to that land."

"These were wrought by a Naiponese smith!" she shouted, shaking her swords in feeble threat.

"Who conspired against his country!" The executioner was wise, and angry. "Your mission was to kill him and destroy his offensive weapons. You disobeyed, so great was your attraction for the alien blades. The glamour began then, the glamour which Huan magnified to hold you. With a proper soul, you could not have been so captivated. With a proper sword, even the Mikado's executioner could not laugh at you."

They had stood each other off a while, glowering, Ugo's footwork and eyes a perfect lesson in watchful balance. He held his sword firmly in two hands, out to his left with point up, and scooted the left foot nearer Tomoe, daring her to challenge. She held one of her swords over head, the other straight out from her side.

They clashed, fell away, clashed again, then stood like frozen dancers back to back. Ugo's sword moved under his arm to reach behind, but Tomoe had leapt forward to evade the point, and turned to face Ugo once more. He turned slowly, with absolute precision, and held his sword straight above his head as if to condemn Tomoe's two-sword style by his singular upright stance.

His certainty burned at her, and she knew she must defeat that self-assurance which marked Ugo's face with serene pride. Even if they must die together, at least she would not die alone. So without regard for her own life, Tomoe Gozen screamed in rage and moved violently to the kill.

Although she moved with the swiftest grace, it seemed that all occurred at a slower pace, giving her ample opportunity to observe every motion and counter-motion. She held Ugo in her sight, but for the briefest instance it seemed that he had winked out of existence, passing as he did through some blind spot in her vision. When he reappeared, she knew that her onslaught would fail its mark and his would not. She raised her swords, crossed to fashion an X, and caught a blow which otherwise would have carved her in twain. The power of the executioner forced her to one knee. She grimaced, tried to push his one sword upward with her two so that she could stand. Sweat broke across her brow, but the bejeweled Ugo could not be budged, and more, he seemed wholly unstressed.

He spoke down to her without strain, "I can spare you, Tomoe Gozen. I am told that if you throw down your swords, and return to the one Way of the Warrior, I am to set you free."

Through clenched teeth she demanded to know, "How can I be a warrior without my swords?"

He leapt back so quickly that she almost fell forward, and certainly in that moment he could have beheaded her had he chosen. He sheathed his sword with care, and removed the scabbarded blade from his back, saying, "You shall have another sword."

She looked at him with scorn.

"A sword made properly for a samurai."

Still, Tomoe sneered.

Ugo said, "Only one hand has drawn this sword since Okio, Master Smith of the Imperial City, placed it in its sheath."

"Whose hand has drawn that sword?" Tomoe asked, half in contempt, half in curiosity.

"No hand that soils the soul," said Ugo. "It has the blessing of the Mikado, who says Tomoe Gozen will be his samurai if she throws down forbidden weapons and takes up this. You will never see the Mikado, but you will serve him with vigilance and loyalty."

Tomoe's face flushed, and she spoke with anger, "I have always served him through the warlords. All samurai are his servants."

"That is both more true, and less true, than you may understand. Already you have served the Mikado better than other samurai."

"Eh?" She cocked an ear, interest gathered.

"Far more. You are too far from the center of Naipon's intrigues to realize the levels of internal conflict. The Shogun vies for the Mikado's power…"

"That is not so!" She could not believe such treason of the highest personage of samurai caste.

Ugo threw the undrawn sword with its sheath upon the ground, and half-drew his own. "It is so! If twice you call me a liar, I will kill you for my honor and for nothing else! The Shogun undermines the Mikado, would reduce him to an honored figurehead. But without faithful warlords and fighting samurai, the Shogun cannot prevail. Today, you helped weaken the Shogun by more than eight thousand of those samurai who were swayed to his will, reducing four powerful clans to a few dozen ruined members."

This made awful sense to Tomoe, and she said, "This is why the Mikado treatied the sorcerer Huan! So that samurai would die!"

The executioner did not reply.

Tomoe rose from her knee, her two swords still in hand. "If the

Mikado kills samurai, how can I hold faith in him? How can I throw down two good swords for one untried?"

Her words were blasphemy and treason, for Huan had filled her mind with heretical notions: the Way of the Warrior was not for the honor of samurai, but for the power of whoever would rule, whether it be Shogun or Amaterasu's godling child.

"This is your choice," said Ugo, and drew his sword full length. He held it upward and to one side, and slid nearer the two-sworded woman.

Anger was intense within Tomoe, but she knew that this was true: the Mikado was Naipon, the supreme ancestor incarnated. Whatever Tomoe did in her life, she did it for Naipon the Eternal Isles, and thereby for the Mikado. Even if bushido were a lie, still must she serve the living flesh of Naipon. Even if a Shogun stole power from a Mikado, still must that Shogun use the stolen power to serve Naipon's highest personage.

She threw down her swords, waited to see if the executioner would still kill her.

Ugo's sword re-entered its scabbard, and he stood impassively, watching. Tomoe picked up the new sword, judged it by its scabbard, drew it and weighed it in her hand, then sheathed it once again.

"You will not feel your prowess for a while," Ugo said, "for you have incorporated much of Ho into your fighting style—ki'ung fu instead of jujitsu, two butterfly-longswords instead of one daito. But when you regain all of your samurai spirit, you will reclaim your previous strength, and more. Until then, you may think you have tied your limbs, for the forbidden style has become a part of you and will beckon exercise, will tempt you with its seeming merits. Never trust it! Never weaken. Never use it again! You will discover that skills born of Naipon are the best borne by samurai."

She did indeed feel unbalanced as she discarded two scabbards and placed one new one at her side. But it was a disorientation she knew would pass with time, once she learned again to find balance at her center rather than at the width of her arms.

"Your honor can be saved by one deed," Ugo began. "Now that you bear a weapon forged, tempered and blessed in Naipon, the sorcerer of Ho will have no more control over your mind. Huan has served the Mikado unbeknownst, but now will be a threat unless you intervene. No one but you can walk unhindered through the walls of sorcery he has woven about his palace."

"I am not the only one," Tomoe amended. "Ushii too has free movement through Lord Huan's palace." Yet she knew Ushii had sworn fealty and could not strike Huan. Tomoe alone was free to act.

"Ushii has another task," said the executioner. "There is still the army of monsters, brought through a door Ushii was tricked into carving to save you from hell. The magician-ninja have said only Ushii can stay the ghouls from their march to the Imperial City. Even if they stray from that course at the moment of Huan's death, they would yet bring wrack and terror to Naipon if left to haunt the living earth."

Tomoe felt responsibility for Ushii's madness, at least in portion, and she hated to see him ill-used now. She asked,

"How can it be that Ushii can accomplish this alone?"

"You will see. You must return to Huan's mansion by route of the battlefield. The battle will be over. Dally if you will, and see the deed Ushii will perform."

"Will this deed cleanse his burdened soul?" she asked.

"He has sheathed his sword in the blood of madness. He will never be whole. Yet if he succeeds at this last important task, Ushii Yakushiji will be recorded upon the Tablets of the Samurai as a most honored and honorable servant of the Mikado."

Tomoe bowed, feeling sorrow but also satisfaction, as well as relief that she could feel at all. Quickly, she started back into the valley.

The executioner called out to her once, and she turned to see him beneath the evening's rainbow of the high falls, the colors of which his own gaudy armor rivaled. "When your strength is centered, Tomoe Gozen, it would be interesting to be sent to you again. I am not certain I would like that day."

The ghouls busied themselves feasting. Beneath the pending, brooding dusk, Ushii fought unaided. He strove without thought or impression, his long shadow darker than all others. His sword worked alone, his body its extension. There was scarcely any balance remaining to his fighting style, the lasting day of battle having left him worn and tired, though maniacal and unrelenting. Yet there remained a kind of grace in the awkward manner by which he stumbled, jerked, and spun around. On every side of him, death was his guard.

When the last fingers of the Shining Goddess played gently over the field, there were but five samurai left of the eight thousand. They surrounded their one mad opponent. The sword of Ushii Yakushiji raced upward in a shower of blood, felling one. It bore left to sever the top half of another samurai's head, that warrior's brain tumbling to the ground with is body left standing. The sword slashed downward at a new attacker, splitting nose and teeth so that the stricken samurai staggered back and fell. It reached behind to stick into ribs, then wrenched loose to swing freely across the front of the last man's stomach, spilling intestines.

There were no more comers, but Ushii could not see this through the red haze of his bloodlust. He fought on, repeating his last maneuvers: the crimson-stained sword slashed upward, bore left, slashed down, reached behind and swung around—all through air, all to naught. He cut and lashed and endeavored to kill the ghost who haunted him, the ghost of Ushii Yakushiji as he once had been.

One magician-ninja appeared from amongst the corpses. Perhaps he had been lying down, pretending to be dead. He stood to bar Ushii's crazed passage, raising his arms so that the grey robes draped down. A brilliant light flashed between his hands, and Ushii threw an arm across his eyes to fend off blindness.

"Ushii Yakushiji," the Priest said, "I command you to be as you were before madness."

When Ushii lowered his arms from his face, he looked around at the eight thousand dead and the half-living travesties which fed. He covered his eyes again, and wept.

"My spell will not hold you long, so be heartened that you may soon again hide your sorrows behind a wall of insanity. I have come to tell you that Tomoe Gozen is free, and now you will do what you must do."

A second magician-ninja stepped out from behind the other, as though the first had multiplied himself, but his duplicate was a woman. She pointed to the ground near her feet and said, "Here, in ancient times, there was a well." Between the two magician-ninja the soil fell away to reveal a deep, black hole, perfectly round. "The well once gave fresh water, but became accursed so that it had to be hidden until this moment. Its waters had been siphoned into hell."

The priest said to Ushii, "Only you, Ushii Yakushiji, can deliver the monsters to their own land once more."

From his armor Ushii withdrew the corked vial, held it to the last moment of visible sun, Amaterasu-on-the-Mountain. "With this?" he half stated, a moving yellow light streaking his face. The holy man and woman nodded as one.

Ushii bit through the brown wax, pulled the cork with his teeth, and spilled the contents in his mouth. He knew the potion meant death, for Lord Huan intended it to be used only as the final resistance, should victory come to doubt. Victory was Huan's; Ushii's mission was fulfilled without this extra magic. And now that Ushii was rational, he knew that with or without fealty to Lord Huan, there could be no honor gained. If Tomoe were safe, he reasoned, then Ushii Yakushiji need concern himself no more with the honor of giri, or duty to his master. He could act instead upon the honor of his personal ninjo, the conscience which told him he must not do what Huan desired, but what the magician-ninja directed.

The two magician-ninja watched him, and they were his ninjo too; like spies, they always spoke truth, the truth that others would have unsaid. A jono priest or priestess sees through lies and illusion, through madness and sorrow. They saw to the heart of Ushii Yakushiji—and he would have been pleased to know they found something good there.

He felt the power of the fluid coursing through his veins almost before it was swallowed. The jono priest took the empty vial and put it in his robe, perhaps intending to study the traces. Ushii experienced a peculiar sensation of strength building, felt it tense and then relax his every bone and muscle. He looked at his hands and his sword, to see how much he had changed.

He turned to walk among the carrion and its eaters, making hoarse commands in a guttural, homely speech. The ghouls bowed to him as though he were a devil-god, and most of them obeyed, for he was bright and golden.

This is all that Tomoe saw:

The same golden warrior who had drawn Tomoe from hell presently walked beneath a sky of pink fading into bronze. He herded the ghouls as if they were strange, clumsy geese and he their holy gooseherd. He waved his shining sword like a gooseherd's flag, and the ghouls were urged toward a hole which looked like the blackest shadow of night without stars, without hope of morning.

One by one, they slunk into this hole, but not without protest. They pleaded and whined in their most awful manner, groveling at the feet of

Ushii the Golden. Some of them were violent.

The golden warrior swept them onward, and down. He cut them when he must, and they gathered up their parts to continue on.

There strode the two-headed monster, and one of its heads was that of Shojiro Shigeno as Tomoe had envisioned in the cave—though the other head was not his horse, as Tomoe had embellished. Ushii's sword barely touched the neck of this stolen head, and there was a look of gratitude on the face of Lord Shigeno when his head fell away and was left behind.

It looked to be arduous work, to get them all, but none could escape because Ushii could be anywhere in an instant and move them back toward the hole. Some of them were bitter and angry, for they had fought their best, and deserved a rich reward. They growled and champed and tried to fight the golden warrior. One of them grabbed a section of armor and broke its leather thongs so that the armpiece came away in the monster's twisted hands. Another pulled at Ushii's legs and managed to remove another segment of armor, while Ushii walked unhindered, dragging the ghoul nearer to its doom.

Although they worried him as dogs do bones, shining Ushii looked to be without concern. He could not be taken by the ghouls. Yet each time one of them touched him, or tore away a piece of his armor, the glistening golden color of Ushii Yakushiji dimmed a little bit.

The ghouls took what spoils they could. Their own weapons had turned back to stones, but they carried off steel swords, those who had hands designed to hold them. Some of them took jackets and other clothes, which ill-fitted their homely bodies. One gathered the ponytails of samurai until Ushii caught the beast and made it throw the prizes down.

Their numbers dwindled, as they screeched and cried and rushed before the sword, down into the hole, seeping like water into the earth. There was one who wailed pitifully, but was a trickster who leapt upon the warrior's front and ripped away the armor and underclothing in its desire to tear Ushii's heart. The strong and muscular chest which had been exposed was somehow impervious to the claws, and Ushii pushed the monster away without effort. It scrabbled toward the hole, kicked in the behind by its golden master.

The strongest were the last to go, and these jumped up and down and whooped and complained, refusing to be herded into the deep earth. Ushii fought them. They could not bear the light of him, and so could not look at him long enough to win a score. They threw rocks at him, rocks which had once been weaponry, and where these struck, small dark bruises erased the gold. Still Ushii did not reveal any weakening. He offered no quarter, this marred but golden man, fading by slow stages but still glimmering in the falling darkness. He was merciless and compelling. His once faithful army struggled to the last, but in the end made every concession.

The magician-ninja had not remained. Tomoe had not seen them go, neither their method nor direction. At the last, no ghoul stood on the darkened field of death. There was only Ushii, all his armor torn away and his garments shredded, the gold gone from his body. A thin moon was rising, dimly cloaking the scene with pale, white death. Ushii was pallid as a wraith, naked but for his sword.

From her distant vantage point, it looked to Tomoe as though Ushii were hunching down into madness, his arms akimbo and his head twisted in a strange way. He looked about with one eye fused shut. He did not see her on the nighted hillside away from the moon's faint light, though he scrutinized the entire valley of dead samurai.

With a final victory-whoop, the deformed and maddened Ushii threw his soul into the well and leapt in after. The well closed behind him, and Tomoe Gozen gaped in horror.

๖ ๖ ๖

She had lived within these dreary rooms longer than a month and never noticed the pall which hung about.

Musty arras lined the hall. Grim, alien deities made of black jade glowered with ruby eyes, sitting in nooks wherever the arras were broken. The cells to either side were dark like caverns, or poorly lit by squat, round candles. The place felt haunted, especially now with the servants fled and no one left to deflect the lingering odor of sorcery.

Tomoe walked this gloomy hall to its end, hearing nothing alive in the few cells she passed. At the end, she lingered and gazed. There was a large room, with it relief ceiling depicting the invented deeds of Huan, heroic fictions which tickled his delight. There were thick carpets and tapestries which absorbed all sound, within or without. This utterly silent place was at once familiar and not—for Tomoe had been here many times, and yet never seen it with clear eyes.

Against one wall was a seat too large to use in comfort, but ornately beautiful, made of carved jade and craftworked gold. In the throne sat

the sorcerer of the Celestial Kingdoms, shriveled in his clothing. A single, serpentine trail of smoke rose from the brazier before him.

Even with this one inhabitant, the chamber gave the impression of emptiness, a feeling of spacious, even eternal desolation.

Huan was locked in a draining trance, breathing slowly, deeply, weakened by the long day of war regardless of the fact that he had not physically moved. He smiled in his slumber, dreaming his dreams of conquest, of power, cloaked in the silvery shadow of these dreams.

The samurai approached the sorcerer. He did not stir. From the tapestries, carpets and relief ceiling, protective spells licked out and tasted Tomoe Gozen, recognized her flavor, let her be. She gathered the old man up in her arms; he was as long-boned and light as a stork. As she had done many times, she carried Huan to his private cell. There she laid him with tenderness upon the narrow couch. His eyes opened the slightest crack, the pupils large and mismatched. He looked at her with childlike trust, the trust of a baby for its most precious and familiar toy. He closed his eyes again.

If he thought of anything at all, aside from the dreams of his vanity's sake, he must have thought the woman was there to guard him through the trio of nights it would take to regain his strength.

She pitied him, this man of sorcery, who sought to grasp all the world like a ripe peach. He thought himself mighty, but had been manipulated by a greater power like nothing more than a black stone sitting on a gaming board. The stone was moved against the Shogun, never comprehending its place.

In Huan's present dream, he might envision himself disposing of the Mikado. From the Imperial Palace in Kyoto he could reach across the Sea of Naipon to harry the coast of Ho, tearing it like a jackal and depleting all Naipon's resources to reduce the Celestial Kingdoms, ultimately, to gigantic provinces of a comparatively tiny island empire.

Dream of your mightiness and of undefeated sorcery, thought Tomoe. *Dream of your immortal dynasty. Sleep without worry, poor Lord Huan, O sad and evil man. Dream of a puppet warrior at your side when you return to your land in a chariot of gold and iron, conqueror of Naipon and Ho.*

He snuggled against the couch and sighed, sounding as he often did like an old woman, looking to be no one's threat, unknowing that his sleep would soon be dreamless and final. His knees drew upward toward his stomach. His spidery, long-nailed hands folded near his throat.

Tomoe's sword rose above her head, centered, poised, invisible in the dark.

Tendrils of sorcery stroked her, in no threatening way, but lovingly. This affection stilled her hands more certainly than would any effort to hold her back by force. The Lord Huan loved her in his selfish fashion, she knew; his magic could do her no harm, for all the terrible way in which he constructed it to keep others out.

If she could blame him entirely for Ushii's gruesome fate or for the slaughter of the clans, then his love would disgust her and her sword would fall with ease and pleasure. But the descendant of Shining Amaterasu was the master of this sport, safe in the Imperial City. Tomoe was not certain that the next stones swept from the board would not include herself, and she was full of blasphemous thoughts: she envisioned the Mikado sitting in his austere palace, child of Light in a darkling's habitat, plotting, conniving, striving to hold or regain power against the military government in Kamakura.

Yet must she maintain fealty with the Mikado, and pray that never again would her duty to a godling monarch conflict with her duty to the Shogun. Perhaps, after this performance, she could flee to the northernfrontier, and serve both governments equally by fighting the vicious Ainu who vainly, uselessly strove against Tomoe's dominant race. Perhaps she would retire from the world altogether, to become cloistered in some mountain place. Or she could throw down her sword to be a strolling nun.

Small as a babe seemed Huan, shrunken like a newborn, curled in upon himself as though the womb were a recent memory. Tomoe was merciful. One swift stroke, and the smiling face did not even move, though the head was completely severed. Still sleeping, dreams fading, Huan's heart pumped blood to soak into the couch and cover. The tendrils of magic faded like the dream; the haunting was over; and Tomoe Gozen was alone.

PART II

The Bakemono's Curse

Something tracked the wandering samurai, something or someone vigilant and unseen. Another might have thought it imagination, after turning many times and swiftly only to see nothing. But Tomoe was not given to gross imaginings. She knew that she was watched.

It began to rain toward evening, when she came to a farmhouse and knocked upon the door. A ragged family of five gathered in the entry and looked her up and down. She was clad well, was Tomoe, not having been on the road so long that her fine kimono and wide *hakama* trousers were tattered or badly soiled; neither were the bright patterns of the cloth yet faded by the sun nor hidden beneath the dust of travel. Samurai with pride intact were fastidious to a fault. Her longsword was held close to her loin by the narrow obi wrapped around her waist. Her big straw hat was lacquered black, and her face dark beneath it.

She was magnificent outside their door, she knew, for it reflected in their eyes.

The samurai stood against the last rays of daylight, an ominous presence, but she smiled at them, and it eased them, and pleased them, and the father said, "Enter, samurai. Enter and be our guest."

Pleasant cooking smells had wafted to her earlier, along the road. Within the plain but unsevere farmhouse, the scent of simple fare tempted and overwhelmed. It was a poor family, to be sure, and it would not be unfelt if they fed strangers; but the area had been neither used nor misused by lords or samurai, so this family thought of the higher classes with admiration rather than anxiety, and were honored to share what they had.

It was a meager meal, but one which Tomoe found completely and extremely adequate. She praised the mother and the daughter who had cooked it, but pleaded that she was full when they offered excessive portions. Tomoe had added her paltry share to the meal, in the form of dried fruit and pickled fish, which was all she had been eating on the road for many days. The pickles especially pleased the family, since this inland country had swamps instead of lakes or sea, and therefore a scarcity of wholesome fish.

Two of the three children were very young. They crawled in Tomoe's lap like kittens upon an amazing, patient wolf. Tomoe stroked these youngsters, and jabbered with them, until it was late and they climbed into a loft to pretend slumber and take careful peeks over the ledge. Tomoe sat with the parents and the oldest sister, listening more than speaking, but telling a little of her adventures when poked.

It was a gracious family, their etiquette somehow resounding with fewer falsehoods than the etiquette of richer households. The warmth of their fire and company calmed her, comforted her, for she had been lately missing comrades dead or far away, and the road had become a lonesome place to tread.

A few months earlier, she would never have supposed a peasant clan capable of filling such a void of friendship; but the road changed a samurai's perspective, causing sometimes a dangerous bitterness, and sometimes a deeper wisdom, but always disillusion. The family made her long for a simpler heritage—but her blood was samurai, and she was bound, if not to a master, then at least to her own line.

Yet even the friendship was illusion. She was a stranger to these friendly folk, an awe-inspiring, transient guest—not kin, not even the same class.

The eldest daughter looked at Tomoe with admiration near unto worship. At an appropriate point of conversation, and at her proud father's insistent prodding, the girl brought forth (with much blushing and seeming reluctance) a fine heirloom halberd. It was a common weapon among girls and women, one which could dismount a warrior entirely, and often best a sword. The daughter held it with care, and had clearly learned from some nearby temple to wield it with skill.

After a while, the eldest daughter went off to her quarter of the floor and rolled out her mat to sleep. The old father continued to ply Tomoe for more words, and the complacent mother listened and smiled. The daughter, like the younger ones, feigned sleep, though the younger ones had by then given in to weariness. At present, only the eldest among the children secretly listened; and later, perhaps, she dreamed of her halberd or a sword.

Few samurai came to these parts, unless rich ones who passed quickly without greeting, with their masters or without, never lingering in the poor land, deigning only occasionally to throw some low-value coin to whatever bold child or admiring adult stood watching from well off the road. Tomoe's willingness to sit with peasants charmed them, boosted their esteem for themselves and for her, although she was virtually a beggar (which they did not notice).

The fire was left to die low; the rain was a pleasant drumming on the roof; and Tomoe was wishing to be given over to sleep. She was about to hint at this desire, when there came a knock upon the door. The mother scurried to the rap, and slid the door aside. Tomoe and the husband looked on, wondering who would come at such an hour.

There against the rainy night was a dark and dirty itinerant priest, a *rokubu* with a bulky wooden Buddha tied by its neck and slung upon his back. The priest was stooped beneath this burden, and looked to have been through many provinces never once setting it down. It was very nearly a part of him, was the Buddha, akin to the bent spine of a hunchback.

The rokubu was homely, unbathed, and disturbing. For all his travel, he was overweight. His yellow robe was turned brown by its accumulation of soil. One of his hands clutched the end of the cord which held the Buddha by the throat and over his back, while the other hand was thrust forward like the beggar all rokubu were—a less esteemed and less appreciated beggar than Tomoe Gozen.

This was a land of uncomplicated people, faithful to the Shinto deities, little concerned with the confounding methods of Buddhists. In fact, the husband did not much like even clean Buddhists, although the mother took some pity and was inclined to share some scrap.

Tomoe was unsettled by the priest's sharp eyes, which scanned the interior of the rude farmhouse and lingered a moment, without surprise, upon the samurai.

To save the husband and wife from further argument or depletion of their small resources, Tomoe withdrew one small, oblong coin of silver and tossed it. The priest's grubby hand scooped it neatly from the air, and, blessing the house in a hard voice, he turned his sharp eyes away and vanished into the wet night.

The next morning, the children saw the samurai off with a few cautious complaints, wishing she would stay, and she almost wished it as well. She lifted up the smaller ones and hugged them in her arms, then put them down and scooted them back toward the house. To the oldest daughter, Tomoe bowed slightly, one hand on her sword, which made the daughter swell with pride, this being the greeting or farewell for samurai and samurai, not samurai and peasant. Tomoe felt guilty immediately upon doing this, for the low-caste girl had the same duty to her birth that Tomoe had to hers, and the girl's bold imaginings ought not be cruelly encouraged.

The mother came up the path in a hurry, proffering Tomoe a bean-filled dumpling for the road—a costly treat for poor to offer. Tomoe in turn left them the remainder of her pickled fish. Then, waving to the husband in the doorway whose eyes were misty with a private musing, Tomoe was again upon her road.

The short time with this family had been like some purification rite. Tomoe felt as though she had left a clean, cooling brook in favor of a parched land—although the ground was still wet from the night's rainfall, outer reality denying the inner feel.

It was not long before she knew she was once again, or still, being followed. In truth, she had fancied eyes at the cracks of the farmhouse the whole night long. She no longer spun around to see who followed, for she knew that someone skilled in *inpo,* the art of hiding, would not in any case be seen. She grew more and more annoyed by the persistent audacity of her shadower, or shadowers (for she suspected more than one).

A goodly distance passed beneath her feet before the sun was very high. The land had dried out in the warm sun, but later became the dank edge of a swamp. The air became steamy by midday, awful to the smell. The road stayed reasonably dry—but on first one side and then both, frogs peeked from amidst reeds in the filthy water which bordered her path.

Further on, the ginkgo trees became dense, their leaves like fans, and even at high noon, the thickening swamp was somewhat darkened.

It was somewhere along this point that Tomoe became hotly annoyed, partly because the miserable humidity beneath the roof of trees had shortened her temper. She wheeled about to march the way she came, sporting a baleful expression. Several paces along, she stopped and called out, "Ninja! Slinking spy! Assassin! Face me with honor, or hunt elsewhere!"

There was no reply. If, as she suspected, ninja were on her trail, they could not be expected to answer a challenge like some honest samurai. The vile pursuer might at this moment be lying in the mud and filth of the swamp, covered over with green and slimy water, breathing through a hollow reed or even a sword's sheath. Or the wretched, furtive spy might be in some tree, invisible to the eye, disguised somehow as a branch—or else squeezed into a narrow badger hole, if there were any such pits unmolested by the marsh soup.

Yet, to her surprise, she *did* hear something, and it made her wonder between two things: was it a trap, or was it someone less skillful than a ninja who shadowed her?

She turned abruptly to the sound, and saw ripples of water rushing from the deeper gloom away from the road.

Tomoe hitched up her long garb and, kicking off her clogs, waded out toward the source of the persisting noise. The water was shallow and about the same temperature as urine, though purplish green instead of yellow. Her feet sank into the vilest ooze, in which things wriggled and might have attached themselves to her were she to stand in one place too long.

A little ways into the swamp, the ground raised to one side, a narrow dry path, and she climbed on this to follow toward the sound, which had grown quite loud. There was splashing and muffled snarling; then, abruptly, there was a watery clearing wherein Tomoe beheld a surprising activity.

There was a ninja all right, who had doubtless come into the swamp silent as a ghost so that Tomoe might never have been aware, except that the ninja had run straight into the snare of some other clever being: a bakemono—a species of ogre.

The ninja was hanging upside down from a strong vine, swinging a wicked barbed weapon at the snuffling ogre who danced around the roped prey, splashing and evading the swinging weapon, feinting with its own sharp claws. The ninja was clad in black shirt, trousers and hood; the ogre wore scales and slime.

Tomoe charged to the very edge of the dry path, stood with sword drawn, and cried out, "Ogre! Flee into your dark habitat lest Tomoe Gozen cut you up the spine!"

The ogre turned about, knee deep in water, and still tall. It had horny growths above its eyes and growing out of its cheeks, and knobby, nailed warts about its chin. Its mouth was too big on one side, stretching nearly to one pendulous ear, a trait rare even in this ugly race. Its arms were very long and thick, and its scaly skin was green and slimy like the algal swamp it lived within. It appeared to be sexless, but might have been male, its organs sheathed. The ogre replied in a harsh, awful voice, "I have caught the ninja fair and square. A rare catch! And I am proud! He is mine to rend and to eat."

Tomoe regarded the ogre casually, and said, "Still, I am today feeling chivalrous, and would like to save a ninja's life."

The ogre was upset. It knotted its huge, three-clawed fists, guarded its captive carefully, and spoke gutturally from its sideways mouth, "A curse will be put to you, samurai, if you cheat me of my dinner!"

"I do not fear the curse of a bakemono," said Tomoe with teasing humor in her tone. "The curses of your race are only good in swamps."

"All the same," argued the ogre, "there may come a time, when like today, you have call to enter some swamp or marshy land. I am a wandering ogre, as you are a wandering samurai, and we might chance to meet again in circumstances auspicious for me. Even if we never meet, my curse will hold in any swamp, at any time until fulfilled."

"Then curse me well, slimy beast, for you go hungry tonight."

Then Tomoe waded quickly into the mire and cut off the tail of the hastily departing ogre. It grabbed its bloodless behind and wailed at the loss of its bottom's brief extension, then turned around a safe distance away to level its curse:

"As I have been denied a tender feast, so shall you be denied some tender friend—for I know samurai value friends above dinners, as ogres value dinners above friends. In addition, for the loss of my tail, which is all we ogres prize as beautiful about ourselves, I curse you with an equal loss: the fairness of your face will learn a scar."

Although Tomoe was disconcerted by the curse, and knew she would be forever wary of swamps if she valued her visage or her friends, yet she laughed at the departing beast. She called it a fool and a coward, especially a fool, because curses could be equally cruel to the perpetrator of the malediction. She thought she heard it whisper, *yes, yes I am a fool and a coward,* but its tone inferred that Tomoe was, perhaps, something far worse, for her chivalry and boldness.

Before it was completely gone, it cried out unseen from some dark vantage point, more bitter than angry, "Samurai are snarling dogs! Ninja are monkeys in trees! The Shogun is a demon-boar, and the Mikado unfit for an ogre's pet! Human kind are less than bakemono!"

Its name-calling complete, the beast ran off, splashing.

Tomoe turned to the ninja who still hung in the tree like a big plum. He glared at the samurai, only his eyes visible from the tight-fitting hood. He still held the barbed instrument, with which he reached up to the vine and cut himself down. He went head-first into the foul water, and Tomoe laughed at that, waiting for the ninja to come up for air.

In a moment Tomoe grew wroth, for the clever ninja did not surface, but had fled unseen. She cried out, "It is true, then, ninja have no honor! You owe me your life and thereby fealty! Come out, shadow-man! Debase yourself before your new master!"

But there was no answer, and mocking all stupid samurai, Tomoe waded to the dry strip of land to make her way toward the road and better light. On the other side of a ginkgo tree, however, she was halted. The ninja was there, upon his knees, and he said, "In our way, we are an honorable caste. I owe fealty to another, but you may ask me one boon, and if it is in my power to give, I will repay my debt to you."

"Go and slay your master," she said.

"I would kill myself first," he answered, which she knew before she asked.

"Then, say who sends you."

"Another boon," he said. "Not that."

"You deny me twice? It must be this; I ask nothing else. It is no joy to be tracked by persistent ninja, who wait only to slay me in my sleep without ever telling me why they were sent. It is only proper that I know who despises me so greatly that they would wish me a dog's un-honored dying. So tell me who it is, then I shall let you go, or you shall cleverly evade me anyway, and I will wait for you to come again, knowing my true enemy by name."

"It dishonors me to tell you," he said. "But it dishonors me not to grant your boon. So you will know the Shogun and no other sends ninja to kill you, and you must know why, for I…"

Suddenly he lurched, and fell forward. As he was falling from knees to stomach, his hands went to his face. His hands bore knives strapped to his fingernails. He tore off his mask, the flesh of his whole face as well, his identity thereby and forever sealed. He lay dead, with a dart in the small of his neck.

Tomoe had leapt to one side the moment she heard the dart in the air, thinking it an arrow or shuriken intended for her. She crouched, and looked into the trees all around. Leaves waved through narrow shafts of sunlight. Many shadows moved. She saw nothing, no one, no other ninja.

Which was more disconcerting, she did not know: that ninja killed each other for the smallest treason, or that the Shogun thought Tomoe Gozen merited the unheralded death of a dog.

Later, on the road, she sensed no presence behind her. Perhaps her destination was so obvious, there being so few towns along this road, that the ninja who had killed his partner thought it a more clever ruse to wait for her ahead rather than follow behind. In any event, even if she saw to the death of one of them, or a great many, there would be no stopping them, and eventually she would not be quick enough, or alert enough, and the ninja would have succeeded in their chore—to the regret of Tomoe Gozen.

In time, Tomoe forgot the curse of the bakemono. How so is hard to say; curses, being the dreadful things they are, are not to be dismissed. But after trampling up from hell, surviving the lick of lightning, fighting amongst demons from the under earth—one bakemono more or less could provide, by contrast, only the most piddling of adventure, hardly worth recall.

It might also be that some vanity, some egocentricity, led Tomoe Gozen to reason how the deities of the upper, middle and lower earth gave less heed to the maledictions of ogres than of human kind. And too, through the many months of travel, Tomoe had beheld many wonders in rapid succession—a merchant's mountainous dromedary which spat acid at highway robbers; a strange, loathsome fish which crawled out of a lake at night and gobbled up the embers of a campfire; a fox which, startled, turned into a red thrush and flew into the sun; a rattling set of bones, anciently enclosed in an amber, translucent tomb; a dragon's scale cast by a magician into a bowl of water, turned into a goldfish for his little girl; and other such—so that she was jaded to the sights and experiences which blended one into the next, none recalled daily, some never jarred to memory at all. With all this, a feeble ogre's swearing was indeed very little.

Then again, throughout the many months, it must be noted that Tomoe—perhaps by coincidence, perhaps by subconscious design—never chanced to tread within a swamp, and made no friend but wandered all alone. It may be, therefore, that some erstwhile corner of her brain pondered and deemed credible the swamp-fiend's epithets. Too, her dreams might have been troubled by things her waking mind forbade to thought; but if so, even those dreadful dreams, themselves unremembered, became fewer and fewer until they bothered her no more.

Finally there was nothing in front or in back of her mind which attributed vitality to the promise of a friend's death or that her face would bear a scar.

Eventually it came to be that Tomoe was untroubled throughout, except by the loneliness of the road, and certain things of government she had learned in passing. And who remains to say, after everything is done, that Tomoe misplaced this memory because some meddling deity was seeing to the curse and wished to make Tomoe unawares.

The ninja, on the other hand, could not be forgotten, for they turned up in least expected moments, which paradoxically made them predictable. She had slain four of them in as many months, and had not been followed for a while, though she knew one of them would pick up her trail eventually. But she had grown blasé even about this, a game to her at last, and one she thought to win.

Deathly winter and bone-dry summer were parted, incongruously as always, by green, erotic spring. Spring gone, Tomoe walked along another dusty road, new and yet familiar; there were many like it. Her straw hat hung to her back, and the sun heated the back of her long, black hair, gathered in a low-fashioned ponytail. She could see a good way down the road, upon which walked but one besides herself.

At first she thought the other samurai was far away. There were only rice paddies, the farmhouses were set far off the road, and there were no trees—so she could not judge distance by perspective. It took a while to realize the individual she walked behind was not off in the distance; rather, he was close but very small.

It was a child so young he could not have been more than two years in military school. The likelihood that he was a runaway seemed, at the moment, remote, for the youngster walked with pride and dignity, as any samurai fully possessed of honor. Had he run off from a dojo, he should skulk in shame. His singular presence on the road, therefore, was a mystery.

As Tomoe closed upon him, by right of her longer stride, she noted that the boy's dress was very similar to her own, though more brightly colored. His hat was thrown back like hers. His hair was done up in a ponytail, sticking up in the manly fashion, and he carried a shortsword or long knife which, contrasted to his size, was not unlike the long daito worn by Tomoe. He was a samurai in every detail of appearance. Indeed, the differences between him and Tomoe were largely of size, at least to a casual observer.

He walked with one fist on his hip, and one arm swinging free, and there was purpose and direction to his gait.

When he placed his hat upon his head, Tomoe was reminded to do the same, lest her brain be cooked by the hot day. Revealed upon Tomoe's back was her family seal, embroidered as the only payment for a recent, brief employment. The round seal consisted of two violent, cresting waves facing each other, a hollow between. It was femininely phallic, as were many family seals.

On the back of the boychild's long shirt was a rooster, wings spread, its feet thrust to each side with claws, its tongue a lick of fire.

As she strode up from behind, she said, "Good day, samurai. My name is Tomoe Gozen of Heida."

He nodded curtly, hand to shortsword, and kept walking. He picked up his pace a bit so that the bigger samurai would not have to lessen hers so much. He introduced himself. "I am Yabushi'take Issun'-kamatoka of Ogmya village."

Tomoe was impressed, though she had not heard of the village. "That is a very large name for a very little samurai."

Yabushi'take Issun'kamatoka turned red with embarrassment, and reluctantly admitted, "Sometimes...I am called Little Bushi."

"Ah, good." Tomoe clapped her hands once, showing relief. "Well, Little Bushi, how have you come to this road?"

"I am 'soldier on the wave'," he said. "I am ronin."

Tomoe showed appropriate sadness. "Alas, I too am a masterless samurai, although I have found minor employment here and there in the past year. I see by our clothing that we have neither of us fared too badly, or perhaps we have not been masterless so long. I would be pleased to tell you my story."

Yabushi could not in politeness or in truth claim he did not wish to hear a story. Yet if he listened, it meant he would be bound to telling his own. After brief consideration, he said, "I would be pleased if you would share your tale."

Tomoe looked woebegone, and confessed, "It has not always been thus with me. Once I served a good master, and then I served one evil, and since them I have served only poor lords for short times and been more often than not upon the road. An important man told me I was the Mikado's own samurai, but I have heard nothing of it since, so I have not gained by the arrangement. Even a great lord could not walk into the Mikado's imperial temple and say, please, I beg instruction. Thus I have come upon hard times.

"Lately I hear rumors that the Shogun sends the most esteemed child of Amaterasu into exile, to an island in the Sea of Naipon, far from his supporters in Kyoto. This has boded ill for me, presumed retainer to the Mikado. I am, alas, hunted like a criminal by the Shogun's ninja agents, though he dares not have me challenged openly for I have not swerved from the Way."

The small samurai was both aghast and impressed by the story.

"The Shogun is an honorable man!" he half protested.

"We ronin learn all too soon," said Tomoe, as if they shared a dreadful secret, "that honor, like power, can be bought for gold, and held by intrigue. As ronin, we are lost of many samurai privileges; we are told we have less honor. But are we less proud than before, Little Bushi? Does Amaterasu shine less favorably upon our faces?" She closed her eyes and turned her face to the warmth of the sun.

Reflections such as these were call *kikenshiso,* doubts or dangerous thoughts. Yabushi was deeply affected, but somehow not appalled.

"Now," said Tomoe, looking upon him once more, "how do *you* come to this estate?"

"It is this way," he began, trying to be as dramatic as Tomoe had been, and looking very sad indeed. "Although mine is a proud family with a good heritage, we are very poor. It happened that there were many daughters. Thus one was sold to a house in Ikiki so that my dojo instructor could be paid for my training and my board. That was two years ago. I have striven everyday to learn everything extremely well, and fast. I have been a student without peer, for I do not want my sister's sacrifice to be without purpose.

"I remember that I loved her very much; and it is sorrowful to me that there is not much more than fondness I recall. I have noticed that the memory of the young is like the memory of the old, that is, I am afraid I do not remember my sister anymore, but the love I had for her remains like a lost butterfly searching for a flower which had been snipped or torn away. Although I am told there is no reason, I feel shame for the plight of my forgotten yet still loved sister. So I have taken my leave of the dojo and go now to redeem her from the house of servitude."

"And your dojo master was pleased to let you go?"

It took Little Bushi a few moments to gather the courage to reply. "It is only about now that he will have found out."

"Then…we are both hunted samurai."

He was undramatically ashamed. "That is so."

"But for a noble cause!" said Tomoe, cheering him up. "Except…how can you redeem your sister? What do you have to give?"

Little Bushi stopped walking. Tomoe took two steps more, then turned and looked at him. The small samurai reached inside his kimono and withdrew a scarf, its four ends tied around a bundle. He shook the scarf, and it rattled. "Two hundred ryo," he said.

This took Tomoe by surprise, and she drew herself up to reveal her amazement. "And how has the son of the poor Rooster clan come by this bundle of wealth?" She barely disguised her questionable feelings and suspicions.

"By honest means," he said indignantly, and drew himself up as she. He thrust the scarf of gold into its hiding place next to his heart, and marched past her. She joined him again, and he explained, "It was sent to me when my grandmother died earlier this month. She had secretly saved and hoarded through many years of labor. It was her last wish that these funds become my endowment, meant to keep me a landed lord in Ogmya village, once I returned from school. I have prayed to my grandmother who is now my most venerated ancestor, for guidance and forgiveness. I believe she understands and endorses what I must do. I will live as ronin instead of lord, but my sister will be free."

They walked together in silence a long while. Once they stopped so that both might pee, Yabushi against a tree, Tomoe squatting in a field. Later, they stopped to eat. Tomoe shared some bean curd which had been packed in a bamboo tube and kept in a small pouch with all her possessions. Yabushi shared his dried plums.

The road took them up a hill, where terraced paddies gave way to the woods. Near a place where the road split in two—the town of Ikiki to the left, some other town on the road that turned sharply right— Tomoe said, "Little Bushi, I think we should go in there." She pointed to the hollow of a living tree.

"Why so?" he asked. "There is yet a little light of day, and I will walk even in darkness to shorten my journey."

"But there are two who follow us, remaining always out of sight."

He whirled around, saw nothing. "You are certain?"

"They may be ninja tracking me, though I have heard them too often and think they must be less skilled shadows. Perhaps your dojo instructor missed you sooner than you thought."

They crouched in the tree's hollow, hidden by shade and gathering dusk. In a while, two rough men walked along the road and into view. Tomoe whispered to Yabushi, "You know them?"

He put his mouth to her ear and answered, "My instructor sends them after his worst students. He must be very disappointed in me to send such insults."

The insults stopped to rest, more because they did not wish to catch up with the child and his friend who they believed were still ahead.

"I overheard our master say," began one of the ruffians, "that the brat has a pouch of inherited gold. What do you think of that, Kobaro?"

The other man picked his dirty teeth with the point of his knife, and said, "I think we can say to our master, 'Poor Yabushi!, we found only this pricked corpse! A bandit must have killed him.'"

Yabushi almost ran out of the hollow tree in anger, his knife-sword drawn, but Tomoe caught his collar and made a sound for silence.

"What was that?"

The two were on guard now, and looked into the woods. They found a sign of passage, and realized their quarry had wandered off the road.

"Be careful, Kobaro! We do not know who that samurai is, who walks beside the brat."

Tomoe stepped out of the tree, like a spirit. Her sword carved down the first ruffian, while the other's eyes went large like eggs and he turned to run. Yabushi barred his path, but the ruffian was not impressed by such a tiny bundle of fierceness. He ran right on past Yabushi and had made it all the way to the road before realizing the child had cut him.

The ruffian put his hand against his bloody side, then looked back at the big and little samurai standing side by side in the woods, seeming supernatural in the gloom of early night. He collapsed and never moved.

Tomoe walked to the dead ruffian and sat upon his butt. From within her sleeve she withdrew a piece of rice paper, a brush, and an inkstone. With these she began to write small characters.

"What do you do?" asked Little Bushi.

"It says, 'Two bad men tried to kill Yabushi who is on an important mission. Yabushi will pray for their souls in his dojo when his mission is done.' There!" She stuck the note on the collar of the ruffian. "If your master is a good man—and I think he is despite who he employs, for he has trained you well—he will send no one for you anymore. He will know you will return."

Yabushi dropped to one knee, palm on hilt of sword and head bowed low. He said, "I am in your debt."

"We are bound by friendship, Little Bushi. No more. And now, I must take this other road, away from Ikiki. For you are no longer hunted, and I am—so my presence endangers you. Take care, my bold friend, and keep secret the gold."

Before he could protest, Tomoe Gozen had vanished around the corner where the second road forked. Crickets sang alongside the road. A solitary nightingale charmed the leaves still. Little Bushi stood unmoving.

Nearly a year on the road alone, Tomoe had grown accustomed to her singularity, and rarely mourned friendships. But the day spent with Yabushi reminded her of other times, better times, when friends were not so rare. When she left him—for the sake of his safety, not because she so preferred independence—depression closed upon her like a cold glove, more tangible than the night. Her feet felt as though they were dragging. Her shoulders weighed too much. Her head hung like a lantern on a pole.

A ways down the road, she came upon a shrine, and went inside to pray for Yabushi's protection, then slept out the night. The next morning she felt a little better, but not greatly so.

For three days she lingered at the shrine. It had been neglected, so she worked its weedy gardens between the torii gate and the small central temple, making the place more fit, pretending herself a farmer as she served the locality's Shinto deity. She was safe for this while, for even ninja would not defile a shrine with blood. But that was not what held her. For the first time in months of travel, it seemed to her that there was nothing on the road ahead which would be different from the road behind or from the place she stood. There was no reason to go on.

Yet there *was* a reason to go on, though not a spiritual reason. She had only been able to find a little to eat in the way of vegetable matter, and one tough hare which she prepared and ate away from the holiness of the shrine. Clearly she would become gaunt upon the spare diet. For the sake of her stomach, she left the shrine after the third day.

Before coming to a village, she stood outside two separate estates along the way. Both had once been rich, but no more. At each, she was told the land-owners had no need of retainers, which meant they could afford none, or else they recognized her as the survivor of Shigeno Valley and did not want her near. But they gave her small coins anyway and wished her fortune elsewhere.

When her year began, she had been too proud to accept coins without toil. But the year taught her the fine distinction between pride and stupidity.

When the village came into view, she stood a long while on the hillside trying to feel less gloomy. The dull quaintness of the farms around the village did not improve her mood. The village itself was more colorful than the norm, made transiently gaudy because there was a festival going on.

Lest someone recognize the crest sewn on her back, she removed her jacket and wore it inside out. She arrived amidst merriment insulting to her own dark mood. People looked at her, and thought she must be famous, or she would not be wearing her shirt as a sign of anonymity. They did not guess she stayed incognito because she was "an unfavored hero." People avoided her path, not so much from any feeling of fright, but because her dampened spirits might interfere with their holiday.

Everywhere there were colorful banners and tents and children running about screaming in groups with flags and paper toys. There were booths selling everything from swords to festival cakes. Games were being played: foot-races, archery, jujitsu. There were fortune tellers and gamblers respectively in small and large tents. The regular shops along the street had their fronts wide open, and the keepers with huge smiles leaned out windows.

There was all variety of music, and dance, and acrobats—and of special merit, a Noh play performed free by four masked actors on a platform. The play was a gift from some unnamed Lord, to the village people and all who visited. The story was "The First Buddhist Native Of Naipon And The Shinto Gods Who Punished Him." The theme was eerie and uncommon, less dull than Tomoe had found most such dramas, but more frightening too, so she did not watch much of it.

Over everything, there was a lot of noise.

"What holiday is this?" asked Tomoe of a passerby, for she was unfamiliar with the local patrons and deities.

The man stopped and bowed several times, saying, "The festival of Great Lord Walks." He scurried off before Tomoe could ask who this "great-lord-walks" might be or what it might mean.

Shinto and Buddhist priests nodded cordially to one another. Lords smiled at peasants. Children were allowed to ride on horses with samurai. The palms of beggars received liberal sprinkle, and teahouse girls were kind to poor farmers. There was a large pretense of prosperity, if not prosperity itself; and joy was all about.

Tomoe might have become infected with all this cheer, and ceased to be melancholy, except that the reminders of her plight were close. She caught a glimpse of a shadow moving along the roofs of shops and houses. Ninja were near.

She spotted another. It was as if they wanted her to see them, as if out of some respect they wished her to be aware that a showdown was pending. Certainly she had earned their respect, killing ninja before. Yet, they may have had other motives. They would know, by reports or fates of others, that she could hear shuriken spinning through air, that she could bat them from flight with the flat of her sword. But here, upon a crowded street, she dared not to do this, for children might take the deflected stars of steel. And if the points were poisoned, as surely they were, even a scratch would kill an innocent peasant.

She pretended not to notice them, although they would know she had. If two had shown themselves, then there must be four. She began to smile, not for any genuine pleasure, but to be misleading, and because she was feeling sly. The ninja dealt in tricks, and she would have to trick them better. Thus she behaved as though the festival were pleasing, and stopped at a booth which sold poor weapons.

"How much for this spear?" she asked, and the seller was alarmed. Samurai never looked at his poorly crafted stuff. He named a low price, which he had not done for any other, and still it took all the coins she had. She bowed as though grateful, and the seller was ingratiating, and later made great truck from the fact that "even samurai" bought his wares.

She meandered to a place where games were being played. People were paying to shoot arrows at targets in hopes of a prize. They were very bad. Tomoe said to the woman renting arrows, "I am without funds today, and in any event do not wish to compete for any prizes. But I would be pleased to increase your business with a demonstration."

The woman happily lent the samurai a bow and three arrows, and as a favor held Tomoe's recently acquired spear.

Hardly taking time to aim, Tomoe made a bull's eye. Several people gathered immediately, to watch her line up the second arrow very carefully. They expected her to split the first, a rare feat. But she surprised them by turning swiftly to the left and in one quick motion shot in a seemingly random direction.

A ninja cried out, lurched from the roof of a nearby building.

Half the gathered crowd fell at once upon their faces. The other half gazed about without comprehending what was going on. Tomoe wheeled around and let the third arrow fly, but the ninja jumped up, somersaulted in mid-air and landed on his feet on the next building. In his hand, he held the arrow. All who saw were impressed (including Tomoe), though even peasants did not like ninja.

A mounted samurai sat high upon his horse, understanding ninja well enough to know *he* was in no danger. His sword was sheathed in a rare, old fashion: across his back. And sheathed it remained. He did not become involved, but only watched.

Tomoe slung the borrowed bow across her shoulder, then snatched the purchased spear away from the gaping woman and pushed her out of danger's path. Two ninja stood on roofs, a third was in a tree. From each of them, star-shaped shurikens spun through the air at Tomoe. All three contacted the wooden handle of the spear, and stuck.

They had thought to prey upon her chivalry, her inability to deflect darts and stars into the crowd. She had outwitted them.

Immediately, three darts followed. Tomoe jerked the spear handle up and down. The darts stuck clear through, their points black with a rapid poison. By this time, the street was littered with prone, quivering bodies. The recent merrymakers looked up coyly, as curious as afraid.

The din of gaiety was subdued. Tomoe Gozen ran amongst the prone bodies, dancing strangely as she went, to avoid stepping on the people, and to twist about left and right to catch the array of tiny, poisonous weapons along the shaft of the spear's soft wood. They came in swift succession from three places, but she caught them all, their shapes varied but mostly like stars, shooting stars, until the spear's handle was so full of them that it could hold no more. By then, the ninja had spent their supply, and Tomoe had reached a narrow place between two buildings, and vanished.

The ninja in the tree signaled the others with hand and whistling. They leapt from the tops of buildings to the ground and, remarkably, kept right on running toward the spot where Tomoe had disappeared. She stepped out of the alley, fooling them again. Her left hand was full of shurikens, gleaned from the spear; her right hand snatched and tossed them overhand and side-hand, one by one.

The first ninja took one in the face, stomach, knee. Others stuck in the tree where the leader-ninja avoided them. When the first ninja fell, multiply wounded, the one behind him had already rushed to one side and made a surprising leap atop a porch, and from there back onto a building's roof.

The tree-ninja had meanwhile leapt from limb to building, thence to another building, so that he and the other were closing from opposite directions. Tomoe could not see them from the crevice between walls.

A smoke bomb hurled through the air, landed behind her, and instantly the alley was filled with unbreathable stench. Choking, she staggered out, staggered on purpose to look more vulnerable than she was. It looked like she was about to fall on her face, but she made a peculiar twist of her body which not only kept her from the fall but also gave her leverage to propel the spear with powerful accuracy at the closer ninja.

He leapt aside fast enough to miss taking the spear through the chest, but still it tore through the muscles under his arm. It tore far enough through that the wooden handle, pierced with poison darts, put infected splinters in his wound. The quick acting poison made his eyes roll up, and he fell onto a porch unmoving.

The remaining ninja was too far away to effectively toss shurikens, if he had any left, and he might. Tomoe had two of them herself, of those plucked from the violently discarded spear. Also, she had the bow from the gaming range. It was a pitiful weapon, and she had no arrows, but she had seen a trick performed on a battlefield once, and it

Wendy Adrian Shultz

seemed presently her only hope. The ninja was preparing some kind of blowgun, and she was probably in its range.

Rolling onto her back, Tomoe braced the bow against both feet, holding the bowstring in two hands. In each hand was a shuriken which she held against the string. When she let fly, the string snapped forth and cut her feet—but the shurikens sped toward the ninja. They would have missed him to either side had he refused to budge, but the could not have known that. Had he veered left, the left shuriken would have taken him. But he veered right, and the right shuriken half vanished into his throat.

He stood a long while, wobbling, only his eyes and lips showing from his cloth mask. He fought the poison and the wound, raised the blowgun to his lips. But blood had seeped into his lungs, the shuriken had struck so deep, and when he blew the dart it went only a little ways, held back by the blood which shot through the tube.

Above Tomoe, who still lay on the street almost as if relaxing, the mounted samurai hovered. He looked down with a pleasant face; with, perhaps, some sadness or emptiness behind the gaze. He appeared to be wealthy. "I am impressed," he said. "I had expected you to die."

Tomoe stood, brushed herself. A nearby peasant took the liberty of brushing off her back, wishing to touch a hero, whoever she might be. The mounted samurai continued, "If you need a friend, or good employment, follow me." He reined his horse around and looked back, expecting to be followed. She did not move. "Come along," he said, a lordly air about him, not expecting to be refused by a ronin.

Forsooth, Tomoe could use good employment, but she said, "I need no friend who would sit, expecting me to die." She walked the other way.

It did not take long before the attentions of overly solicitous folk grated. She was the talk, and the mystery, of the festival. To escape, she slipped into a *kodan* house.

The kodan stories, war stories, had already begun when Tomoe slipped in, fleeing the raucous, attentive crowd. She came without notice, for the various young samurai, who made up the largest percent of the small audience, were enamored of the elderly samurai's story.

This was one of the oldest tales, about the twelfth Mikado's son. But Tomoe was surprised by the manner of its present interpretation, more sensual than expected.

She sat near the wall in back, upon her knees. With hat shadowing her face and loose, colorful garb somewhat disguising her figure, she looked little different from the male samurai, who were a young and beardless lot; although anyone who looked carefully would know at once that here was someone older, well tested, and of greater dignity. Also, the garb did not completely disguise her sex, was not meant to. Still, the audience was distracted by what they came to hear.

The old storytelling samurai was strong for his years. Although he moved slowly as if his bones might ache, he moved also with grace, punctuating his tale with pertinent movements of his hands, to indicate a dancer, a sword-thrust, someone in their bed. The young, sexually unlearned samurai were especially fascinated by the ribald nature of portions of the recitation, and doubtless some preferred this kodan house for no other reason. Yet the teller was good on other levels too, his lined face wrinkling up or stretching apart to make any number of distinctive characters in the story.

"So Yamato-dake came alone to the island of Kiushiu," he continued, "and saw that it would be difficult to breech the walls of the guarded castle. The rebellious conspirators were many, and he but one, and the question was how to get to the central palace and slay the Mikado's sworn enemy, Nomonaka.

"Yamato-dake decided on a disguise—a disguise which even the wary Nomonaka would not suspect.

"The young prince was not yet in his seventeenth year when he undertook to avenge the insult to his father, and already a renowned hero. His was the body of nubile youth, very slender but more round-cornered than angular. He was still without beard, and much envied by the women of his parents' court for his fairness and grace.

"Thus he went to the pleasure house of the nearby village, where the skillful ladies fawned upon and admired him and vied for his attentions. Modestly, he told them, 'Beauties supreme, I am unworthy of your observance, and, alas, am sworn to a fortnight of celibacy for my patron deity. I would beg a boon, however.'

"The young women were very eager. 'The boon,' said Yamato-dake, 'is to possess one outfit from among your store of pleasurable clothes.'

"The ladies all giggled tremendously, but were not surprised, for they had thought right away that Yamato-dake would have been as pretty a girl as he was a boy. They found the most daring dancer's costume for him, and painted him nicely, and Yamato-dake enjoyed this very much. Then he went away from the laughing ladies, who begged him to return when his fortnight was over, so they could show him pleasures such as geishas show other geishas. They begged him thus, it may be supposed, because they desired his beauty. But also they must have been extremely curious what kinds of conquests the temporarily womanly prince could make, being as he was celibate and looking as he did so virginal and sweet.

"Prince Yamato came to the front gate, where the sentry was alert and made threatening challenges to the dark. Yamato-dake stepped into torchlight and stamped his foot, saying in a haughty girl's voice, 'I want to see your boss!'

"The sentry espied the girl and judged her comely. Yamato-dake was of exceeding beauty, it cannot be over said. The sentry asked the seeming-girl what business she had out so late and all alone.

"'I am a dancing girl from Kuji,' Yamato-dake said, for the dancing girls of Kuji were famous even then, 'and I am on a Wandering for the love of my patron deity. I have walked a long way, and desire to sleep in the richest house of this country.'

"The sentry laughed at this audacity. The disguised prince said, 'I can earn my night of lodge by dancing.' Then Prince Yamato began to dance a little bit, to show the guard. He was impressed a lot, and thought to himself: 'My boss will like this girl for his sport.'

"So the sentry took the dancer to the innermost part of the castle. There, young geishas were serving saké and playing samisen. Yamato-dake saw also that enemy chiefs had gathered from various smaller islands.

"The sentry groveled before his boss, begging a reward for delivering the gentlest flower of Kuji. The boss was swayed indeed, for the Kuji dancer looked very nice to him. He rewarded the sentry with all the other geishas, who went away with him to another place in the castle.

"'Dance for us,' boss Nomonaka commanded, and the prince danced with the gracefulness of a sweet girl. Dancing was not so different from swordplay, and Yamato-dake had happened to learn both, the latter from his father and the former from his mother.

"So well did Yamato-dake dance, he captured the hearts of half the chiefs but especially of Nomonaka. The flames of desire were high in the heart of the boss, so that when Yamato-dake was through with dancing, Nomonaka pulled the beauty harshly to his chest.

"'Come with me now!' he demanded. The dancer giggled and blushed and struggled meekly, saying, 'I cannot. I have never.'

"Hearing these words of innocence, the flames burned higher in Nomonaka, and he dismissed his envious visitors, dragging the dancer into private chambers. There, he urged his prize to a soft grass mat, put his arms about the lithe beauty, and held tightly. He demanded the dancer hold him similarly. Yamato-dake obeyed, wrapping strong arms around Nomonaka. The seeming-girl began to squeeze.

"At first the boss laughed at the surprising bear-hug of the dancer. But then he could not breathe and began to struggle. He squeezed in turn, and it became a kind of contest which boss Nomonaka was not winning.

"There was terror on Nomonaka's face, his face which was red with blood squeezed still within his veins. He felt his own heart stop and the life go from him.

"Presently Yamato-dake went to the chambers of the guests, these being chiefs who conspired against the twelfth Mikado. They gathered about and welcomed who they thought a girl; who was in tears; who said she had been much abused by the cruel Nomonaka, and she had therefore batted him on top of the head with a pot and rendered him incogitant.

"One of the chiefs ran to see, and returned quickly to say, 'It is true, he lies unconscious on his mat. He will be angry with this beautiful girl and have her slain, and that will be a waste.'

"The beauty fell upon the floor wailing for aid, and the chiefs, taking pity, put Yamato-dake in a sack which they carried with them to the outer gates. The sentries were surprised to see the chiefs leaving so soon, but dared not bar the way. A certain guard, suspecting some conspiracy, ran to tell his boss that the chiefs were leaving under cloak of darkness.

"Though unmarked by any wound, boss Nomonaka could not be roused, and so the sentry gathered that his boss was not asleep, but dead. He called the alarm.

"Nomonaka's faithful retainers were after the chiefs, and there was a battle at the crossroads which Yamato-dake heard from inside the sack.

"When the battle was over, someone opened the sack, and it was a chief. They had killed all the men from the castle, and lost only one of their own number. But they were angry, having learned during the battle that Nomonaka had been killed.

"'They thought we killed him,' complained the chief who opened the bag. 'But it was you, and we no longer believe it was an accident. Yet we will let you go if you pay us well, here upon the road, for having saved the life of a murderess!'

"Yamato-dake allowed the first chief to embrace him, and in that moment stole the big man's two-edged sword and killed him. The other chiefs fought bravely and with skill, but fell before the sword wielded by the apparent damsel.

"The last chief died in agonizing slowness, but managed to say, 'Lady, you are special! I would feel your cheek to mine before I die!'

"And granting this final wish, Yamato-dake placed his cheek against that of the dying man, and let him part this life with a lover's passion in his heart."

When this story was done, the young samurai were aroused, for they were yet pretty boys themselves, with dreams of valor, and more attached to one another than to any girl. They were full of praises for the old kodan teller, and begged him for another tale. He was flattered, a little bit inflated, and in an even greater ribald mood.

"Now I will tell you a story not unlike the first," he said, "the story of Tomoe Gozen, who—akin to Prince Yamato who played a woman— became a warrior so that she might play the man and conquer all the geisha houses of Naipon."

The young samurai hooted uproariously, but suddenly it ended. A samurai stood among them fierce and strong. Even had she not turned her jacket right-side out, revealing her crest; even had they not already speculated as to the identity of the mysterious samurai who earlier slew four ninja; even then, by her anger, they would have known who she must be.

The storyteller grew palest, for he was not a youth to be excused for prankish insults.

Favor was a fickle goddess, and the favored hero of last year's tales became unfavored in the next. Ever since the death of eight thousand samurai at Shigeno Valley—many slain by Tomoe who served a foreign lord—Tomoe had become the brunt of disrespectful humors which poorly disguised underlying hostilities. But a samurai's pride is strong, and even these youths knew they had erred in applauding the old man's joke. They were not surprised that her sword should dash among them before they could take a breath—they were only surprised that they had not been killed by the many swift strokes which kissed their beardless faces with a breeze.

It took them a moment to realize, looking amongst themselves, that they had all been deprived of their proud queues of hair, lost to Tomoe's strokes.

The storyteller's hair was too thin to merit shaving, but she said to him, "Grandfather, you have a spider on your shoulder." He looked quickly at his shoulder and saw lying there not a spider, but his own ear, cut so quick and clean that he had not seen her blow or felt its effect. He gasped and grabbed the bleeding side of his head, stanching the flow with his shirt sleeve.

Tomoe Gozen walked out into the street, which seemed even gloomier than before.

In the morning, she found Yabushi.

Shortly after leaving the kodan house, Tomoe had discovered a camp of four retainers to some lord whose crest she did not recognize, and who they would not name, though it seemed he must be rich for he clad his samurai well. Tomoe's own crest was more famous and, now that she wore her shirt properly, the samurai whispered among themselves and avoided her.

Oddly, they all bore an ancient kind of double-edged sword, and carried them across their backs in heavy sheaths. It was so unusual that Tomoe could only suppose these men followed the man with whom she had had a brief exchange yesterday. He had not been a lord, but perhaps some lord's favorite; and he too carried his sword across his back. If it too were two-edged, she had not seen.

These four were staying in the village primarily to display their abilities in an exhibition for the festival. Tomoe would have liked to see two-edged swords in use (the legended Yamato-dake used such a sword, though they were centuries outmoded since his day); but the bearers were so unfriendly she made no note to witness their exhibition.

With minimal words exchanged, they had let her spend the night at their camp; but with her identity known, she received only those cordialities which were absolutely expected, none extra. She might have shared their breakfast, as that also was minimal between samurai, but she chose not to impose herself further. Their entire manner had been less than inviting.

Rising earlier than the others, Tomoe exercised in darkness, upon a street which had been busy the day before and soon would be again. Banners flapped unseen in the darkness, while she stretched and forced her muscles, and practiced graceful assaults that none could see beneath the fading starlight. Near the time of sunrise, she smelled fresh fires in hibachis and fireplaces, and over them, pots of stews and rice; but hunger she put from her mind.

After exercises, having stressed her body an extra bit, she walked slowly to the village edge, letting her body cool. She stood apart from the festival gear and the transiently quiet town, and watched Amaterasu grow out of distant mountains and low clouds, as Naipon had grown out of the primeval ooze at the beginning of time.

When she started back along the street, early risers were about, preparing their exhibits and stalls, opening their businesses' doors and shutters, carrying feed to horses, speeding here and there upon errands of unspecified urgency. Unwealthy comers who had camped outside the village in discomfort straggled back onto the festival street, theirs joints stiff, looking discouraged that nothing yet was happening on this the final day. It was not a busy street, but enough so that the seclusion Tomoe had savored before the sun arose was entirely dispelled.

And then she saw Yabushi, where he did not belong.

In an isolated yard, the samurai child was surrounded by six unwholesome men who were laughing. They looked to be themselves of samurai caste, but dirty and uncouth. They were *sanzoku*, well below ronin—bandits lost of their bushido. Such as these were bound to one another by their own misfortune and vileness. They soiled the name of samurai.

Little Bushi had his shortsword held high, threatening them to keep back. His eyes watched his field. His feet moved with swift, even ease. Always, he kept his back to a tree. His guard was perfect.

"Come now," said one of the sanzoku, sounding coarse and wicked, leaning on his sword. "We heard you at the geisha house. You said you had gold to buy a girl. Hand it to us. You are too young to need a geisha, and we will put your money to better use."

For answer, Yabushi dashed forward and then back to his tree. One of the six whooped and clutched his groin, for the small fencer's overhead swing had reached as high as the crotch and unmanned the despised sanzoku. He fell on the ground and rolled about in pain, lamenting his best part.

The other five were swift to ready their swords, curses of vengeance on their lips and in their eyes, angered to learn the baby rooster had spurs.

At that moment Tomoe shouted some blasphemy, reviling those who ganged up on one small person. Suspecting a rear attack, the five sanzoku were unsettled long enough for Yabushi to escape from between them and run to Tomoe.

The five sanzoku left standing were less willing to attack, being cowards from the start and not liking the sword and face of Tomoe added to the child's. But the sixth sanzoku, lying on his side and curled partly in a ball, looked up from his agony and cried, "One and a half to five! The odds are very good!"

Thus the ruthless brutes were encouraged to continue. Tomoe and Yabushi stood back to back. Doubtless, in this case two could handle five, for samurai did not become sanzoku because of their immense skill and courage. But Yabushi and Tomoe never had the chance to prove this.

A strolling nun, who Tomoe had never seen before, dashed into the fray with her staff. She wore a tabard inscribed with prayers over her kimono, yellow upon red, and went barefooted. Her staff served as *bo*, a fighting stick held horizontally in both hands. She smashed two of the sanzoku in the back of their heads before they knew someone came from behind, and they fell as one, unconscious. Two others turned on her at once, but the ends of her pole smote left and smote right, and the two sanzoku staggered back and ran away, their front teeth broken out. The fifth had fled to the side of the sanzoku Yabushi had previously cut, and helped him escape the Buddhist with her stick.

This done, the woman swelled with enormous pride in her work, stood with bare feet placed wide, and sported an almost foolish grin of good humor on her tough, tan, beautiful face. Her bo was once again only a walking staff, its tip upon the ground, and she looked innocent of violence.

Yabushi complained, "We did not need your help! We could have defeated them ourselves!" He kicked at one of the two unconscious sanzoku abandoned by their friends.

"I believe you," said the nun, smiling more broadly at the boy. "But your swords would have killed the louts. My stick only punishes a little."

Tomoe put a hand on Yabushi's shoulder, for he was storming with anger. This intervention insulted his strength and the strength of his friend, Tomoe. It hurt his samurai pride. Children and women, he had noted, were often thought to be in need. But Tomoe said, "She did not help us, Little Bushi. She helped them."

Yabushi was appeased.

Hereafter, it was difficult to be rid of the nun, whose name she gave unasked: Tsuki Izutsu. She followed after Tomoe and Yabushi, asking pointed questions about faith, thereby discovering that Yabushi's instructor taught both Shintoism and Buddhism and kept a reliquary for both within the dojo. This struck the nun as adequate if not perfect. Tomoe, however, was averse to Buddhism, and Tsuki Izutsu seemed to put it in her mind as her duty to straighten Tomoe's path.

"Zen is popular among the more influential samurai," said Tsuki, sounding like some tempting devil.

"So is rich food," said Tomoe. "It makes them fat and slow."

Tsuki enjoyed Tomoe's response immeasurably, but added pointedly, "The Mikado himself is a student of Buddhism."

"And in exile," said Tomoe, then caught herself lest she sound blasphemous for judging Amaterasu's descendant. She said, "The Mikado demonstrates *ryobu-shinto*, the Two Ways of the Gods. It has nothing to do with Zen."

Tomoe wished Tsuki would simply go away, so that the two samurai would be left to speak in private. Tomoe wanted to know how Yabushi had come to be in this village, when Ikiki was where his sister had been sold; it was not a topic for uninvited ears. Tsuki, unfortunately, could not be rebuked by subtle methods, and her strides were too vast to be outpaced.

"What do you know of Zen?" asked Tsuki.

Tomoe stopped—Yabushi too. The bigger samurai looked at the strolling nun harshly, and replied, "Not much and enough! Buddhists preach of a hierarchy of souls, with human next to the top. Shintoism means that all things bear an equal soul, every tree and rock and fish and fox and farmer and samurai and god. Material wealth, strength, power—these may fluctuate; but souls are absolute, and every soul has the same worth."

"There is only one soul," said Tsuki, eyes glinting as by some private joke. "And that One is ubiquitous."

Tomoe had not asked to argue theology. She said, "Not all Buddhists say that."

"Not all Buddhism is Zen."

"I will tell you this:" Tomoe began, in a tone as lecturing as Tsuki's, "Shinto is a religion not of tracts, but awe. Everything has importance. We do not bow down. We dance."

"When have you danced?"

"Mine is the dance of the warrior."

Tsuki liked this answer, too. Tomoe continued, "Buddhists say it is wrong to kill. How can a samurai believe that? Are we the greatest sinners?"

"We are all wretched in the world," said Tsuki, looking for a brief moment less than happy. "To tread the very grass kills insects, to have eaten a piece of fish—and who is to say a grain of rice has less feeling than some animal, than you or I. We cannot help but sin! The air we breathe has life which we soil. But Buddha has shown a way to flee the endless cycle of painful lives and deaths, to gain union with the Whole."

"Shinto is less cynical," countered Tomoe. "Life and death are inspiring gifts, not sufferings to escape."

Yabushi stood beside these women, half ignored, watching and hearing their exchange with a bemused expression too mature for his years. Maybe he was thinking ironically: They fight like children.

"Zen, too, is against scripture, is not a faith of tracts," Tsuki explained. "Knowledge exists naturally, not in a Buddhist text, or in any other. When you lose yourself in your sword, when you are one with your bushido—that is Zen." Tsuki thought this brilliant. "Zen *is;* it cannot be taught."

"Then teach me nothing," said Tomoe as she took Yabushi's hand, intending to leave the woman standing.

But the pest endured, walked beside them, asked, "You are perhaps both hungry?" She beamed annoying pleasantness, while stern-faced Tomoe looked forward and refused reply. For one thing, Tomoe did not wish to be beholden to the nun for a meal, and thereby saddled with her longer. For another, she did not wish to be cornered in a discussion of the religious significance of digestion.

Yabushi, however, was done with anger, and had warmed to the gentle nature and humor of the strolling nun. Also, he was extremely hungry, having saved his two-hundred ryo exclusively to redeem his sister, spending none of it on food or other personal requirements.

"If you have food to share," said Little Bushi, "we would be honored and grateful to accept."

Tomoe made no contradiction.

Tsuki had no food, but she did have means.

The festival was beginning to gather pace. The strolling nun, in her long strides, approached a rich-appearing booth by herself, and said to the man selling cakes, "Most beneficent food-vendor! I can see by your necklace that you love Buddha. Can it be that you are generous to Buddha's poorest questers?"

The man was fat, probably from his own cooking. He might be less rich than he had made himself appear for the festival, yet it could not be entirely that he was less than well-to-do. What success he had achieved was very likely due in part to his refusal to feed beggars, who otherwise and gladly would eat him poor. But the nun was very beautiful, and to the fat man this made a difference. He bowed to her and returned to her her winning grin, while handing her a cake.

Tsuki turned around and motioned to Yabushi, who ran forward to take the morsel away. Tsuki smiled at the vendor once more. "Jizo-sama, protector of little children, will reward you for your kindness to my friend," said Tsuki. "There are many blessings on your house, but only an anger-sprite in my tummy."

The vendor smiled less hugely, and did not bow so low. Still, he gave the nun a second cake, and when she turned around, Tomoe was there to take it. Tomoe imitated Tsuki's grin, and Tsuki liked that very much, though it might have been a mocking insult.

Tsuki said to the vendor, "Not every servant of Buddha, as austere as I have become, has a famous retainer like Tomoe Gozen. I must feed her lest she grow mean like a hungry dog. I am Buddha's most fortunate strolling nun, albeit a starving one."

Without any smile at all, without the slightest nod, the vendor proffered the third cake, and looked around and about for some other vagrant in the nun's charge. But there were none additional, and Tsuki scurried off with her staff and her final prize, blessing all upon the street.

Nun and samurai sat down together in a miniature park. In the park were small, carved stone houses. There was a bridge too minuscule to use, not that it was needed to cross a brook no wider than a step. Brilliant flowers blazed in the shade of maple trees.

There in the shade, three lovely beggars feasted, the women and the child; and there, the cheerful, prying ways of Tsuki Izutsu uncovered the plight of Yabushi'take Issun'kamatoka, who had warmed completely to the nun, and told her all.

"In Ikiki they told me, 'We recall your sister. She was always saying:

I am a samurai's daughter! and would not mind the wishes of our guests.' It seems the geisha house in Ikiki transferred claim on my sister to the geisha house of this village—but they told me when I arrived this dawn that she is not here, never arrived, vanished on the road from Ikiki. I am myself witness to the treacherous nature of that road." He sighed heavily. "I do not know where any road will lead me now."

Little Bushi's lips quivered as he said these things, and directly two silver tears fell from the same eye and streaked his cheek. "Brave warrior," said Tsuki, who touched away the streak. "I have a certain power, and can divine for you the whereabouts of your sister. To do this, I need something which belonged to her. I am afraid to ask if you possess one such item, since you say you have not seen her in more than two years, and scarcely remember more than the memory of her. Yet I cannot help you after all, unless you have upon you a thing that once was hers."

Yabushi reached into his kimono and withdrew the bundle of gold ryo. He untied the scarf, and spilled the content in his lap. The coins shone like pieces of the sun. The scarf he handed to Tsuki. "This was hers," he said. "She gave it to me a month before I left for the dojo, before she was taken to Ikiki and never seen again."

Tsuki fondled and wadded the silk, closed her eyes, rubbed the scarf on her eyelids. That was all she did. She handed the cloth back to Yabushi, who methodically restacked his ryo and wrapped them up again. Reluctantly, he asked, "You saw nothing?"

"I saw it all," she said quickly. Her usually happy features were drawn up in a sad way.

"She is dead?" Yabushi asked, his eyes round.

"She was kidnapped by an ogre," said the nun, "and lives as his wife in a swamp."

Tomoe started. She tried to recollect something she could not, something of dreadful importance. But it had been erased, like a slate, whatever it had been. There were only vague images of what had been written—written in chalk, deathly white. Written in snow, which melted, and fell once more, with no message.

"We must go save her!" exclaimed Yabushi.

"We must! Yes, we must!" agreed Tsuki.

Yabushi leapt to his feet; Tsuki climbed her staff. They brushed crumbs from their kimonos. Tomoe still sat on the ground, staring at nothing, thinking: *We must not.*

卍 卍 卍

There had been others who left the festival early, those with small journeys or larger, those desirous of homes before dark. But only three trod the marshland road, for it was hardly ever used anymore, unless by folk in a desperate hurry (and the greater the hurry the better, people said). Yabushi had been in precisely such a hurry when coming from Ikiki, anxious as he was to find his sister at the road's other end; so he came through the marshland despite warnings of mysterious disappearances throughout the past year, and of a vampirish kappa who was not very large but magically ferocious.

"I did have trouble on this road," Yabushi confessed to Tomoe Gozen and Tsuki Izutsu. Tsuki did not wear her prayer-tabard, which was rolled up and tied to her back; so she was clad in a simple but colorful kimono, as were Tomoe and Yabushi. Yabushi continued, "But I had been told in advance about the kappa lurking in the black waters along the way, so I made preparations. Before entering the marshland, I sought cucumbers, which is the only thing kappa love more than human blood. I found seven. When the kappa came for me, I gave the cucumbers to him as a gift. He was so pleased he promised not to suck the blood through my anus, but instead would guard my path so that oni devils and their bakemono captain would not get me."

"Did you see oni or bakemono?" asked Tsuki, shivering.

"No. I do not know if the kappa helped me, for he never showed himself again. But I must say that the only other trouble I had was a fear of awful noises of many sorts."

Tsuki laughed at that, but it was a more nervous laughter than her usual, for she felt much the same about their current path.

"Even in broad of day," said Tomoe, "this place smacks of ghosts and danger. Perhaps the kappa *did* protect you."

Tsuki bowed close to Yabushi's ear and said, barely loud enough for Tomoe to hear (and that was on purpose), "Buddha protected you."

As Tomoe had remarked, even with the sun angling on the marshland and its road, it was an awful place. It was more than a common haunting, too. The road seemed to carve through an entirely different world, as unlike the village as rivers are from sand. The shadows were green and wavering, like some underwater habitation. The sky was pale jade instead of blue. Anything could happen in such a place as this, and take one—or three—unawares.

The road was half overgrown from a year of minimal use, and it was sodden in many places where swamp waters encroached. There had been no repairs.

The very vines reached out to grasp passers, vines alive with vine-slender snakes whose heads wobbled and whose breaths stank. In the water, things that looked less like frogs than they ought bobbed up and down as though watching the small procession's every move. And those bulbous eyes were made for just such observation. Perhaps they were the spies, the ninja, of this ghastly land, merely disguised as frogs.

Tomoe Gozen knew she was not alone with one fearful consideration: How much worse will this road be come dark!

Dusk was some ways off when the two samurai and nun turned to the sound of a wagon creaking and harnesses rattling. People were coming.

Most who used this road traveled in haste. But the five men on horses and wagon moved lethargically, as though they were in dread of arriving home.

The five men were samurai. Four were those who had begrudgingly allowed Tomoe a space to sleep one night. The fifth, evidently their leader, was the self-same man who had expected Tomoe to die and offered her occupation when she did not.

"Trouble?" asked Tsuki softly, guarding Yabushi, which he allowed because he liked her.

"I think not," said Tomoe. "I know them."

Tomoe, Tsuki and Yabushi stood off the side of the road, pressed into the foliage, and let the slow wagon and riders pass. The wagon contained tent gear beneath assorted paraphernalia for Noh plays: wooden masks, gaudy costumes, and set-pieces. Tomoe was surprised to consider samurai as actors, for these four men must have been the ones who performed the Noh play with the strange theme. The fifth was perhaps their director. She wondered all the more about what lord these men must serve, so odd they were with their double-edged swords sheathed on their backs and their second occupation in theater, so much stranger must their master be.

They looked less magnificent in the green shadows of the marshland forest, and the shadow of their own gloom. They were tired and sad, it was certain, as though the festival had meant as much to them, or more, than it had to common peasants.

"A downtrodden lot, eh, Yabushi?" said Tsuki, good-humored even in the eerie land. The leader may have overheard.

When the wagon and riders passed, the leader hung back. He looked down at Tomoe with the same expression he had given her before, that is, pleasant, but sad or empty. Only his voice was different from before. It shook with the weight of secret sadness, and that made Tomoe wonder more.

"Be glad you did not join me after all," he said, "for I had somehow forgotten, or refused to recall, that the festival was for two days only. But I offered you my friendship as well, and that at least you might have taken, though in the end it is perhaps as well you did not."

Tomoe flushed. "What right have you, who would have watched me die, to sound bitter about me?"

"I have no call whatsoever," he confessed, his voice louder. "All the same, I wish you had at minimum attended our exhibition today. I would like to have impressed you as once you impressed me."

Yabushi and Tsuki exchanged glances, puzzled by these exchanges. Tomoe said, "What master do you serve, who enriches the lives of peasants with warriors who are actors or actors who are warriors, but makes those very men unhappy to return home?"

"I cannot tell," he replied, a warning to his tone. "He is only, The Great Lord."

Tsuki boldly interrupted, "Only Buddha is the great lord!"

The mounted warrior glared at her, and she silenced. He said, "There are many Buddhas," and Tsuki could not deny it. Returning his attention to Tomoe, the sad warrior said, "Please, before I am away, I would beg to know your name, although I cannot properly tell you mine."

"You mock me?" asked Tomoe, who knew herself famous whether for better or worse. "Your men hosted me one night, and refused to talk to me, as have many other samurai in recent months. You will already know that I am Tomoe Gozen, survivor of the Battle of Shigeno Valley."

"My pardon, honorable Tomoe. I plead innocence for myself and my men. We are poor in knowledge about the world. If they were not friendly to you, it is because we are always reticent in matters regarding samurai."

"But you yourselves are samurai."

"No. We are not."

"You are Noh players then?" Tomoe was incredulous.

"Not that either. We are..." he seemed to search his mind for an appropriate introduction. Unhappily, he decided, "You might say, we are of the *haniwa* clan."

For a samurai to call himself haniwa was hugely demeaning, for haniwa were hollow, clay warriors found in lords' tombs of an earlier era. She was not certain if he detested himself so much that he considered himself hollow and of clay, or if he reckoned her a fool to be made fun.

Tomoe begged to differ, "Haniwa is no clan. Haniwa are things."

"Then we are things," said the sorrowful samurai, or non-samurai if he preferred. He turned his mount and hurried away, spurring the steed to catch his men, retaking his place among them and their wagon.

Tsuki Izutsu touched Tomoe Gozen's hand, which had grown inexplicably cold, and she said, "That was a strange conversation."

"They are strange warriors," replied Tomoe, and they went upon their way. They followed in the track of the five men and their wagon's wheels. Soon, those men were out of sight and beyond the range of hearing. Even their tracks disappeared after a while, as if they had never been.

"There it is!" exclaimed Yabushi, pointing. Being the only one familiar with the road, Yabushi had taken the lead. Down the road a ways was an abandoned boat, which the small samurai had wondered at on his earlier passage here. The boat lay upside down, half in the marsh waters, half on the road, overgrown with weeds but largely intact. Doubtlessly, it had belonged to some unfortunate victim of the marshland's trouble.

As samurai, nun, and samurai neared this vessel, a kappa vampire stepped out from behind it, trailing vile green algae from his feet.

"We meet again, friend Yabushi!"

The monster was no taller than the small samurai. It bore no clothing except a belt to which was strapped a shortsword. It was obviously male. Tomoe half drew her long daito; Tsuki readied her stick; but Yabushi said, "Let me. I handled him before," and the two women held back.

The kappa asked, "What have you brought me today?"

Yabushi looked his dubious friend up and down. The slender kappa was not entirely unhandsome, having many qualities of a normal child, though he might well be older than many a grandfather. Only his greenish tinge and the depression on his hairless pate betrayed his non-human condition. The depression on his head was filled with water from the swamp in which he lived, for if he was without water altogether, he would lose his magic and become weak and helpless. If left dry a long while, he would die. Yabushi answered the kappa, "I paid you seven cucumbers before. I have nothing more today."

"Be generous, my friend," the kappa begged, and bowed very low. He was careful not to spill the water in his head's indentation.

"I have one dried peach," said Yabushi, but the kappa immediately declined. "You are too greedy, my kappa friend. Who has ever given you more than seven cucumbers?"

The kappa clenched his hands together in the manner of woe, and spoke with immeasurable self-pity, "But I did not eat even one of them! Seven oni devils attacked me after you left, and took my cucumbers away! Oh, life has been miserable since they ventured into this swamp!"

"Then the oni are your enemy, not I. I am not responsible that they take your wealth."

"The oni are my enemy, it is true." The kappa insinuated himself nearer. "But they are very big; I am small. They serve an even bigger bakemono, who I would not happily anger. He has become famous among ogres. He acts like a human lord, keeping samurai and a bride. There is no ogress who will look at him, without a tail, so he has taken a human wife."

"Oni live in mountains," said Yabushi. "What is the bakemono's hold on them in the wetlands?"

"I was about to tell you that! A year ago, or nearly, he found a magic sword, none knows where. He came to this swamp with the oni he had captured with the sword's magic. He made them his sworn samurai, for he says, without a tail, he is more human than bakemono and must live as men. He is not glad of it, be sure. Even for a bakemono, he is very much insane. Be that as it may, his oni-samurai brandish swords bigger than mine, which you can see is a very little sword like your own. How can I challenge them to regain my cucumbers? But you will notice that Yabushi is exactly my size, and in any case a worthier opponent."

The vampire drew his sword, slender like himself, and Yabushi quickly drew his own.

Tomoe Gozen and Tsuki Izutsu started forward, meaning to slay the minuscule monster. But he pointed his sword at them and they froze to the spot, unable to approach. They could only watch.

Wendy Adrian Shultz

"No tricks on me," said Yabushi.

"No tricks," agreed the kappa. "After all, we are friends." Then he attacked the child samurai viciously. Yabushi beat him off.

The tussle went back and forth for a fair length of time, with neither gaining advantage. But a kappa is untiring, and Yabushi began to sweat. Luck alone helped him: the kappa slipped in his own slime, spilling a portion of the water in his head-hole. The kappa was weaker when this happened, but it merely evened them again, for Yabushi wearied more.

By skill, he almost poked the kappa, but failed because the kappa lurched aside, in the process spilling more of his water.

"I yield!" said the kappa. He gave in for fear that he would spill the rest of his water, and then might be slain by Yabushi or by his friends who would be able to move freely if the kappa lost his magic. "You have defeated me, Yabushi. I am your slave."

Saying this, the kappa sniggered.

Yabushi pulled some extra strength together, never letting on that the kappa might have won had he held out a short while longer. The little samurai kept this shortsword pressed to the kappa's throat, and said, "The bakemono's wife is my sister, whom I have come to save. You will take me to her."

"I will!" agreed the kappa, and he and Yabushi vanished utterly.

Tomoe and Tsuki were free of the spell and stumbled forward, since they had been frozen in mid-rush and retained their momentum. They hurried to the place where the boat was upturned, where the kappa and Yabushi had been fighting. "Where!" exclaimed Tsuki. The ground was soft and much-trampled by the swordfight, but no tracks led away.

"Gone," replied Tomoe.

Tomoe stood at the prow of the boat, keeping it away from branches and snags, while Tsuki stood in the back using her staff as a pole to push through the shallows. It began to rain, at first lightly, and then quite hard; by the time it relented a little, the boatwomen's kimonos were soaked through and through, giving them each the aspect of miserable, half-drowned survivors of a shipwreck.

The sun was very low; her light hardly filtered into the marsh at all. Reeds hindered passage and ability to see far ahead. It was a hopeless quest, to find the bakemono's house in so vast a place, to find Little

Bushi on the doorstep where the kappa must have dumped him far from friends and aid. Salty tears streamed down the faces of samurai and nun, but the cold rain hid the fact, except for eyes which were red from strain and sorrow.

"How can we see in here?" asked Tsuki, her happy nature completely doused.

"We will find him," said Tomoe absolutely. She loosed the boat from an unexpected loop of root. Tsuki pressed the boat onward.

As spears of silver rain struck the murky waters, a mist was raised upon the surface. The women came out of the reeds, and could at last see a long way, by the dim light of day. The water looked like smoke. A little island rose out of the surface-mist, and on this stood a woman. She did not appear to be wet, despite the rain. She watched the women in the boat and did not move for a while.

"Yabushi's sister?" asked Tsuki, striving to sound hopeful.

Tomoe did not think so. The woman was very far off, but Tomoe could make out some elements of her face, which was more beautiful than any face Tomoe had seen in all her life, with one exception, and that the face of a jono priestess which few were blessed to see.

"Little Bushi never said she was so beautiful!" gasped Tsuki, seeing that visage for herself. "She is like a kami spirit, divine to my eyes."

It was true there was something more than ordinary about her beauty, something suggestive of divinity. This was disturbing, for gods could be kind or cruel, or both at once; they were unpredictable. Oni, kappa and bakemono were better visions, even all combined, for at least these were earthly apparitions, and mortal, to be understood and battled.

The heavenly lady raised her arm slowly, motioned for the boatwomen to approach. They did this almost without choosing to.

The mist swirled up around the woman, hiding her. When Tomoe and Tsuki reached the island, there was no one on it. They discovered that the island was a floating accumulation of vegetation, not strong enough to hold human weight.

"There she is!" cried Tsuki, pointing in a new direction, then began pushing the boat harder. The elusive beauty had motioned them to follow once again; and once again the mist engulfed her before the boat had reached the rotted, crumbling remnant of a tree which rose up in her stead, shaped vaguely like a woman.

"Now there!" shouted Tsuki, and would make the chase again.

Tomoe grabbed the limb of the broken tree, the limb which was like a woman's arm with broken fingers. The samurai held tight, so that Tsuki could not push the boat toward the wraith-woman anymore. "We must not follow her," said Tomoe. But the woman beckoned with her thin, pale hand, and Tomoe changed her mind, saying to Tsuki, "All right. We will."

This time they found a bloated corpse floating in the water. It was a woman's corpse, the clothing rotted off, her anus distended in the manner that told how the kappa sucked blood. She was half decayed and horrible smelling, and in no way resembled the creature whose divine beauty allured.

Twice more they changed their route to follow her. Twice more she vanished, or turned into something else.

Darkness fell with suddenness. The woman, the mirage, made no further appearances. Either she was a diurnal wraith and could not come out at night, or she had intended only to cause the boatwomen to become lost. At this, she had succeeded admirably.

No longer confounded by the sorcery of the mysterious vision, Tsuki Izutsu and Tomoe Gozen regained their wits, realized they were lost, and complained to one another about the terrible assortment of trouble residing in the haunted wetlands.

"Next," suggested Tsuki, trying to recapture her quelled gaiety, "a black whirlpool will be sucking us into the under earth!"

"Do not say so!" said Tomoe, who preferred the strolling nun to remain somber if this was her finest jest.

They pressed on through the dark. And as Tomoe had promised earlier in their venture, the night was worse than the day.

They searched on for Yabushi, guided by the vaguest vagrant starlight and a pale gibbous moon, which shone sometimes between rain clouds, grey upon black night.

The bedraggled voyagers on the mockery of a sea began to despair of ever finding Yabushi or his sister. They despaired of ever finding their way out of the marsh. Despaired of the noises and the half-formed shapes. Despaired of their very lives.

Patches of fog walked amidst the swamp's grim trees, ghosts for sure. The voices of frogs were more coarse and horrid than any they had ever heard, seeming one moment to croak the name: "Tsuki! Tsuki!" while in another moment others answered, "Tomoe! Tomoe!" Directly the hairs on the women's bodies prickled with dread of the supernatural.

Tsuki squeaked and held her breath when something started

thrashing around in the bottom of their boat. She stabbed downward with her stick, poked a hole in the damp, poor vessel.

"Only a frog," said Tomoe. It had escaped uninjured, while the boat began to fill with water. Directly, samurai and nun were wading waist-deep in foul water, rain falling all around. "Amaterasu's brother keep us!" said Tomoe, referring to the cloud-veiled moon.

"Buddha bless!" countered Tsuki, and drew a circle in the air before her.

The limbs and hanging mosses of swamp trees stretched down to stroke them as they passed. The rain and wind caused the leaves and water to sound like ominous laughter. The rain thickened, and there was no place left in the sky for star or moon to peek through and light their way. Awful things slithered between the women's thighs, obscene and thrilling, then slid away. But samurai and nun contained themselves through all. They did not cry out. They spat in the eye of panic and experienced only the dread of their own stubborn persistence. They dragged on through muck and mire, fear and misery.

Night shades toyed with their senses. Weariness heightened their susceptibility to suggestion. Everywhere in the wet wilderness, monsters were in abundance, but none came forth to fight. Tomoe had lost her clogs and tabi-socks in the clinging mire, so felt the cold silt squish between her toes, as did Tsuki who was ever barefoot anyway.

Ahead of them, a patch of fog luminesced. It began to take on a firmer outline, and Tomoe wondered idly if her sword could cut a wraith. But it was only a ghastly old woman next to a lantern hanging from a tree. She was wrapped in a shawl of misty grey, hunched in ragged clothing and leaning on a gnarly cane. She stood on a raised, dry knoll, watching the two women struggle through mud and water. She said nothing, made no call, beckoned in no way.

Soon Tomoe cried out, "Grandmother! Do you live in here?"

The crone cocked her head to one side and did not reply aloud, but the wind around her hissed like a serpent, "Yesss. Yesss."

"Let us go away from her," begged Tsuki, tugging at Tomoe from behind. But Tomoe thought the old woman could be trusted, although she might be ugly and eccentric. The kappa had been handsome in his peculiar way; the beautiful kami spirit had misled them entirely. Things were never as they seemed, not in the whole world, and especially not in these wetlands.

"An ugly crone might be a friend," suggested samurai to nun. "I would guess she has dry lodging near."

They waded up, out of the worst of the mud. The old woman looked Tomoe over, deemed her fit, and nodded. Then she looked at Tsuki and scowled. With speed remarkable for any age, she raised her gnarly cane to strike the strolling nun. Tsuki Izutsu's walking stick again became a bo, and she fought the old woman, blocking the blows of the gnarly cane, having her own blows deflected. Tomoe was awed by the old woman's fighting ability, though possibly she would not have fared so well against the nun were not Tsuki, like Tomoe, frazzled by the arduous day.

"Grandmother, please!" begged Tomoe. "Please stop!"

The old woman did so, letting Tsuki off, but said, "Beware, Buddhist! This country is a Shinto haunt!, more so than all of Naipon." Then, turning to Tomoe, the old woman scolded, "You keep bad company, samurai!" But Tomoe defended her friend.

"The Buddhists mean well, for all the harm they cause, and this one means better than others."

It was difficult for Tsuki to mind her tongue, but she did. The old woman took the lantern from the tree's twisted limb, and motioned, saying, "Come with me. You too, Buddhist. Follow my trail precisely and you need not get more dirtied."

They followed the old woman through the rain, keeping their feet on her trail, splashing into mud if they failed. After a while they came to an old, old shrine, half as old as time. Mist clung to it like fungus. The small central temple glowed from within, pulsing. Inside, a lit hibachi was the cause of the glow. On its rack sat a pot filled with steamed rice, gobo root, and some sweet-smelling spice or substance wafting rich and inviting.

"You expected us, Grandmother?" asked Tomoe, appreciative of the odor and the large portions of steaming food.

"You make more noise than the oni devils," said the old woman, and mimed them with sarcasm: "'Yabushi! Yabushi! Oh, poor Yabushi!' Splash, slop, splosh." She stamped her feet.

Tsuki Izutsu did not like the interior of the shrine's temple. By the torii gate she had recognized this place as Shinto. She lowered her face, but brooding eyes looked up evenly. She said, "You have, perhaps, also heard the child?"

The old woman was deaf when Tsuki spoke. Tomoe repeated the query, and there was a better but still poor response: "The boy is half

Buddhist, pah! Has Naipon forgotten who made the land from jelly? A big egg without any shell, that was all that floated in the sea. It was made into Naipon the Eternal Isles. What did the Buddhas ever make, but silence beneath a tree?"

"He is half Shinto, too," said Tomoe politely. "So you might help us halfway?"

The old woman sat her gnarly cane aside, which visibly eased Tsuki who relaxed her grip on her staff. They all squatted around the hibachi. "First eat," said the old woman, committing herself to nothing.

It was a peasant tradition—and the old woman was clearly a peasant, more ragged and wretched than most—to tell stories while sitting about the hibachi to feast. Tomoe wondered who would tell a tale to whom (she did not feel up to it herself, after the tiresome day). She asked, "Who are you, Grandmother, to live here all alone? Are you priestess to this forgotten shrine? What kami do you serve?"

"To answer," said the old woman, "I must tell a story." And thus the old woman fulfilled the tradition with this tale:

"Izanami, mother of the eight hundred myriad of Shinto deities, loved the mortals of the Eternal Isles. She taught them the Way of the Gods that they might become wise and valorous, just and merciful, loving and artistic. When she had done this, the Moon darkened, the Sea slapped, the Storm rose fast, and they said, 'Mother! You have made these mortals into gods!' And the eight hundred myriad deities grew wroth with their mother.

"The deities drew up a scroll of official condemnation and read it aloud, 'Thou so Loveth the Children of the Eternal Isles, therefore, Descend, and abide with Them!' Izanami made this appeal, 'Can my own offspring truly condemn their mother, who has never done them evil?' Then spake the eight hundred myriad of deities in a single voice: 'You have dragged your mortal vesture in the mire of earth. Goddess of mortals, go down. Go among them to dwell in the abode of death, where your immortality will wither and you become as dust.'

"And thus Izanami came to Naipon to dwell a mortal."

This seemed a scriptured sermon, which surprised Tomoe, for Shinto had no texts. Tsuki had listened with curiosity and dread, eating all the while from the bowl in her palm. Tomoe had eaten half her bowl of rice and gobo, tasting also something sweet which she did not recognize, but liked. She stopped chewing long enough to ask, "You serve Izanami, goddess of death and of love, in this decrepit shrine?"

"The story is not finished!" the old woman said sharply, then went on,

"Amaterasu also loved the mortals, and said to her mother, 'Upon each night, you will age one hundred years, to fulfill the letter of condemnation drawn by your other children. But each morning, on my rising, I will melt away those years as I melt away the darkness. Therefore will you never die, though cloaked in mortal vestments.'

"Izanami was glad, and said, 'Many are the children of my loins. Of all these multitudinous offspring, the fairest is you, O Shining Amaterasu.' And thereafter Izanami lived and wandered a never-dying mortal, young by day and elderly by night."

Tsuki Izutsu had set her emptied bowl aside, and started to whisper some warning to Tomoe, for the nun had understood the tale better. But she closed her eyes instead, and did not speak. Tomoe had finished her meal as well, but their hostess had touched nothing, having told the tale without eating.

The story closed, the old woman raised herself with the aid of her gnarly cane, and looked down into the faces of Tomoe and Tsuki. The women did not rise as had the crone. Tomoe realized she was irresistibly drowsy; and though it was expected she would be tired, this seemed an unnaturally compelling sleepiness. Tomoe said, "Grandmother, we are on an important mission." Her eyes were weighted with a thousand ryo. "How could you feed us sleep?" She was disheartened, because her trust had been misplaced.

Tsuki Izutsu sat crosslegged with eyes shut, breathing deeply, already asleep as in a trance. Tomoe Gozen struggled to her feet; an ordeal it was. She staggered and fell down, her rice bowl scooting across the floor, rattling unbroken. She lay with her head in Tsuki's lap.

Tomoe and Tsuki shared a dream.

They were nowhere near the shrine.

In the swamp was a rich lord's mansion. It was set on a hill surrounded by marshes, high above the water level. An ornate iron gate held miraculously against moisture, devoid of rust. Beyond the gate was a carefully laid path of flat stones and wooden slats, leading through pleasant gardens without a vagrant weed or untame bamboo to be seen. Beautiful lanterns atop posts cast their warm glow throughout the nighted gardens. From the leaves, moisture from the recent rain clung like glistening stars, and dropped like meteors. At the far end of the path stood the mansion. It had a carved, teakwood door and no hint of windows, but in some way it remained no less friendly.

Tomoe and Tsuki did not question why so beautiful a house should come to be built in the midst of a dismal land. They did not even think to wonder how they came here in the first place. It was a dream, after all, and no one could question a dream.

The two women stood in water to their knees, gazing as might beggars through the gate to a wealthy estate. The gate was invitingly ajar.

In the gardens they saw the five warriors who had declined the name of samurai. They were practicing their skills. Tomoe witnessed some of what she had missed by not attending their festival performance, and was impressed. As might be predicted, their two-edged swords were handled quite differently than any modern sword, since they could be swung forward and back with sharp edges in either direction. The style of these warriors was yet, in its way, as conventional as any other, but their footwork and motion was more reminiscent of a dance or a play than the deadly game it truly was.

When Tomoe waded out of the marsh and went through the gate, Tsuki followed, although she murmured discontent and suspicion about Shinto magic and a dream. Tomoe approached the exercising warriors, and shouted up the path, "You must come with us!"

The leader was taller and more slender than the others, almost regal, like a prince, but deathly white as she had never noticed previously. He looked at Tomoe and the nun, and asked, "Why must we?"

"Because," Tomoe answered, "seven oni guard the home of the bakemono and you must help us kill them. You five and we two will make the number even."

"How do you know where they are?" asked the leader of the non-samurai.

Tomoe was not sure how to answer. She said, "I do not know how I know it, but I do. This is only a dream. Anything is possible in a dream."

"It is not a dream," said the non-samurai leader. "Do not say it is. We dream, my men and I, the whole year long. We wake from dreaming for three nights and two days during the festival of Great Lord Walks. Do not say *this* is the dream, or we will be sadder than we are. When the sun rises, we must return to dreaming for another year—and perhaps someday the dreams will have no interlude, if the festivals should ever end."

The other men had continued their dance-fight until they came to still postures to the right and left of their leader. They had silently sheathed their swords, and stood listening, nodding dour agreement as their leader spoke.

"You *must* help us," Tomoe insisted.

Tsuki dared not add, though she might have dared to think, "Yes, you must. If there is some curse on you, which makes you sleep so long, a good deed may free you. Buddha is merciful."

She had not said these words aloud, but the warriors stepped back from her in alarm, and the leader replied, as though she had spoken, "Buddha is weak! The Great Lord loved Buddha, and still does, yet we are imprisoned in the haunted marsh of angry Shinto gods and monsters!"

"Then fight the monsters of Shinto!" Tsuki cried angrily.

Tomoe was confused, and was tempted to say, "No, appease them! Make them love you again!" But she did not say this. Instead, she said, "Nonetheless, you must help us save the sister of a young hero, and the hero himself, who has been delivered to the bakemono by the clever kappa."

The non-samurai leader looked away. He said, "Once, I offered friendship. You turned your back on me."

In the doorway of the mansion an old man appeared. Old did not describe. He was ancient beyond reckoning. But he was strong for all his evident years, his spine straight and supple, his eyes bright and serene, every wrinkle tracing a visage of wisdom. Tsuki saw him first, and was overcome. She fell to her knees, and cried out, "Venerable! Great Lord!"

The non-samurai turned around and fell upon their knees before their master. Only Tomoe remained standing.

The venerable spoke more to Tsuki than to the others, "I am the one the villagers call Great Lord Walks." His voice was very gentle. "But not the great lord you suspect, Tsuki Izutsu, favored of the North Land Buddha. Soon, you will obtain what I cannot; you will blend with the universe; you will achieve sublime oblivion. But before then, you have deeds to perform."

He looked harshly at his warriors, though harshness from him was but a loving pat. "Haniwa-san," he said, using the suffix of respect usually reserved for equals, despite the fact that Great Lord Walks was both the elder and the master. "Haniwa-san, you and your men will help the strolling nun and Tomoe Gozen. Remember, you must return to me by dawn."

Obedient as would be true samurai, the five warriors followed after Tsuki and Tomoe who fled back down the path, upon a desperate errand.

Here the dream parted a little bit in a strange way, so that they did not see how it was they arrived at the awful lodge of the bakemono. Suddenly it was before them. The night's mists separated so that the moon revealed a house of mud and filth, windows barred with bamboo, one candle shining from a single window.

In the light of that only candle, Tsuki, Tomoe and the five non-samurai saw Yabushi's sister. They saw how sad she was. Her sadness made the five warriors seem happy by comparison. Her sadness could drain all the happiness from the world, and not fill the well of her unshed tears. Pretty she was, though not in the way of the supernatural beauty who had led Tomoe and Tsuki madly through the marsh. Hers was a different kind of loveliness, a tragic kind which allures no one, but makes all look on empathetically.
Two women and five men did look on, did feel empathy, were stricken to the very center of themselves.

Tomoe led the others, sloshing through the reeds, each trying to make less noise than various things which hopped and croaked around the area. They saw into the lit window better. They saw Yabushi lying fevered on a pallet. His sister doctored him and wept without tears.

"The vampirish magic of the kappa made him ill," whispered Tsuki. "If we can get him away from the swamps, he may recover."

Tomoe motioned left and right so that Tsuki and the five men began to spread out and surround the bakemono's lodge. Yabushi's sister looked up with her sad, sad face, and saw dark shapes moving among the reeds, with even darker visages staring at them through the window. Not knowing them as friends, she cried out and slapped the shutter tight against the bars of the window, against the haunted, horrid night.

The noise wakened the oni, who slept in trees, despising the wet ground. They lived in the marshland only because their master bid them do so, not because they wished. In the mountains, they were feared monster-warriors, skilled with a variety of weapons. Only the yamahoshi, or warrior-priests in mountain sanctuaries, were capable of besting them regularly. It was to be hoped that the swampy ground would hinder their considerable abilities.

Seven oni fell straight away from heaven, it seemed, though really from the swamp trees around the bakemono's lodge. The battle was engaged.

Two purple-skinned oni landed side by side, each with a *kusari-gama* sickle-and-chain. The weighted ends spun around, whirring like the wings of gigantic insects. The oni stood monstrous against the night. When they let loose of the chains, the ends shot forth into darkness and wrapped around the arms of one of the soldiers said to be of the Haniwa clan.

The two oni pulled him forth, a fish from the sea. It was a struggle. The warrior fought hard to hold his place. Though both arms were entangled in the chains, he did not drop his two-edged sword. He showed no fear, but went through the motion of struggle as though it took place on a stage: calmly, precisely, according to script.

When the oni had drawn their captive in range, they raised the sickles on the other ends of their chains, in opposite hands. But the warrior parried form one side to another, swinging his sword on a horizontal plane between his two purple attackers, then brought the sword around in a vertical circle and plunged the point into the heart of his right-hand captor. It dropped its sickle, clutched its bleeding chest, and stood with life going slowly out.
Oni died hard.

The warrior and the uninjured oni were left standing in a tug-of-war at each end of the chain. Sword and sickle were held high, against each other. The second sickle, dropped by the dying oni, dragged in the mud, its chain still wrapped around the warrior's arm, offering the fierce oni too great an advantage.

A second warrior was coming across the top of the bakemono's lodge, preparing to leap at the oni's back, deciding the battle.

Elsewhere, Tsuki Izutsu met a scarlet oni, redder than her own kimono, and it bore a barbed *yari* spear. She parried its thrust, held the *yari* by its barb, then slid her bo loose, swung it around—hard into the oni's stomach. It began to double forward with pain, but she caught it in the chin, making it throw its head backward. The barb of the yari had caught hold of the yellow prayer-tabard Tsuki had rolled up. The end of her pole thrust fast against the underside of the oni's jaw, and it stumbled back with such force that the packed tabard was torn from her back.

A human neck would have been snapped from the blow that Tsuki delivered, but the oni shook its ugly scarlet face and came again. Tsuki said through gnashing teeth,

"It is wrong to kill even you!" Her pole slapped it in the ear, sending it off balance before its own spear point was delivered. She added,

"But I will do it unless you run away!"

She shook her pole in a specific fashion, turning a triggering mechanism with one hand. A long spike protruded automatically from the end of the pole which was aimed toward the oni.

The oni understood her meaning entirely, though some people claimed oni were stupid. It believed her, too. It gazed at her a moment, disbelieving human kindness of any sort for oni, maybe worshipping the moment. Then it turned around and fled through reeds and darkness.

On another side of the lodge, two soldiers worried at a single violet oni. They could not break through the guard of its *kama* scythe, with which the oni hooked, blocked, or captured every slash of the two swords. It grunted and snarled and slobbered, green eyes glowering hatefully from its violet visage.

In a muddy area away from the lodge, the leader of the warriors, who had been called Haniwa-san by Great Lord Walks, was similarly worried by two blue-tinged oni. He was pitted against an *ono* axe and another of the grim kusari-gama sickle-and-chain. He dodged the whirling chain as it was released in his direction; he dodged in the direction of the other oni, and with a quick swipe of his sword severed the oni's hand so that axe, with hand, fell into the mud.

A third oni, bright red, came running through the night with a nun's promise fresh in its mind. It hurtled the barbed spear through the air and caught Haniwa-san in the leg. Haniwa-san fell, as the scarlet oni kept on running.

The oni with the sickle-and-chain was still gathering in its chain, to start it whirling again. The second blue oni who had lost its hand went howling into the night, chasing after its red cousin who had thrown the spear so effectively. Haniwa-san sat in the mud, and wrenched the barbed spear loose from his leg, tossed it from his sitting position after the two craven oni. He never knew whether he made his mark, having to turn his attention elsewhere.

Haniwa-san rolled out from under the downward slash of the remaining oni's sickle, regained his feet, and though poorly balanced on his hurt leg, fought on.

His two men with the violet oni held against the tree were finally succeeding in breaking the guard of the kama bearer. Its neck was already cut deeply on the right side. One warrior let the wounded oni catch his sword with the scythe. Sword and scythe held each other immobile. The other warrior took advantage, and hacked deep into the left side of the oni's neck, a score deeper than the previous cut.

The oni's head started to topple off. It dropped its kama scythe and attempted, with a little success, to hold its mostly-severed head in place. The warriors left the violet oni to die its slow death, and hurried toward the place where their leader limped and battled against the sickle-and-chain. Surrounded, the blue oni knew it would lose.

Unlike bakemono, mountain oni could not speak. This one dropped its kusari-gama and fell upon its knees, silently pleading mercy with clenched palms.

"Run away then," said the leader. The oni stood and fled. The two men hurried to hold their tottering leader, lest he fall from the leg.

Tomoe Gozen was meanwhile entertaining the seventh oni, a head taller than herself, albino, broad-shouldered, and lacking nose. It bore a sword of spear-length, and its guard was good though the sword itself was rusty and ill-cared for.

The white oni's weight pushed its feet deep into the muddy ground, giving Tomoe her best advantage against a sword so big only a devil could wield it. Due to the samurai's smaller size and greater swiftness, the oni had already taken several minor wounds from Tomoe, and offered none which she accepted. It had lost a lot of its thick, black blood from the dozen scores; but oni were indeed hard to kill. It fought on, never lessening in ferocity, red eyes glowering.

Tsuki Izutsu appeared beside Tomoe. Her bo, its spike withdrawn once more so that Tomoe yet knew nothing of its additional value, outreached the oni's overlong sword. She cracked its ribs, smashed its fingers so that it dropped the sword, then bashed it in the temple. It wailed the inhuman cry peculiar to oni. Tomoe Gozen leapt forward and thrust her sword into its throat, cutting off the cry in a gurgle and rush of blood, cutting through the neck bone so that the oni's head flopped sideways. It fell down, still gurgling, death slowly enveloping it.

"It was already defeated!" stormed Tsuki. "You did not have to kill it! It would have run away!"

Tomoe panted and glowered, her eyes angry like an oni. She answered, "You let one go?"

"I did. So did our warrior friends. Three in all."

"Three alive," Tomoe said, pondering. "That is bad. They are held to the bakemono by magic. They may return."

The five warriors were gathered together. With the help of one of his men, Haniwa-san came forward to Tomoe on his hurt leg. The clangor of weapons had ceased to echo through the nighted marsh. Frogs and other creatures made no sound, having themselves fled or hidden, so the silence was quick and eerie. Four corpses of the bakemono's oni-samurai were adrift in the rank water, or face-buried on muddy ground, already decomposing. The reason no one ever brought an oni's body home to stuff was because they rotted almost as soon as they finally died.

The seven victors had suffered no casualties, and only one injury. The injured leader asked, his voice quavering more from hope than pride,

"Are you impressed?"

There was a little anger left inside Tomoe, because the warriors, like Tsuki, had let some oni go. But she was indeed impressed, for the victory was undeniably a good one, without loss of friends. She bowed low from the waist and replied, "I am amazed."

Haniwa-san bowed in turn, standing on his own. "Thank you," he said. "Thank you." Then his men braced him again. He said, "We must hurry, so I bid you farewell for myself and these men. Amaterasu comes soon, and it is our last day without dreams for a while. Perhaps you will come again to the Festival of Great Lord Walks, and join us in our exhibition."

"Perhaps," said Tomoe, thinking not. Her road was too vast.

Without further formality, they went away to rejoin their lord in his mansion. They left behind the two women and four smelling corpses. For the five warriors, the play was over. For Tsuki, Tomoe and the captives in the lodge, it was not.

The bakemono had stepped out of his mud lodge, appearing not too upset that his oni-samurai were defeated or slaughtered. He bore a forked sword, a sword with two separate blades sprouting from the hilt. In the candlelight behind him, Yabushi's sister sat on her knees, bowing and praying over her dying brother.

The bakemono-with-no-tail scanned the bloodied mud and water, then laughed horrible deep laughter.

"So we meet again!" he said. "You do remember me, samurai?" He turned his naked butt to her, and slapped his own behind, both to insult her and to remind her of her deed.

Tomoe Gozen answered from afar, "I had forgotten you before, but now I remember." The veil cast on her memory began to dissolve like mist. "You cursed me more than a year ago, and thereby bound our fates together. Yabushi lies in your lodge dying of kappa-fever, for you said I must lose a friend as you had lost a dinner. And when you and I engage in battle, you will probably leave a scar upon my face, using your two-pronged sword. For that too was in your curse. I might have been afraid one time, but no more. Samurai are aware that our friends, and ourselves, will be killed and scarred. It is part of the Way of the Warrior. That being so, your curse was foolish after all. In the end, you have only guaranteed that I kill you."

Bakemono are instinctively cowardly, which was partly why this one never came out to join the battle. But he did have the sword, rumored to be magical, and apparently the rumor was true if it helped him contain seven oni from the mountains. He cried almost hysterically that, "The gods who heed curses did not figure this!" he shook his magic sword, its two blades humming as he did. "With this, I cannot be defeated!" His crooked mouth approximated a smile.

Tomoe was about to say that, perhaps, the gods figured the sword quite well. But the first ray of sun seeped into the marsh, and Tomoe Gozen awoke with her head in Tsuki Izutsu's lap. She opened her eyes. Tsuki was already awake, smiling down at Tomoe, stroking the samurai's face and hair.

"You had a dream?" asked Tsuki.

Tomoe sat up, looked around for the old woman who was nowhere in the shrine's small temple. Sunlight angled in from outside.

"I did!" she answered. "We must find the place again!"

Samurai and strolling nun searched the swamp a long time, sometimes swimming where the water was deep. They had grown used to the foul wetness and the eerie trees and small animals, and were unafraid. But they searched a place labyrinthine and huge, a frustrating task. Real as their dream had seemed, real as it must have been, there was yet no recollection of a single proper direction or landmark.

When Amaterasu was high in heaven, Tsuki cried out, "There! That dry hump of ground! That is where we saw Great Lord Walks and his retainers!"

Tomoe looked hard. "But there is no mansion."

"I recognize it anyway," said Tsuki. "It is the one place in these wetlands seen by Buddha. I know it."

There was no sign of a gate, not even a flake of rust where it had been. They could see no walkway of stone and wood. A single post was discovered amongst the weeds, set there long ago perhaps to hold a garden's lantern; but of the garden itself there was no remnant; of the mansion, no sign.

On the highest part of the dry hill, under an accumulation of brush, they uncovered the entrance of a tomb: a tunnel angled downward into darkness. Outside this entrance was a wagon tongue and the broken fragment of a single wheel. Tomoe kicked amongst the rubble, and found an ancient wooden mask, its paint long worn away, the wood itself eaten in places by worms. It might have been some precursor to the masks worn in Noh dramas.

All about were the bones of horses, dead so long there remained no measure of flesh for insects to nibble.

There may once have been a wooden seal at the tomb's entrance; but if so, it had long ago been stolen, or reduced to dust. Tsuki and Tomoe entered the unblocked corridor, ducking because the ceiling was low. The way led down a steep, stone ramp and into a single large chamber. The chamber was lit by a hole in the center of the high ceiling.

In the single room, amidst the rubble of the deceased's belongings was a sarcophagus. It was carved with old symbols not used in five or six hundred years.

"Buddhism came to Naipon half a millennium past," Tsuki said. "Great Lord Walks must have been the first to embrace the new religion." She peered into the sarcophagus, which had no lid, and Tomoe joined her in this occupation. Therein lay only bones and dust, and one colorless scrap of linen bearing no resemblance to the great lord's colorful costume they had seen the night before. Tomoe stared at this contents a long while, but Tsuki turned away, upset. Tomoe's eyes lifted, looked into a dark corner where the narrow shaft of light from the ceiling barely touched.

"Look there," said Tomoe, whispering, for voices were loud in the deep, small room. Tsuki followed the direction of Tomoe's hand. In the shadows away from the shaft of light were five small haniwa figurines made of clay, their mud-carved swords across their backs.

Tsuki fell upon her knees before the little statues, and lifted one gently. It had a flaw in its leg. Tomoe looked on as Tsuki Izutsu recited ancient prayers which meant nothing to Tomoe. When the nun was finished, she set the statue down and looked up with moist eyes and charged: "Your gods are cruel, Tomoe."

"To give life to clay?" she asked softly. "They begged us not to call their final night a dream, for their lives were more than that. They were glad of their life, which would not exist but for Shinto magic. If the gods of Shinto are cruel, then stomp those fragile figurines into dust! Then, come the next festival of Great Lord Walks, the first native Buddhist of Naipon will awaken alone, and have nothing to send the peasants he assuredly loved. The gods are unfathomable. But cruel? We cannot judge them."

The faintest laughter responded to Tomoe's words, and it was not the laughter of samurai or nun. The sound came from above, and the two women looked up to see a third woman: the beautiful kami spirit, peering down the light-hole into the tomb. She was only there a moment, then went away.

Although Tomoe and Tsuki hurried out of the tomb, they could not see the direction taken by the kami spirit. Tsuki said, "I think that the kami is one-and-the-same with the old woman. Do you remember the story of Izanami told us before we slept? Young by day and old by night..."

"We will pretend not to see her if she comes again," Tomoe suggested. "We must find the bakemono's lodge, and not be diverted. In the dream—if dream it can properly be called—I think we started off that direction from this hill." She pointed, started forward. Tsuki followed Tomoe back into the mire.

The marsh was more tangible than it had seemed during the dream, and far less fearful by day than night. Still Tomoe entertained doubtful thoughts, remembering a saying: that those who have commerce with the dead (as she and Tsuki had with the unnamed great lord) soon join them properly. She wondered if the goddess Izanami came to protect or confound. The dream of the night before could have been conceived a gift, as its weaving spilled into reality of a wakeful sort and wrought defeat for the oni devils. Izanami was an ambiguous deity to be sure, more so than others, who all appeared devious to mortal vision. As overseer of love as well as death, Izanami was at once sought and feared, and in every case, required. On whim, Tomoe spun around and shouted over the wetlands: "Izanami! Because we love him and he is so young, do not let Little Bushi die!"

Tsuki drew little circles before her with a finger, and the search went on.

🌀 🌀 🌀

Night came again, and with it all the fearsome sounds and splashings to left and right, before and behind. But nun and samurai ignored all things impertinent to their quest. They trudged on.

At least they were spared rain; but it made little difference, they were so soaked and muddied face to toe. Moonrise was helpful, lighting their watery path; but also it cast half-shadows in their way, which they felt they must avoid.

The two heroic women moved like wraiths across the wetland. Were others on quests in the same swamp, they might have chanced to see this pair, and fled another way, or else ignored them, having also grown used to ghosts.

Nun and samurai could have searched thus for many days, finding nothing they desired, the marshes were that vast. Pools were linked to pools; they joined with beds of peat and muck, were laced with natural dams of mud and bridges of fallen timber. Nothing was familiar from the night before, or the day before. Nothing gave up clues. But gods walked the islands of Naipon, and would not allow fate to go unmet.

Izanami-the-Old appeared before them with her lantern in one hand and her gnarly cane in the other. She appeared so close at hand, so quickly they could not have expected her. They were blinded by the lamp, so that Tsuki could not see to deflect the crone's blow. The gnarly cane smote her twixt the eyes, and Tsuki Izutsu fell limp across a log, unmoving. Before Tomoe could act in anger, the elderly Izanami said, "It is that way, the lodge. It is beyond the rushes and those trees. You must meet the bakemono alone."

Tomoe lifted Tsuki's head, saw that she was only sleeping, breathing evenly. Indeed, the blow between her eyes had not been so terrible, but more like a brush or a kiss, and should not have caused unconsciousness.

In that moment, Izanami's lamp was blown out by a cold brief breeze, and Tomoe Gozen could see the goddess no longer.

She came then to the bakemono's lodge, where old Izanami had indicated. From within came crying. Yabushi's sister had finally found her tears, pouring forth in torrents. The young woman's voice wailed like a wind. Tomoe wondered: Is Yabushi already dead?

"O Bakemono-with-no-tail!" called the samurai. "Tomoe Gozen of Heida has come to steal your head!"

The door flung open at once; the bakemono had been waiting. He stepped out without hesitation, looking fierce and certain, swinging his two-pronged sword with violent meaning. It was the source of his bravery, and clearly he expected Tomoe to fall back from the sight. Tomoe made no delay. She leapt onto the slick mud which surrounded the lodge and struck the bakemono's sword with her own.

At contact, the sword rang like a tuning iron, resounding like a bell. Tomoe struck over and over. The harder she hit her opponent's sword, the louder it rang. The marsh filled with the sound of the bakemono's weapon. The sound surrounded Tomoe Gozen like a thick, cold jelly. It made her slow.

Once, the bakemono could have killed her, she moved with such lackadaisical maneuver. But in his eagerness, he slid in the mud and fell upon his tailless rump from clumsiness alone. There, Tomoe might have killed *him*, had she her normal speed. But the knell of the sword held her. She swam through thickened air, while the bakemono scooted away from her with ease, stood up, and came at her again.

Held as she was in the sword's spell, she could not move fast enough to break the bakemono's guard, poor as that guard might be. It was all she could do merely to counter his blows; and even with that much success, she only increased the spell by making the ringing louder.

The bakemono caught her final blow between the two prongs of his sword, and held her to the spot. Tomoe grimaced, then grinned, for she realized that if she let the bakemono hold her long enough, his sword's knell would quieten. Then she would regain her swiftness against the brute.

The vibrations coursed through her bones, a sensation not unlike the time when she survived a stroke of lightning—only this time, it was endured far longer. The vibration blurred her vision, shook her skull, threatened her with unconsciousness. But she held fast, would not let the bakemono withdraw to strike again, until the sound was lessened. Perhaps he realized her ploy, but he was slow and dumb and could think of no way to untangle his double-sword from her daito without further danger to himself.

After long moments of patience, the vibration seemed to be dying down a bit, but not quickly. The bakemono put his full weight behind the magical weapon, intending to press Tomoe, by far the smaller of the two, onto the ground. But she braced her legs carefully, and neither of them moved.

From the corner of her vision, Tomoe Gozen saw a movement, and then another. Two bright blue oni devils, bound to the sound of the sword, had returned to their master. One of them had a blackened stump where its hand had been, and it carried a large rock in its remaining hand. The other bore a long, thick branch, brandishing it with wicked force.

Tomoe could not move at all, for she had become frozen by the too-slowly fading knell. The bakemono's weight at her front, and a pair of oni approaching from the side, Tomoe Gozen was prepared to die.

The strolling nun was not prepared to let her. Tsuki Izutsu plodded through the swamp, one hand to her eyes which smarted in an odd way. She staggered, stumbled, but came on. She fought the Shinto spell with a Buddhist prayer on her lips and came, as had the oni (but with different intent), toward the sound of the ringing sword.

The two oni of brilliant blue turned upon the nun. She raised her bo, its spike protruding, but she was too dazed by the touch of Izanami's gnarly cane. She did not see the rock flung through the air. It struck her in the ear, bringing blood from her head in a large rush. She dropped onto her knees in the dirty water, as the second oni leapt forward. It knocked aside her bo with its log, and thrust the log down upon her over and over again. The sound of splintering bones burst through the sword's knell. Tomoe heard the sound and was helpless.

All the while, Yabushi's sister had been crying inside the lodge. Upon Tsuki's fall, the mournful crying ceased; and Tomoe thought the timing was very inappropriate. The very trees should weep, with Tsuki murdered!

Tomoe's vision blurred from her own tears and the strain. Anger drew aside. Sorrow weakened her. The bakemono's pronged sword had faded in sound the barest amount, while he put every bit of his muscle to the task of forcing her down.

The points of the sword moved toward her, one on each side of her own sword. She had no way to guard. She could not move. Slowly, those points pressed against her forehead, harder, deeper, and blood joined with the tears in her eyes. The vibration stopped, transferred into her brain where it sapped all remaining vitality.

At that moment, the bakemono lurched back, leaving only the two deep cuts on Tomoe's forehead. She fell away, drained by the sword's magic and her own stress. She lay on her back, unable to move or groan. But the bakemono did not deal the final, easy blow.

He stood tall and rigid, terror in his huge, black eyes. He dropped the sword. When he folded forward onto hands and knees, Tomoe barely saw from the angle of her vision that Yabushi'take Issun'kamatoka had launched himself from the doorway of the lodge to thrust his shortsword far into the bakemono's upper spine, finding even the heart.

Little Bushi, pale as death, clung to his own sword, clung to the bakemono's back, and wrenched the blade back and forth.

There was a third oni in the reeds, who had seen its two comrades slay Tsuki Izutsu, the nun who had spared an oni's life. The oni, redder than blood, rushed forward with its spear, and struck first the back of the oni with the log, and next the stomach of the one-handed oni who had thrown the stone. The red oni pulled back with pieces of liver and lengths of intestine on the barb of his yari spear.

The stricken oni scream hideously, ran a little ways into the swamp, then fell to their slow death and swift decomposition.

Tsuki drifted face down in the water, blood spreading away from her body. The oni lifted her with surprising tenderness, and it wailed as had its fellows—for if oni ever loved, how could one help but love Tsuki Izutsu? It bore her away into the night, wailing its awful, wordless lament.

Bakemono died not much easier than oni, though their heads might be taken as trophies, since they did not rot swiftly like oni. Yabushi's sister helped the boy pull his blade from the bakemono's spine, and helped the little samurai stand because he was still weak from the long sickness. The bakemono's curse had dictated only one friend of Tomoe Gozen die within a swamp, and therefore Yabushi had regained a portion of strength at the moment of Tsuki's death. He did not yet realize the connection; when he realized, he would regret her sacrifice, suspecting that Tsuki had let herself be slain for precisely this cause.

The bakemono rolled onto his back, thick fluids widening from the rent he lay upon. His black eyes blinked several times; and by his fear, it was evident that he knew he was dying.

Yabushi and his sister approached the bakemono. Weak as the small samurai felt, he yet handled his sword with purpose.

"Please do not take my head!" begged the bakemono.

"Why should I not?" Yabushi snapped, supported by his tall, slender sister. "Bakemono eat people. You caused one of my friends to die, and injured another. You have been an especially poor husband to my sister whom you stole."

"But I want to keep my head," he whined, and started to bawl. "It is true bakemono eat people, but so do human folk eat fish, and snakes eat mice. It is how we live! And had I not allowed my wife to nurse her brother back to health, I might stand this moment a victor. So I am not wholly evil. I beg you reconsider. I have already lost my tail. Let me keep my head! Please!"

Tomoe grunted, trying to regain strength. She turned her face from the mud, peered through a haze of pain and said, "Be merciful, Little Bushi. A poor trophy is a coward's head anyway."

Yabushi said to the bakemono, "I have more reason than you to be unhappy; and my sister has a greater need for vengeance than you ever did. But you will have your way. I will still cut off your head, but will leave it in your keeping."

"You are kind," said the bakemono, sniffling. "Kind enough to grant one more favor?"

"What favor?" asked Yabushi, annoyed by the wheedling coward, and by his own pity for the dying beast.

"I wish to be cremated and buried in an urn with my grave marked, as is done for human folk. Then, perhaps, I will be reborn a man."

Tomoe heard this, remembering a time when the bakemono said that bakemono were *more* than humankind. She, too, pitied the ogre, who hated himself so well.

"With what name would I mark the grave of a bakemono?" asked Yabushi. "Bakemono have no names."

"I have a name," said the bakemono. "I invented one." His tears fell harder, for much as Tomoe and Yabushi pitied him, he yet pitied himself more. "Kwashiorki is my name. It is good?"

"Kwashiorki," said Yabushi, trying the sound. It was ugly like a bakemono, but Yabushi said, "It is fine. You will have your grave."

Trusting the word of a samurai, the bakemono grew calm.

With the aid of his sister who held the bakemono's head up by pendulous ears, Yabushi cut all around the neck. The bakemono did not complain, accepting this painful demise. His executioners twisted the cut neck until the bones broke loose, and Kwashiorki breathed and wept no more. They folded his arms to hold his head. Then the sister of Yabushi went to built a fire for the cremation.

Tomoe Gozen's poor vision faded more, and then there was darkness without sound.

There were obscured recollections of a pyre outside the lodge, made from coals fetched by Yabushi's sister; of weird faces watching in amazement from the nighted marsh as a monster received human rites. The bakemono burned like dry sticks, the fire raging in the darkness, and finally going out. The dank of the ground quickly cooled the ashes. The child samurai and the slender woman gathered the grey ash into a pot which would serve as urn.

As these tasks were performed, an old woman nursed Tomoe, while Tomoe alternately leered mindlessly, fought imagined wraiths, cried out in agony, and wept tears from emotional nightmare. The old woman seemed like someone from Tomoe's childhood: a dimly remembered, nurturant aunty, or Tomoe's gruff, mischief-making grandmother, who was still alive and still a fighter. Later, she seemed not nurse, but the vengeful dame of a bakemono, and Tomoe was afraid. Finally, she was only a strange witch with a gnarly cane whom Tomoe had met twice before.

When the ashes of the bakemono were gathered, and the sun began to rise, Tomoe discovered herself no longer attended by an old and all too mortal hag, but by a beautiful goddess of eternal, heavenly beauty. There was no gnarly cane, but, instead, a shining, handled object quickly tucked into the robe of the goddess before Tomoe could tell what it was.

Yabushi's sister strapped the two-pronged sword to her back, then tied the sealed pot of ashes by a rope around her neck with a wife's care of a husband.

It then transpired that Tomoe attended the actual funeral, for she was carried to the site. Yabushi and his sister each held a leg; the goddess bore most of the weight on her own back. Tomoe felt weightless, as though borne atop a cloud, her eyes only occasionally opening and seeing sun through the leaves of the swamp's trees, feeling her back against the warm, soft comfort of a deity's shoulders. Her head bobbed, and now and then she saw the woman and child holding her feet out of the mire.

All this while, there was a persistent buzzing in Tomoe's head, remnant of the sword's strange touch.

She was brought, with the bakemono's ashes, to a dry hill where the goddess blessed the pot as a proper urn. Then the bakemono was buried near the tomb of Great Lord Walks. Little Bushi planted the narrow grave marker on the plot, the name of Kwashiorki burnt into the wooden slat. The goddess made a strange promise, that from the slat would grow a tree which would be known among the gods as Kwashiorki's Shade. Tomoe was not certain that she approved of the fuss, when Tsuki Izutsu's corpse had been carried off by a raving red oni, a proper burial never given *her*.

After the burial ceremony, overseen by the goddess, Tomoe was carried further. She was taken away from the bakemono's grave, and to the Shinto shrine.

There were fragments of conversations among these memories, words shared between the two mortals and the goddess after the building of the pyre and before the arrival at the shrine. The content of these exchanges seemed more vague than dreams, certainly more vague than the Dream of Seven Oni, which had been in some fashion real. Tomoe constantly fell back into comatose slumber, especially when considering the import of the conversations she overheard.

She half overheard, or dreamed, or imagined that Tsuki Izutsu was not actually or precisely dead, but joined with some greater thing which the goddess abhorred but which Yabushi and his sister thought wonderful. In another sense, Tsuki may have chosen her own moment of going, having understood the workings of the bakemono's curse, knowing that only this sacrifice would save Yabushi. Contrary to this, perhaps Tomoe Gozen was personally responsible for Tsuki's death; for Tomoe had implored the goddess save Yabushi, aware that someone else would have to die in his place if the request were to be honored. This was too terrible for Tomoe to believe, and her conscience was eased by the possibility that even gods could gamble, and none of the playing chips *or* the players were wholly responsible, unknowing until the last moment who was to live and who to die.

A larger fate, which ruled even gods (presumably at their bequest, lest certainty destroy Them with attendant ennui), was the source of Tsuki's demise, or absorption.

Thus, caught between anger at deities who saw to Tsuki's end, guilt for seeing to it herself, and awe of the imposing force beyond the very gods, Tomoe slipped in and out of half-consciousness. When she finally awoke—a real awakening—it was within the shrine's small temple.

Her head burned from the double cut, but had been cleansed of any matter which might have cause purulence. Her clothing had been somewhat cleaned as well, but were torn and ragged. She wondered momentarily how bad a scar she would have, but was not upset by any prospect.

Near her stood Yabushi, no worry on his brow, for he trusted the goddess who bowed over Tomoe. Behind Yabushi stood a tall woman, a twin-bladed sword strapped to her back. She was somehow less beautiful without her sorrow, for the sorrow had made of her a remarkable tragic portrait. Now she was an averagely attractive woman, calm like her brother, proud. These siblings must have absorbed something of the goddess' healing presence, for neither seemed adversely influenced by all that had transpired; both were renewed of vigor, as Tomoe was not.

In all probability the sister knew she was still required as a geisha, for she had been legally indentured. But given the circumstances and the unlikelihood of her retrieval without Yabushi and his aides, it was likely that she could be redeemed cheaply, and Yabushi would retain a good portion of his small inheritance after all. Further, since the young woman was the proprietor of a sword of limitless worth, it could be that in the end the poor Rooster clan would be wealthy.

It was seven days after Tomoe's awakening at the shrine before she was able to piece together all that transpired in the aftermath of adventure. By then, she had left Yabushi and his sister in the village, having held them good-bye, having seen especially that Yabushi would have safe passage to his dojo. Then the weary samurai trod once more upon the lonely road, toward a colored twilight, with all the half-memories of semi-consciousness whirling through her head. She thought especially of the crone-cum-goddess who had nursed her, and of returning to reasoning wakefulness in the shrine.

On that waking moment, the goddess bowed to Tomoe Gozen's prone body, and placed her lips twice upon Tomoe's forehead.

The kisses burned, and healed. The pain increased a moment, then was gone entirely, and a month's healing was done in the span of those two kisses. Tomoe was given temporary respite, or peace, which lasted until she was on the road again. Only then was she given to these thoughts, these efforts to reconstruct the last hours' daring enterprise.

Before the goddess had vanished from her shrine, she had brought forth from her robes a bronze mirror. It shone like the sun. She held it before Tomoe who arose, cured by the perverse medicine of Izanami's lips. Tomoe beheld her own reflection, and the twin-scar on her forehead: two white, ragged, vertical markings which looked like waves of the ocean facing one another in stormy combat. Viewed one way, the scar was like Tomoe's family crest, embossed upon her brow. Viewed another way, it was like the third eye of certain Buddhas, which was shocking to see in a Shinto place, but good homage to the nun who gave her life.

"Thank you, Izanami," Tomoe had whispered, and reached to embrace the goddess…but the light of the mirror expanded, then faded, and Izanami was gone.

These days later, upon the road, Tomoe found that she had become introspective for a while, remembering all of this.

"Tomoe Gozen."

Sitting beneath a tree, resting from the road, was an itinerant priest, a rokubu, vile and filthy as some of them could be, or more so than others. Generally they carried images of Buddha eternally upon their backs, held on by rope, and never put them down. This one had not merely set the burden aside—he had hung the Buddha from the tree by its throat.

"You know me," answered Tomoe, stopping before the priest who called her by name. She trod the road unshod, having lost her clogs and tabi socks in the marshland days before. The rokubu had set out a fine, new pair of clogs and tabi, perhaps as a temptation only, perhaps to inform the samurai that here sat a rokubu of more than a beggar's means.

"A disfavored hero," he said, qualifying his knowledge of her. "And you know me as well, though not by name. Mine is never spoken."

"I know you," she admitted. "A year ago I slept in a peasant farmhouse, hosted by a family. That was at the beginning of my *musha-shugyo.* You came to the door to beg."

Musha-shugyo was a kind of schooling unobtainable in dojo or academy. It was had only on the road, gleaned from harsh experience. This hard-knocks university was not chosen by the will of Tomoe Gozen, for disfavor had necessitated her route. It had been useful nonetheless, though perhaps its use was served and no longer best required.

It was often the case that seeming coincidence marked the beginning and end of some precise phase of an individual's life, framing certain events as it were. It was possible, therefore, that this fat, vagrant rokubu had come again because Tomoe's musha-shugyo was coming to a close. The rokubu said, "It was kind of you to spare me this *mon* when first

we met, poor though you were." He held his hand up and open so that the samurai standing over him could see that he held a coin of small worth, perhaps the very coin she had given him. "I see by your ragged state today your need is greater than mine."

In fact, Yabushi had offered her a gift from his ryo, and when she refused, a loan. She refused that too. But the rokubu's mon she accepted. It seemed to her a ritual, for why else would he have saved it? And why this gift of quality shoes, except that she needed them for faster travel; would a rokubu care if she could go quickly or not?

There was many a "why" about the rokubu. Coincidence would not serve to explain two meetings in widely separated regions at critical stage in the samurai's development. There had to be a reason for his planting his buttocks along her road on this particular hour.

For some reason, she did not doubt that he could have met with her anytime, anywhere. How she felt this to be so, she could not ascertain. Rokubu were not more clever than ninja. Far less so. And she had evaded ninja for several weeks at a time. But this rokubu was different from other beggar-priests, and she was certain the moment and manner of their meeting was his choice.

She suspected he was a jono priest, a magician-ninja. Certainly he was not truly Buddhist, or the idol would not be hung as from a gibbet, a whimsical but damning insult to Buddhism. Too, he had spoken cryptically about his never-spoken name. Jono guarded their names and their faces. This one did not guard his face, it was true, which she admitted was not in keeping with her feeling that he was jono. But the magician-ninja used sorcery; perhaps this one had other faces. She hated to think what he *might* be…if not jono.

"My blessings for the coin," she said, tucking it away. "My gratitude for the shoes," for she took for granted they were hers.

The rokubu nodded, and pressed his palms together. He said, "One mon and clothing for your feet are not all I bring to you. You may have already guessed your road changes today. You are no longer ronin, if you were ever truly so. You are sworn to Lady Toshima, who has need of you."

"She sends you?" asked Tomoe, her interest captured. She had set herself down beside the priest to put on the tabi and clogs. The rokubu's own feet, barely revealed beneath the hem of his robe, were naked and excessively dirty.

Hard, cold eyes sparkled with harder, colder humor. "No one sends me," he said. "But I come."

The coldness pressed at Tomoe, and she nearly cringed from the chill. She remembered the cold rain of the night she first met him.

"Then why?" she asked, not one "why" but many.

"This past year," he began, looking at her from those strange, penetrating eyes, "Goro Maki has been guardian to Toshima and her mother. That was Lord Shigeno's final command. But Goro has been mightily unhappy, so that Toshima gave him leave of the world."

Taking leave of the world meant that Goro Maki had shaved his head and become a priest. Perhaps in some unfathomed way, the rokubu *was* Buddhist, an obscure variety to whom sacrilege against idols came easily; or else how would he know Goro had done this thing...

"Goro loves the Shinto gods!" Tomoe said. Shintoism had no monasteries, so the rokubu's news struck harshly. It meant Goro had become a Buddhist.

"Not all Buddhists malign Shintoism," said the rokubu, his foul breath wafting toward Tomoe. His reassurances eased her somewhat, for all his personal vileness. "He has retreated to the mountains, among the yamahoshi. They owe allegiance to none! They study everything; teach it to any who swear to an ascetic's life."

"Like your own?" she said, and his eyes glinted once more with icy humor.

"Worse than mine," he answered.

At least the yamahoshi were martial priests. Goro had therefore not put down his sword, which was encouraging. Still, he must have been very sad indeed to leave the world. Tomoe wished to know, "What made my friend unhappy?"

The beggar-priest made a gesture of unknowing, though probably he did know. He said, "Maybe he was bound by samurai codes to avenge the death of his warlord. However, suppose the killer of Shigeno was a friend! To escape his duty, he might have preferred to end his life as a samurai and start anew as a monk."

"You are cold indeed," said Tomoe, stricken, "to bring these tidings. I have lately come from a Shinto haunt, and know the gods are real. Perhaps Buddhist gods are real as well, and you are some god of mischief."

She had said this in wicked jest, then wondered if it were true.

"I may be that," he said. "I may not. In whichever case, you are needed by Toshima. She and her mother are left without retainers, and the Shogun has her watched. He does not like the stories she has written since last you saw her. They are coy stories, damning of unnamed officials in high office. Things would have gone well with her but that she is compelled to intrigues!" The rokubu laughed, half sinister and half appreciative. "The Shogun no longer suffers her to write. He has decreed she take up brush no more, or else join the Mikado in exile. She is proud, and has chosen the latter course, though knowing the Shogun fears her glib texts will find their way back to the main islands nonetheless. She may not survive to see exile."

"To what port must I go?" asked Tomoe, quick in her resolve.

"If you are swift, you may reach Hojikai Harbor before she is gone, and join her as is proper for her last retainer. The shoes will speed your course. But if you go, you may return to the main isles of Naipon only on penalty of death. You will be exile-by-association, and the Shogun would have you challenged if you ever returned."

"The Shogun has no champion who can slay me," said Tomoe, not meaning it as a boast. The rokubu's ill-words were fondly heard, for she would rather be challenged openly than be hunted anymore by ninja. Even if she were defeated in the contest, it would at least not be a dog's death without notice. Yet it remained that to the knowledge of Tomoe, the Shogun had no champion good enough. Therefore Tomoe might return to Naipon anytime she wished, be challenged honorably, win honorably, and cause the Shogun immeasurable dishonor if he harried her longer.

The rokubu lowered his face, closed his eyes, his hands still folded as in prayer. He said in a barely audible voice, "The Shogun has a champion," and when Tomoe did not ask, he volunteered: "Ugo Mohri."

Tomoe Gozen started. She had learned much on the road, but she was not at all certain she could yet defeat Naipon's best disciple of bushido.

Ugo Mohri was her nemesis, not because they disliked each other, but because they would want to meet again and test one another, this time each with proper swords. He had toyed with her before, but she had used a foreign style of fighting unfit, she learned, for samurai. It must eat at him to wonder if he could beat her still. It ate at Tomoe Gozen.

If Ugo Mohri had remained with the Mikado, the duel could never be, for the Mikado would not desire it. But Ugo was faithless—had managed to preserve his position when the Mikado fell. No doubt it had taken the full year to arrange this good grace, which was why Tomoe had not heard of it before.

"You will hesitate to sail?" asked the rokubu, knowing she would not.

"I will serve Toshima always. But I will not fear returning to Naipon. When I face Ugo Mohri, he will know that we are equals; in anticipation of that meeting, I will train to make it certain. And on that day, I will stand as reminder of his unfaith with the Mikado, a graver weakness than he may yet believe. He himself named me the Mikado's samurai. I may become the Mikado's vengeance!"

Blood had rushed to her face when she said this, but it quickly drained away, and Tomoe added without the ostentation, "But Toshima did not send you, priest. It may be that she does not wish my service anymore. If my unfortunate slaying of Shigeno ruined Goro Maki, so might it have ruined Toshima's love for me."

"You need not think it. By her intrigue, and because of her kinship with the Mikado, she learned in advance that the Battle of Shigeno Valley was inevitable. If I am not mistaken, she tried to convince you to run away with her in some fashion? She would have kept you from it all. You thought it a childish crush, but Toshima was wiser. It was at her bequest that the Mikado sent two magician-ninja to guard her father; and she personally directed the jono-priestess to protect you also. What she had not foreseen was that you and Shigeno would meet on the battlefield. The jono could not protect you both, so it was left to fate. She blamed herself more than others."

"You know a lot," said Tomoe with a hint of antipathy. She had long believed the culprit of Shigeno's downfall was the Mikado—but the Mikado had granted immunity. Certainly the sorcerer of Ho who brought the war could not be blamed, manipulated as he had been from the Imperial City. And though Toshima might blame herself, she could hardly be held to fault for wishing those she loved protected.

There was only one felon in the end, and that the hand which slew— the hand of Tomoe Gozen. What wonder Goro Maki would wish a grudge match against her. Goro's honor and dedication to his bushido would have dictated he seek out Tomoe regardless of friendships, and fight even loving her. But again, Toshima would have intervened. Since Goro had been directed to obedience to Shigeno's daughter, there would have been only one way out of the dilemma: seppuku. Toshima would have guarded against suicide as well, directing her protector to a mountain retreat instead, denying him his pride and his status, forcing him into retirement more cruel than honored death.

Toshima had inherited the Mikado's manipulative prowess. And like the Mikado, it had lost her much when every tile was played. She was no betrayer; she played the game for the game's sake, not for spoils.

"Your intent?" asked the filthy robuku, interrupting her reverie.

"I will go with the Lady into exile. Mischief you may bring, but I thank you for it, for much of this I did not know before, although it makes good sense, and good sense to know. Tell me, am I bound to you in some way—I would return to you the favor."

"I require nothing," said the rokubu. "For news and mischief, you need do one thing: resolve to play the game well, and use the pieces given. That you would do anyway, unto death, even without me. But you surprise me Tomoe! I thought you would ask me about the jono priestess, for it is true as you say, I know much."

Tomoe's heart leapt. "Tell me of her."

"Of who?" he asked, acting innocent.

She did not like to be teased. She said hotly, "The jono priestess, whom you mentioned."

"There are many priestesses in that strange sect. Which one do you mean?"

Tomoe stood abruptly, angered. She said, "So! The conniving rokubu does not know everything! If I told you her name, it would be the biggest treachery of my life." This said, Tomoe Gozen drew forth her sword, slashed, and sheathed it again, in one quick motion. The rokubu never blinked. The Buddha, hanging from the tree, fell to the ground, free of its noose. Tomoe said, "A Buddhist friend of mine, gone from this life, would not have liked him hanging there."

She bowed to the rokubu, then went away.

PART III
The Invisible Path

An enormous bronze Buddha hovered in the air, held by winch and pulley. The wharf creaked and bent beneath the relic's bulk. Forty laborers strained to center it off the end of the dock, to lower it gently onto the junk. It was the Mikado's own Buddha, so they were careful. Slowly, it lighted on the thick, wooden pallet in the center of the junk's deck. Laborers crawled over it like ants, removing ropes, placing the moving apparatus into the hold, for it would be needed at the voyage's end.

The junk's hull sank low in the water, to the very limit of its endurance, held down by the heavy bronze.

Toshima's mother oversaw the project. Old beyond her actual years, her hair was already greying, and once-stately Madame Shigeno was losing the straightness of her spine. She was strong nonetheless, and hurried along the dock with lively step, squawking orders like a raven. Toshima herself walked along the beach, potentially her last walk upon any of Naipon's major isles, which was sad to think. Beside her strode the samurai, recently arrived, to Toshima's delight and surprise. She peered from behind her fan with undisguised happiness, in spite of the sorrow of the voyage, and stepped with a more girlish bounce than she had affected in a while.

They stopped between the two big rocks, out of sight of the wharf, leaned against the smaller of the rocks, side by side. A crab scuttled sideways, digging its way out of sight. The women looked at one another, and Tomoe thought without saying: *Toshima, you have changed, as have I.* The last month, if not the whole year, had obviously worn on the Lady. She was tired, and more somber than before, but also matured, for all her girlish act.

It had been a long time since Tomoe had true commerce with Naipon's nobility, and Toshima seemed almost alien. On the road, the samurai had grown used to seeing peasant women hardened by toil, or fellow travelers weathered by adventure; and women such as these had given Tomoe an untraditional concept of beauty. Yet Toshima remained beautiful too, it could not be denied. For the first time, Tomoe wondered what the Lady would look like without cosmetics. It could be arranged to find out. Unlike most samurai, Tomoe might share a bath with the Lady.

But that assumed luxuries. The small island to which they were being sent would have few of those. Baths would be swift, cold experiences in rushing streams—not calm exercises in warm, enclosed chambers with maidens to stroke, cleanse, and loosen muscles.

"You have acquired a scar," said Toshima, and reached out to touch the smooth, white marks on the samurai's dark forehead.

"A good scar, as they go," said Tomoe.

"That is so. It looks like two waves of the sea. Surely you are luck for the voyage."

Tomoe turned her face away from Toshima's touch, could not see the junk or workers or wharf from where she leaned upon the rock. She said, "It is not a good season for seafaring."

"The Shogun knows," said Toshima, and smiled a sardonic rather than seductive smile. Indeed, thought Tomoe, the Shogun might welcome the loss of these voyagers. The junk provided was in horrendous disrepair, an insult to Lady Toshima, and dangerous. It was hardly suited to transport under best circumstances, and might threaten to crumble into flotsam by the weight of the gargantuan Buddha which the disenthroned Mikado had commissioned sent.

The danger of the trip should have been enough to satisfy the Shogun, but Tomoe quickly suspected other measures were made as well. She heard the sound of someone slinking near; only a ninja could have been more still. Apparently the Shogun was not so certain the voyage would prove sufficiently fatal.

Tomoe caught Toshima's eyes. The Lady had heard the movement too. When Tomoe reached for her sword, Toshima touched the swordwoman's hand to stay the draw, and whispered, "I cannot believe they dare."

Four samurai stepped out from amidst the rocks upon the beach, two on each side of the narrow space between boulders where the Lady and her samurai rested and talked. These four men bowed low, grandly respectful. They were bigger than most samurai, dressed well but not richly. Toshima stepped away from the rock, chin raised, and demanded, "Is the honor of samurai preserved by killing me?"

"Not you, Lady," said the nearest. "But you must take no retainers with you into exile. We come for Tomoe Gozen."

One of the samurai grabbed Toshima from behind, held her with arm around her throat, pulled her from the path of promised battle. The other three drew their swords. Tomoe had not drawn her own, but said coolly,

"The Shogun must despise you also." She drew her sword at last, and added, "For he sends you to your doom."

While Tomoe guarded against three swords, Toshima was not idle. She reached into her hair and withdrew a long steel pin. A moment later, it was lodged in the spleen of the man who held her. He let go, staggered back, trying to remove the needle. Toshima turned to face him with her fan wide open. He was not prepared for her attack, was directed not to kill her anyway, and least expected that her fan would be razor tipped around its edge. She slid the fan along the samurai's neck before he realized. Blood pumped forth in gushes from the big vein.

In the same moment, Tomoe had slain her foremost attacker, and was left with only one murderous emissary before, and one behind. Trapped between unyielding boulders, it was difficult to move and to guard both front and back. Lady Toshima threw her fan at the back of Tomoe's rear attacker. The fan spun through air, struck deep enough into the samurai's shoulder to stick there, weakening him, but not stopping him.

Tomoe met the forward blow with one that countered, then slid her sword smoothly behind and broke the attack of the injured man at her back. With dizzying speed, the sword came forward again, before her attacker could complete a new maneuver; and again, she slashed backward in time to keep the other man from pricking her kidney.

It was difficult to do more than this defensive action, in her confined space. Few could protect their own front and back while simultaneously launching an assault.

The rear attacker was losing strength as blood flowed down his back from the sharp edge of the fan. Toshima brought forth another pin from her hair, threw it like a dagger. It sped past Tomoe's shoulder, took the front attacker through the eye. The man squealed, dropped his sword, then fell to the ground when Tomoe's sword cleaved through his shoulder. She whisked about, broke the attack of the other instantaneously.

Toshima retrieved her fan and the second pin, knelt to a tidepool to remove the blood. Tomoe cleaned her sword on the jacket of the last to fall. Only one of the four still lived, the one losing blood from his jugular and with Toshima's other hairpin in his spleen. Already he was pale from blood loss, too weak even to plead a more honored death by the sword. But Tomoe understood his eyes, and her sword licked down to where he sat, cutting through the bones of his chest and exposing the heart.

The women walked away, did not look back, told no one of the encounter. On the wharf, Toshima looked at the great Buddha sitting in the decrepit junk, and reminded, "A dangerous voyage ahead. It would be best to wait a month."

"If we could," said Tomoe, and smiled for the first time that day. She added, "But we would have to kill too many if we stayed."

Three days at sea and no untoward incidents, Tomoe Gozen almost found relaxation, despite the serene, impudent face of the Buddha which watched her every motion. Or so it felt to be. No matter where she walked in front of it, the eyes seemed always on her, though she could not properly say she had seen them move.

The junk glided smoothly over calm waters, the wind a gentle nudge against the slatted sails. Tomoe stood aft, to avoid the Buddha's eyes, and looked into the clear, green waters. The sun was at a good angle to see deep into the sea, and Tomoe thought she beheld a white highway and a temple. When she looked harder, she saw less. A patch of cloud passed before the sun, and when the cloud moved on, there remained nothing of Tomoe's illusion of a seafloor road.

Buddhism provided the sects for richer Naiponese, but the sailors were poor, therefore as disturbed by their cargo as was Tomoe. They paid homage and apology to the Shinto gods of the sea and wind several times a day, and gazed never on the bronze visage of the Buddha. The prayers may have held sway for these three days, but toward evening of the third, billows of angry clouds erased the sunset, waiting ominously in the distance. The sailors began to batten down their supplies, in preparation for ill weather.

That night, there were no stars, for clouds engulfed the sky. The junk's sails were folded tight, making of the craft a sleeping beast. Firebrands burned fore and aft, reflecting orange trails out into the sea. There was no other light. The voyagers watched the sky with terrified anticipation, but there was no wind, no wave, no obvious cause of alarm. Only the atmosphere was noticeably changed, seeming stifling and thick; and the sailors wrought their own atmosphere of dread.

The Buddha's bronze visage was black upon the night. A fire brand reflected in its eyes, nowhere else.

Then, way off over sea, a sound arose, the sound of all voyagers ever taken by the sea, their souls bound to the underwater land of the Dragon Queen and the mythic city of sea-dead, sea-folk, and horrifying gods. The sea-dead rose from slavery on rare occasion, to become the bitter, hateful Divine Wind.

Rain refused to fall. No wind touched the ship. But they heard that terrifying wind growing louder, and the sailors fell in anxious prayer, clapping their hands and chanting: "Protect us! Protect us! Oh Heaven do Protect us!"

Toshima's mother came up from the junk's bowels, lit joss sticks from a firebrand, placed these lengths of incense in the lap of the Buddha. The pungence wafted along the deck, and out upon the sea.

White fire blazed momentarily in the distance, briefly lighting the roof of roiling, tortured clouds. Moments later, there was a deep, throaty growl—as though the Dragon Queen had waked, had breathed the fire.

Still, the rain would not fall. But the wind rose fast and screaming, and sailors screamed back in fear. The calm sea became a hell of angry fists, reaching up higher and higher with each blow upon the complaining hull. One fist reached up in fore, another aft, and doused the brands. The Buddha's eyes continued to glow, not with fire, but with icy blackness darker than the dark. Tomoe wondered if the seated figure would suddenly stand, but it did not, for no Buddha could ever rule the sea.

Buddhas captured naught but human minds.

Tomoe held Toshima onto the deck as the junk rocked and twisted about. An invisible sword—the wind—slashed the folded sails, tore the mast from the junk and flung it into the sea. Sailors screamed louder, mourning for themselves.

Toshima's mother stood before the Buddha with her hands held high, shouting a charm or prayer of entreaty at the huge bronze figure who watched her dispassionately. Woe be to the world if the gods should ever war on each other, so the Buddha remained passive. A wave swept over the deck, soaking all in spite of the lack of rain. Madame Shigeno alone had dared to be standing, and only the prematurely old woman was washed away. Toshima struggled to escape Tomoe, to crawl to the edge of the deck where she would have cried out uselessly for her mother. But Tomoe held fast, lest her mistress go over the rail. The Lady kicked in tantrum.

The deck of the junk began to crack, the pressures of the stirring sea pulling the wooden hull in various directions. The wood cried like a man. The Buddha, sitting on its heavy pallet, added to the tensions. It fell through the deck and punctured the bottom of the hold.

Sailors were already trying to launch fishing boats over the side, but the living sea reached out with cruel fingers, snatched the boats, pulled them away and down. Braver sailors flung themselves to their doom. Others clung to the rails and to life and begged the sea to spare them.

The junk was sinking fast, drawn down by the giant Buddha and the sea's grisly insistence. Only the head of the Buddha protruded from the junk's bowels, its shoulders below the broken deck. Something must have pushed at it from below, for the statue began to rise...then fell once more so the junk split near in two. Then the sea enveloped the whole of the junk. The Buddha's head was last to sink from view, gone perhaps to decorate some hall of the Dragon Queen's country, for the folk below could not make their own ornaments and stole even their cities by sinking lived-on islands.

In the raging waters, Tomoe clung to Toshima. The Lady used her fan like a fish's fin, and it was difficult to say who was keeping who afloat. They saved each other, or at least held one another back from swifter death. They gasped each time a wave passed out from under them, filled their lungs with air, then held their breaths until the clinging sea let them up once more.

Wenoy-Adrian Shultz

All was darkness, or nearly. Tomoe's eyes strained to see through salty sea, black as squid's ink. She could not tell up from down when submerged with Toshima, and was not certain if what she was seeing were vagrant stars above, or city lights below. The sky, she knew, was shrouded with clouds—but what fire could burn on the bottom of the sea? There was no logical answer, so Tomoe closed her eyes.

Again, the sea parted from them, and the women choked for air, clutching one another tightly. Tomoe could not see the Lady's face, for all was held in darkness, but she remembered with some irony that she had wished to see Toshima without cosmetics.

Almost as if some chiding deity were granting this request, lightning split the sky with a fiery gulf, and Tomoe saw Toshima's face twisted with fear and agony, frightful as a devil's mask, wet hair clinging like tendrils around a horrifying visage.

Then rain fell at last, so that sea and sky were one, and Tomoe knew they were lost, forever lost, and cursed the awful sea.

It may have been that the sea did not hear Tomoe Gozen's hateful charge, its own racket had been so miraculous. Or the sea may have heard perfectly well, and had set itself about the preparations for a more grueling death for a samurai and her mistress.

Vomiting seawater, Tomoe fought her way upward from a coma deep as the waters. She was entangled with Toshima in lengths of kelp and rope—rope from the winches which had been stored in the junk's belly. They were adrift upon the Buddha's pallet, with no other remnant of the lost voyage in sight.

Toshima lay akimbo amongst the rope, breathing easily and therefore commonly asleep. Tomoe fathomed how it had to have been: the Lady managed to drag both of them onto the pallet, in spite of the tangle of hemp and seaweed which had caught them. Certainly Tomoe had no recollection of herself achieving this temporary salvation or respite. She had been stricken alongside the head by a fragment of the splintered junk. That was her last memory.

The sky was startlingly clear and intensely blue, fading toward light green on the empty horizon, where sky blended with jade waters. The sea was calm. There was no breeze.

Inspecting Toshima, Tomoe saw that the Lady's neck was already blistered from sleeping face-down in the hot sun. Tomoe, hardened by her career, suffered less from the exposure. Carefully, she untangled herself from the ropes, and gently unwrapped Toshima as well, turning her carefully. The Lady stirred, groaned, woke in Tomoe's arms and nearly smiled, but cried out in agony instead.

Her arm was swollen. It was not broken, but badly wrenched. It hurt to move it even a little, but with Tomoe's aid, the injured limb was soon bound between Toshima's breasts, immobilized by the Lady's obi sash which served as bandage and sling.

"Alive at least," said Toshima, her voice husky from so much salt-water swallowed and coughed up. They were grateful for their lives, but shared doubts about their fortune when looking in all directions to see nothing but blue and green horizon.

"We can fashion a sail," said Tomoe. "My sword can serve as mast. My jacket can hold the wind." But when the makeshift sail was fashioned, there was no wind to fill it. Neither did they have a paddle. There was no wrack from the lost junk, aside from their immediate selves, and therefore nothing they might adapt as oar. Eerily, there was not even a natural current to move them on. It was too quickly evident that they could not hope to use the pallet-cum-raft as more than an island of slow, suffering death.

For a long while they sat on the raft, looking at each other, then at their knees, but never at the surrounding sea. They did not speak. They listened to their own breaths, and the tiny waves lapping around the edges of their minimal habitation. In a while, Tomoe began to handle the rope in a diverting manner. Slowly, her eyes grew more and more intense with considerations. Finally, she said,

"We can make a harness of this rope! I will draw the raft with the power of my own limbs."

It was true Naipon bred strong swimmers, being as it was a land of many rivers, lakes, wetlands, and surrounded by oceans and seas. Martial training had given Tomoe stronger arms and legs than most good swimmers could boast. Her will as much as her training rendered her adept at arduous tasks. All the same, it was a terrible thing to set herself to perform, a thing she would not have proposed were there other choices.

Toshima helped as best she could with but one good arm, and soon the two women had fashioned a harness which Tomoe fit over her head and around her shoulders. The further ends of the rope were attached to one edge of the square pallet, which perforce became the prow.

The horror of the night before had left Tomoe less than trustful of the sea, but she entered it, and would long endure it. She swam to the rope's length, took the tension, and pulled. The raft moved slowly at first; but because the sea was calm, it did not battle her strokes. Soon, she was giving Toshima the swiftest ride possible by the power of a single swimmer.

The sun was their only marker. They made way toward the north, where Tomoe expected the greatest concentration of islands.

The first day in the water was tolerably unpleasant; the second educated her more fully in regard to the sea's willful cruelly; and on the third, Tomoe's body began to reveal the horrific effects of extreme fatigue and long-term exposure to the sea. Had Toshima not discovered, by accident, a source of nutrition and unsalted water, certainly the torture could not have gone on so long.

Toshima hung her arm off the back of the raft, inadvertently providing a rudder. She gasped, injured by ongoing exposure, hunger, dehydration. Fish swam slowly beneath the shelter of the raft, and one chanced to brush against Toshima's hand. Fitfully, she snatched at it, captured it, bit into it's living flesh, madly desirous of an end to her famished state. She was surprised to realize she had bitten into a bladder which was neither salt nor urine, but part of the specie's biological system of ballast.

For the second and third day of Tomoe's long swim, Toshima provided food and drink by the determined speed of her reaching arm. On the fourth day, constant exposure to the sea stole Tomoe's ability to swallow, and the fish vanished in any event, learning their danger in Toshima's proximity. Thereafter, both women were expiring with increased rapidity.

Though stronger, Tomoe suffered more. Every muscle shouted for release. Her very bones commanded rest. The sea sapped the warmth from her body despite the relative warmth of the surfacemost layer; her arms, hands, face and feet wrinkled until she looked like a hideously diseased crone. Eventually the cramps were too awful to endure, and she was repeatedly forced to climb onto the raft and lie in exhaustion. Toshima was helpful during these periods. Tomoe would lay belly down while the Lady walked up and down upon the samurai's back, bare feet massaging warmth in, pain out. Tomoe groaned with near-ecstasy, emptied her mind, succumbed to total relaxation and illusion of renewal. But she would not allow these moments to persist. Soon, she slunk over the edge of the raft, returning to her dreadful mission.

The harness abraded her shoulders until they were red and raw. She tried to swim with enough clothing to protect her torso, but wet cloth hampered her, and she was forced to remain naked while in the water, which at least meant dry clothing waited each time she climbed on board.

Once, a strange fish swam beneath the shade of Tomoe, attached itself to her by means of a sucker disc. She was so numb that she did not notice it until, climbing onto the raft for another brief period of rest, the suckerfish let loose and stayed in the water. It had bitten her, and sucked her blood, but the wound was superficial. She watched out for such fish thereafter.

A wind began to rise, and Tomoe's jacket billowed forth—but the gods only teased and toyed. The wind grew still once more. Tomoe slid yet again into the evermore horrendous waters.

She could no longer speak. Her tongue had swollen. Sometimes, she could barely breathe. Although Toshima's sharp eyes kept vigilant watch, as night drew across the fifth day, no isle had betrayed itself in any direction. There seemed no end for Tomoe's labor.

The Lady had been burnt by the sun until every exposed portion of her body was bright red and peeling. Her arm had swelled and darkened. But she did not complain, for looking on Tomoe's misery, she counted her own grief minor. Each time the samurai climbed onto the raft at dusk, she was completely drained, looked to be death's sister.

Sleep brought little peace, for Tomoe could not remain oblivious to the complaints of her every muscle. She suffered terrible chills, although she had reclad herself in all her clothing and Toshima held her close. Later she was fevered, and Toshima stripped the samurai completely, and splashed sea water on her burning body and her face. Twice, she awakened gagging on her own swollen tongue. Toshima kept awake half the night, seeing that Tomoe did not choke to death in her rough, uneven sleep or die of chills and fever.

The next morning, the task was taken up anew. After five awful days, she did not imagine the sea could cause her worse misery. But her tongue grew larger still, blackened, could not be moved. Mucus drained from her nostrils, slicked her face. Her skin shriveled more, and whitened, until she looked no longer fully human, but like a member of the sea-dead, as though the sea prepared her in advance for an eternal existence as a thrall-corpse for the folk of the Dragon Queen's saline country.

Numbness had erased the pain at least, save only for the cramps which came and went; but weakness was making her less effective in drawing the raft. She could feel so few parts of herself that she was sometimes unaware that she was moving her arms and legs, and sometimes she forgot to do so, floating in a daze until Toshima's shouting broke through to her vague awareness.

Regularly, she was set upon by cramps which caused her to pull herself into a ball, and sink helplessly below the surface. When this happened, Toshima drew her forth like a fish, struggling to get her onto the raft. Each time, she begged the samurai to give up the hopeless intent, to let death come less painfully than this.

Tomoe could not talk, could not even draw her black tongue back into her mouth; but if she could have spoken she would have said: You and I will not be slaves to the sea-folk. We will not dwell in the Dragon Queen's city, our cold flesh monstrous among monsters. I will bring us to some island, if only a rock incapable of sustaining us. We will die on land, and be attended by better gods than these!

With this unsaid, but grimly considered, she slipped again from the side, and Toshima lamented, as though Tomoe were already drowned. Lady Toshima scanned the horizon constantly, ever with hope, but not much of that. She also watched the strained, wretched swimmer, lest the woman cramp up, and sink away, and die before the desperate Lady could draw her up one-handed.

The sun treated Toshima as harshly as the sea treated Tomoe. Tomoe's aqueous task kept her from dehydrating, while Toshima lost moisture from every pore. She tempted herself to devour salt water, but refrained.

The Lady's face was blistered, and the blisters drained yellow fluids. She might have mourned her ruined beauty, but for the tortured face of Tomoe, leached of faintest coloration, shriveled to the texture and appearance of liverwort except around the eyes, where her lids were puffy near the point of sealing off her vision. Whenever Tomoe climbed on the raft to rest, Toshima would massage her while both shrank behind the slim shade of the samurai's jacket, which still hung upon the sword, a useless sail. It was Toshima's moment of rest too, for touching Tomoe was no hard task; whereas while Tomoe labored, Toshima must do so also, lest the hitched samurai drown or some island go unseen.

"Punish my vanity, Amaterasu!" Toshima cried, and took up her own task beneath an angry sun.

Several times, a panic-stricken Tomoe returned to the raft, having hallucinated monsters in the sea, for eventually her mind was affected. At last, however, she swam blindly, her eyes so swollen, while Toshima tugged the lines like the reins on a horse, directing the path ever north. When a monster truly appeared, Tomoe could not see it.

Toshima shouted half-hysterically, pulled viciously on the reins. Tomoe was still powerful enough to keep Toshima from drawing her back to the raft.

"Tomoe!" she screamed. "Stop swimming! Let me pull you in! A shark is coming!"

A swimmer's long strokes emulated a dying animal thrashing in the water, easy prey to a shark's point of view. The beast was rushing toward the thrashing samurai. Tomoe's ears were plugged and swollen, but somehow she heard, and turned to swim toward the raft, barely evading death.

The shark lingered. It swam around and around the raft, puzzled by it. They tried to wait it out, but it would not go. Yet good came of it, for it was the longest period of rest Tomoe had taken except during the difficult, restless nights. It was probably a good thing she acquired this forced luxury, although rest brought them no closer to any goal—presuming some goal existed in the north to be achieved.

The blackened, lolling tongue of the samurai began to lose some of its excessive size, so that she could hold it in her mouth at least, though it was still too large to allow speech. After a long while out of the water, her eyes were less swollen so that she, like Toshima, could follow the shark's patterned cruise. Feeling returned to her hands and feet, with Toshima's persistent rubbing. Tomoe's nose, however, managed to increase mucus production, so that nose as well as mouth would not allow easy breath. When the samurai began to convulse and gag, Toshima struggled to force breath into her throat, blowing down Tomoe's nostrils and into her mouth.

The shark fin disappeared periodically, but always manifested itself again.

More time passed; and had there been anything more edible than rope, Tomoe might have regained her strength. She could breathe easily at last, but the stress had greatly reduced her energy. By perverse will alone she maintained a semblance of prowess.

The jacket had been the whole time a useless sail, so Tomoe took it down, tied it around Toshima's face to protect her from worse burn. She seemed grateful to have it hidden. With her eyes peering out of the wrapping Tomoe made, Toshima looked a little bit like a jono priestess. For a long time, Tomoe gazed at the Lady, thinking of a certain jono priestess named Noyimo—and perhaps it was a good thing, in that moment, that Tomoe could not speak.

Impatience extended a blinding hand over Tomoe's common sense. She stood from a crouching position, dizzied by her own sudden motion. She looked about until she saw the shark again. Then she pulled her sword out of the raft where it had been stuck as mast and, incredibly, dove into the water.

Toshima gasped, cried out, but could only watch thereafter.

Sharks were the bullies of the sea, and like all bullies, cowards in their hearts. Something thrashing on the surface appealed. Something swimming beneath the waves like a healthy animal gave it pause. The longsword of Tomoe Gozen was wedged between her teeth, steel whiskers below puckered eyes and flat nose. She swam upward at the beast's belly, but it turned aside to see her better, dodged to plot its own attack.

It changed direction unexpectedly, came at her with razored maw open, but bit only her sword, which she had brought to hand. Absurdly, Tomoe took a standing posture, and slashed the beast above her from jaw to belly, successfully gutting it. It swam a distance away, trailing its intestines, excited by the smell of its own blood. The creature knew no pain, but actually began to feast upon its own entrails. When its tiny eyes saw Tomoe again, it came at her with extreme haste. It barely missed her feet as Toshima helped drag the samurai on board.

"Foolish woman!" scolded Toshima, then averted her eyes when Tomoe tried to smile, looking uglier than before. Gazing out to where the stricken shark was shaking and rolling in the throes of death, Toshima was surprised to see many sharks coming to feast upon their kin.

"Worse than before, Tomoe! The blood attracted others!"

On the end of Tomoe's sword was a length of intestine, which she removed carefully, and cut it in half with the sword's keen edge. She handed a piece of it to Toshima, who accepted it; but Tomoe could not even chew without chewing her tongue as well—so that finally Toshima took the piece of intestine, chewed it for the samurai, and forced it from mouth to mouth as a mother bird feeds its infants. Both women gained what nutrition they could from the meager meal.

When the sharks had finished their cannibalistic feast, they sped away to other errands. Tomoe crawled to the edge of the raft, renewed somewhat by her minuscule meal. But Toshima stopped her, said,

"Wait. The sharks left too quickly! Something may have…"

Before she finished her speculation, the surface of the water broke, and a huge spiny globe began to rise. Tomoe watched the monster without much concern, thinking herself again imagining. The gigantic globe fish rose half out of the water, its little eyes beneath the surface, looking back and forth. It's tiny fins paddled furiously. It was a whimsical monster, and apparently harmless, its spiky body mere defense.

"A blessing!" cried Toshima. "Even the ruler of the sea despises sharks, and you have slain one. The Dragon Queen rewards valor!" Tomoe still stood on hands and knees, prepared to enter the water when the hallucination dispersed. She did not restrain Toshima from quickly removing the harness. Toshima threw the rope toward the spiny globe fish, catching it on one of its spines. The fish remained half above the surface, beating its hummingbird fins rapidly, whisking the raft along at a much steadier, swifter clip than Tomoe ever managed. It took them north.

The tracks of foot and knee and hand revealed the passage of two plodding, stumbling, bedraggled survivors out of the sea. The crooked track led from the water's margin to grassy, higher ground. Amidst tall grass, Tomoe and Toshima lay at the side of a freshwater stream, sick from drinking too much too quickly. It was some while before they regained the strength to move along the beach of the island on which they had been deposited.

They found an abandoned farmhouse, proving the island inhabited, or at least inhabited in some past year. The house was very old, in ruinous condition, and looked on first inspection to have been unused for generations. On closer inspection, they thought it must have been used as a camp periodically, or at least a minor supply depot, for the house was stocked with food, clothing, and folk medicines in neatly labeled apothecary jars.

It was mysterious, for the food consisted only of rice, pickles and salted fruit—suggesting that whoever used the place came rarely, keeping only that which stored indefinitely. The clothing, too, was a riddle. It was all sewn for someone of largish size, but it was not all the clothing of a farmer. In a closet hung the yellow robe of a priest, and beside it, a carpenter's pocketed smock; and here again, the motley costume of a strolling actor. As the women moved things about to clear floor space, they found a box containing a carefully folded black hood, black shirt, and black trousers. The sight caused Tomoe to exclaim hoarsely over her barely moveable tongue: "A ninja house!"

For only ninja would need the variety of disguises held here, or an emergency sanctuary with healing drugs, itself disguised as a ruined farmhouse.

From amidst the jars of remedies, Tomoe chose one designated for burns and abrasions. She applied this to Toshima's sunburned hands, face and neck, with the gentlest strokes of her fingers—fingers softened by the long swim, so that the touch hurt Toshima less. After tending to the suffering Lady, Tomoe applied the same ointment to her rope-burned shoulders and torso.

They were still too sick to explore much of the house, but Toshima managed a little. She struck tinder ablaze and started a fire in a hibachi. She bid Tomoe only rest, for the samurai's muscles were yet stiff and needed to be exercised with complete trepidation. Tomoe acknowledged her own need, and let Toshima fetch water from the stream, boil it for rice, and serve a meal as to a lord.

The samurai was impressed by Lady Toshima's stamina, but disconcerted over the swift manner by which her mutual ward set up household in the ninja-farmhouse. By nightfall, the main living quarter had been cleaned and set aright, and not by Tomoe's instigation.

"We cannot live here," said Tomoe, lying on a grass mat and covered by another, her head resting on a wooden pillow, her eyes staring up into darkness.

"Where can we go?" asked Toshima. "We are thrust here by the will of the sea. It must be our home for a while. The sea is visible from our porch, but it may be a long while before we sight a friendly junk to end our marooned state." Her arguments were convincing, but by her inflection it was obvious she anticipated rejection—personal rejection more than rejection of her plan.

"This is no farmhouse," said Tomoe, "and we do not know how long before a ninja comes to use it."

"A long while, Tomoe. If the ninja who once used this place is even still alive, or gave it to an heir, it is still clearly unused now."

Tomoe was too weakened emotionally as well as physically to argue, and too aware of Toshima's unstated intentions to shatter a foolish dream.

As they were indeed castaway, it would be cruel to break the dream which sustained the Lady through hardship. But was it less cruel to let her think Tomoe shared some slight joy of the circumstance? Would it be in the long run more wicked to insinuate through silence that Tomoe held budding pleasure of the prospect of Lady and samurai living farmers' lives, and loving one another? For it *was* love which made Toshima's voice shake and made her fear rejection.

In the night, Tomoe felt a tentative touch. The Lady's hands were no longer soft, though already her burns were getting better, and always she was gentle. Tomoe tried not to stiffen, not to be a sorrow or a disappointment. Toshima's hand moved along Tomoe's skin, which had regained its firmness and was no longer white and wrinkled, but retained its ultra-softness from days submersed. It was a strange sensation, to feel her own softness, and the lady's roughness, the reverse to be expected. It was not erotic, and Tomoe regretted that, for Toshima certainly meant it to be.

In truth, Tomoe had been attracted to women, had loved women. It was tangentially encouraged by her society. Naipon was of limited size, and marriages were arranged for women in their middle twenties, for men in their thirties, so that successive generations of heirs were insured but not so close together that the land grew too populous. Upon marriage, women were expected to be virginal—yet skillful, pleasing lovers. How else to learn proper lovemaking and to preserve a relative chastity, except by the exploration of their own bodies and the bodies of women friends?

The sutras which educated in these matters illustrated much of womanly love. Though rarely discussed, it was inevitable that women gain required skills in this fashion. Thereby, each betrothed would be a proficient lover at wedlock, though having always been (after the given fashion) chaste. It did happen, of course, that women occasionally became more attached to each other than to their eventual husbands, or in some way made themselves altogether ineligible as wives and lived with other women. This was at all times discouraged, and discussed even less than the original matter.

Eventually, Tomoe responded, but she did so by rote, as though comparing her posture to a painting regarding the very subject. She felt a little, but not a great deal. Perhaps she was too weary. *Certainly* she was weary. Toshima's massaging hands soothed muscles which still ached; her hands were welcome, but did not arouse. But Toshima was aroused. Encouraged by Tomoe's relaxed state, the Lady moved her whole body near, raised herself over Tomoe, became Tomoe's blanket, the grass cover cast aside. The moisture of Toshima wetted Tomoe's thigh. The Lady sighed quietly, contentedly.

In the dark of the ninja-house, Tomoe wove a private fantasy, a fantasy of a jono priestess named Noyimo, face bright like the sun. Suddenly Tomoe was aroused, incredibly aroused, and her arms swept up around Toshima. These women had been weakened by the previous days, but it only made them slower and more gentle about their endless, endless endeavor.

Food and care and rest were miraculous healers. In the early dawn, Tomoe Gozen felt revitalized, and went about the investigation of the island which was perforce to be her home. Emotionally, she was not completely strong, but she hid this from herself, refused to admit that mind as well as body had been driven hard upon the sea. She focused attention on her sudden environment, not upon the uneasiness that trembled beneath consciousness.

The island was of reasonable proportion, with two slumbering volcanic peaks, large grasslands, a forest which spread itself up between the ridge which joined the mountains, and several streams which suggested lakes in the highlands. It was a mystery why a nearly idyllic isle would not have encouraged settlement.

Directly, Tomoe learned that a city *had* been established, but abandoned for some inexplicable reason. Ruins came into view when she first topped a rise. From her vantage point, she could see down into the rubble-strewn streets.

The architecture was unlike that of Naipon. Buildings were tall and square and made of stone and masonry instead of wood. It was, in fact, more tomb than town—a city of oversized mausoleums. Yet she knew from her ventures on the mainland that there were indeed peoples nothing like Naiponese, peoples who preferred the permanence of deathly stone over the natural beauty of wooden structure; and, impossible as it seemed, these same people paved roads for fear of native soil; and they graveled their yard where gardens ought to grow; and worst of all, such folk imprisoned their whole cities inside plain grey walls, despising open space. For her own reasoning, Tomoe would have liked to assume the city was left because it was so adverse to living things. But it was not a people of her reasoning who built this place, and therefore her own disdain did not explain the exodus which had given the place over to decay.

At first she was not encouraged to go down and explore the brooding, colorless city. Certainly she would not live there; she would rather risk the ninja-house. She might have gone away and never looked at the city again, even from a distance…except that her eyes captured a motion.

A figure clad in long grey robes moved about the streets. The robe flapped against a wind which rushed between the buildings like a tide. An old woman, Tomoe guessed. From the distance it was difficult to be sure; and the figure had only been visible a bare moment before slipping into a monster's maw of a doorway.

Curious of this one inhabitant, Tomoe hurried down the slope, entered the arched city gate.

Here and then, she chanced upon a vagrant weed which had upset the pave, or a vine which clung with inexorable tenacity, tearing down the walls with the patience of eternity. More rarely, she saw the quick movement of a mammal which had taken residence in the cracks, armies of insects marching single file across established intersections, or a lone bird in a squat, homely tower. In larger part, the city was ignored by all things living, the natural environment choosing to heed the surrounding walls and keep away.

As Tomoe rounded a street corner, she saw a hem of grey robe, grey as the city of stone, vanish around a further turn. The clogs Tomoe had discovered in the ninja-house clacked upon the paved ground, and she considered taking them off, but decided stealth was uncalled for; for the old woman might suspect a sneak to be an enemy. The samurai ran noisily to the corner where the woman had disappeared, and saw again, but barely, the grey garment's hem pulled out of sight.

Hurrying to that corner, Tomoe discovered a blind alley, with no window or door or passage of escape. Yet the old woman was not there.

"Good day, samurai."

"Huh!" Tomoe turned quickly. The old woman had come up behind, and stood with her head held at an odd angle, gazing wistfully. Her face was brown and creased. From the corners of her upper lip, long white hairs grew, had been cultivated into fine, soft, slender, snowy whiskers. One eye was clouded over, but the other was perfectly clear. She peered from the sharp right eye, grinned toothlessly and foolishly, and said, "Skittish, samurai? No danger here. I welcome you to Kyoto."

The woman was mad. Tomoe said, "This is not Kyoto."

"Did I say it was?" She raised her arm in a sweeping gesture, and introduced the city again: "Here is Kamakura. Death City! (Its beauty is a pretense)." She whispered that last.

"A city of death, indeed, old woman. But it is not Kamakura."

"Kyoto," she said again. "City of Sloth. City of Avarice and Waste."

"Old woman, I think you are very crazy."

"Tch!" She stepped sideways like a crab, lithe for all her age. She giggled like a little girl, albeit a slightly ill-sounding little girl. "We are all of us mad!" she said, waxing philosophic. "You are mad! I am mad! All the people here are mad!"

"There are no other people," said Tomoe, keeping her voice even and low.

"Ah! Then you are not yet mad enough!"

The woman was confounding, and Tomoe was becoming dubious about the wisdom of conversing with a madwoman. Birdlike and slender, her whiskers swaying in a breeze, the woman was the very epitome of aged innocence. Tomoe returned the intense gaze, and asked carefully, "Old woman, can you tell me what city this really is?"

"Naniwa!"

Tomoe grumbled. "It is not Naniwa!"

"Whore City! Naniwa! Sailor's Delight!"

"Old woman, this island is not Naipon. It is a littler land than that, with two peaks and only one city, one not of Naiponese design."

"You think me feeble? I know it!"

Patience, Tomoe lectured herself, and tried another tack. "You live here?" she asked.

"I? No!" the oldster said indignantly. "I would live in a Whore City? Do I look like a whore? I come to scoff at whores! To scoff at the avaricious; the self-indulgent; the fools who plan but never act. I scoff at them all who live here." She looked about the towers and walls, cried out half in anger, "Death City! Whore City! City of Greed! Of Sloth! Ah, the decadence..." she gazed at Tomoe once again and spoke with less volume. "Would I live here? I live there!"

She pointed with bony finger, and Tomoe looked toward the higher volcanic peak.

"I am a hermit," she said. "An ascetic. You may call me Keiko. A pretty name? Ah, and once, long ago, I was a pretty girl." A tear appeared in her one good eye, but she brushed it away, reinstated her humor with a loud boast, "Still am!" and danced around a bit, like a young girl, then asked, "Your name, samurai? No! Do not tell me! I do not need to know! I will call you Tada. Because when I saw you looking down from the hill, I said to myself, 'Tada!' Too long since I saw a living soul with my right eye, though I see too many with the left. You are less fool than these others, my eye portends." She swept her arm wide, indicating those "others" on the empty street, believing as she did that this was one or several populous cities on Naipon. Loneliness must have driven her to unfortunate imaginings.

"If you need help, old woman…"

"Keiko! Keiko!"

"Keiko," Tomoe said, correcting herself. "If you need help, I will give you aid."

"I? Need help? Tch! You are madder than I thought, samurai!" She looked at Tomoe askance and said, "Not dangerous, are you, samurai?" and eased away a bit, as from a raving slayer.

"If need commands," said Tomoe. "I am."

"Good!" Keiko declared, and hopped close, kicking Tomoe in the knee, dancing around her and daring the samurai to strike back.

"I live with a friend in the abandoned farmhouse," said Tomoe, unperturbed by Keiko's unpredictability. "You may come there if you please."

Keiko stopped dancing, looked horrified, stepped further back than she had before. "Not there! Not there!" She turned and ran away, her speed exceptional, her knowledge of the winding streets wonderful. Tomoe might have caught her, but found herself led into a street end's cul-de-sac against the city's high wall.

Toshima stood anxiously in the doorway, her face scabbed and heal-ing. It would be a few more days before she regained her beauty, but she had remained unconcerned about that. Presently, her eyes were bright with excitement, but also with a hint of alarm.

"Tomoe! Tomoe!" She waved for the samurai to hurry, but Tomoe kept her pace. At the door, Toshima sounded breathless as she exclaimed: "This is not a ninja-house!"

The samurai looked at her, questioning.

"Come! Come!" Toshima tugged at the samurai, pulling her inside, still speaking. "I heard noises behind the walls—I heard them last night too, while you slept so deeply. After you went out, I began to look around the house. I expected some small animal, but all I found were corridors. Many! There are hollow spaces between the walls, and another space between ceiling and roof with a hidden gymnasium and storage for all manner of weaponry!"

What Toshima had observed was entirely in keeping with the nature of ninja houses. Tomoe listened to the Lady, did not comment. Toshima continued to pull the samurai, bringing her to a specific wall. There, Lady Toshima pushed on one of the woven grass panels in a certain way, and it slid aside, revealing not merely a passage, but something far less explicable.

When the door slid away, Tomoe's senses were assailed by a coldness more spiritual than physical. She heard a whining sound, vague and distant. The space beyond the panel was like a window into nowhere, absolute void beyond.

"Jono!" declared Toshima. "Jono magic!"

"Jono live in temples, Toshima. Dark, austere temples of occult learning."

Toshima looked deflated, said, "But once jono were ninja."

Tomoe was adamant, and strangely unsettled. "Jono are no longer akin to ninja. They do not skulk, do not disguise their places like this. It is true they walk invisible paths, but those lead from temple to temple. This is not a place for priestess or priest, this would-be farmhouse. And it could not be the abode of a novice jono, for none of that sect leaves a temple until they earn high rank. I do not know who would live in a common ninja's house with jono capabilities. I fear who might."

She continued to gaze into the black hole behind the wall, trying to pick out words or meaning from the barely audible whine, the sound of a thousand tiny creatures shouting in high-pitched voices. As she listened, it seemed she heard an even fainter dirge of other voices, deeper than the human ear could properly comprehend.

"It is not dangerous, Tomoe. Do not look so frightened. I entered this very door. It is cold and strange inside, but nothing attacks."

"That was a terrible risk," said Tomoe, more appalled than impressed by the Lady's courage. "You should not have done it."

"But I did." Toshima quickly unwound her obi from her waist, tied one end to the outside of the panel, urged Tomoe to follow her inside. "It is easy to find our way back if we hang on to the end of this," she said. But Tomoe would not budge toward the Door into Nowhere. Lady

Toshima grabbed her feebly, encouraged her, chided her reluctance. "It is safe," she insisted, then added in a teasing tone, "I will protect you."

She held Tomoe's hand, and they entered the black door-way. Immediately, Tomoe was engulfed in wintry chill, half the fault of her own dread. The hairs of her body stood and prickled. The sound of miniature, almost chirping creatures grew louder, yet kept its ambiguity; and at the periphery of her vision she thought she half-saw things like bats or small winged people fluttering madly about. The less tangible background dirge had become a soundless rumbling in her chest; and gazing intensely into blackness, she saw motion, like the after-images of light, shaped in some manner like shambling beasts, swaying back and forth as they made their noiseless death-chant.

Tomoe would have stopped, gone back along the length of the Lady's sash—the sash which had apparently stretched longer than long, seemingly endless. Toshima pulled the samurai onward, toward the furthest end of the lengthened sash. Tomoe squeezed the smaller hand for comfort and made no attempt to disguise her loathing of the passage.

It felt as though they walked upon nothing, and might at any moment be dropped into infinity. There was no light in any direction, discounting the mottling effect of the after-images and phosphenes. There was no sign of the door behind them, or the other wall of the farmhouse ahead. With unexpected suddenness, Tomoe found herself drawn into the lesser darkness of a cavern which suited the natural senses far better than their method of arrival.

Toshima still held the end of the obi, which stretched back into the cavern's darker recesses and vanished. Carefully, she set the black length of cloth on the floor of the cave. The Lady then pushed Tomoe toward the mouth of the cave, where there was light aplenty. All around the interior were strewn evidences of habitation—including a firepit near the mouth, with coals still smoldering.

"An old woman lives here," said Toshima, leading Tomoe to the light. They gazed down from the top of a volcanic mountain, a smaller peak visible across a forested chasm. In the lowlands was the ruined city Tomoe had visited earlier that day.

"When I found myself here previously," Toshima continued, "there was an old woman sitting on that rock, digging in the firepit with a stick. But at the sound of my approach, rather than turning to see who was coming, she leapt up and ran outside. I tried to call her back, to reassure her I was no ghost, but she would not linger. She held back the briefest moment, and shouted without looking my direction: 'I do not look upon who comes through that door!' Then she ran on down the steep mountain trail spry as a kid goat despite her age, heading toward the ruins."

"I met her also," said Tomoe, her voice without emotion. "I met her in the city, which she thought inhabited. She had no fear of me. Strange, she would have no curiosity about you."

They returned to the rear of the cave, and Toshima took up the end of the sash from the floor, using it to guide herself and her samurai back to the presumed-farmhouse. It seemed a farther trip back, distances being entirely warped and inconsistent upon the invisible path. In a while, they arrived in the house, and Toshima rewound her obi about her waist.

"I think we should not go through there again," said Tomoe, still holding her forced calm. "The old woman's name is Keiko. She does not like this house, or anything in it. We should leave her be."

"There are other paths we might try," said Toshima, her suggestion offered in an entirely tentative manner, for she clearly did not wish to frighten Tomoe more—and despite an air of calm, something of Tomoe's fear was yet evident. It was that fear, completely aside from the excuse of not invading Keiko's mountain retreat, which urged Tomoe's command against the supernatural openings in the wall. Toshima said, "I went into some of the other paths, but they must lead to far places. The length of my obi took me nowhere. I thought I was lost once, but my trick with the obi is fail-safe. I thought we might make a long rope, and see where the other paths eventually take us."

"Please, no," said Tomoe, her calm unraveling. "We must move from this house, go away from it. Live in a cave like Keiko! You have done without much comfort already, Lady. A little less will not injure you!"

"Why do you shout at me so? Why do you fear the magic? It is less deadly than your sword!"

"I do not like it! Last night, I dreamed of a place like Naipon, but without magic. I would rather live there! I killed your father, Toshima! I killed him because of magic, not because I willed to! A year later, I met a woman named Tsuki Izutsu and I was not kind to her, and regret it, for magic killed her also, and we can never meet again."

Tomoe stomped from the panel as Toshima closed it. But she feared to stomp far, not knowing where the other doors were hidden. She stood in the center of the room, afraid to move in any direction, afraid even that the floor might hide some foul, black opening—and fuming about her own embarrassing fears.

She verbalized her fears, half to rationalize them, half with the conviction that she was hugely justified. "The Dragon Queen's monster brought us here! Something plots against us, Toshima; I know not what. Only, we are not in this place without interference. Who is to say what would come through those paths to snatch us away to some terrible land? Perhaps the Dragon Queen herself conspires against us, though surely we are beneath her notice. Perhaps she has a servant, or a worshipper, versed in jono magic—and that servant bears you or me some grudge. We are dishonestly manipulated, I know it!, possibly because we are faithful to the Mikado, or for some reason we do not suspect." Her mind raced with its reasoning. "It could be the animosity of the Shogun which brings disaster upon us; though even the Shogun does not play with sorcerers. Our enemy may be unguessed."

"You see ghosts where there are none! You are like that old woman!"

"There *are* ghosts! There are foes! I will tell you what I think, Toshima: even the jono have enemies. We have both had commerce with jono, and might be used against them..." Tomoe was not certain how much she dared suggest. Surely Toshima had suspicions, too. She had directed two jono to protect her father, and one of them to protect Tomoe, but only Tomoe survived that terrible Battle of Shigeno Valley. In that, there was intrigue, not fortune. The intrigues might have begun even before Toshima's birth, when a marriage was arranged between Shigeno and a woman of royal lineage: Toshima's mother. Despite this marriage, Shigeno held greater fealty with the Shogun. The Mikado insinuated through Toshima's contacts that Lord Shigeno would be spared. The Mikado even sent jono, ostensibly to be Shigeno's guards. But in fact, there was nothing to gain by pardoning the warlord from death.

It was possible Tomoe invented these ideas, in her desire to be less than wholly responsible for Shigeno's death. But it was also possible that neither jono nor the Mikado felt a need for the great warlord's continued exploits, whereas Tomoe might in some way be of service to the jono cult, to the Mikado, or both.

Toshima had followed Tomoe's thoughts, having much the same knowledge to work from, and a little more. She said, "You think yourself important, samurai! *I* asked the jono priestess to defend you. You think she saw to your safety for some cause of her own, but you are important to none but *me!*" She rushed to Tomoe and clung to her, but the look in her eyes was as much like hatred as love. "Your vanity exceeds all, samurai! To think your life weighed better than that of my father!"

The samurai twisted away, ridden by guilt, and crushed beneath the sudden knowledge that Toshima had indeed held Tomoe in some manner responsible for Shojiro Shigeno's death. But Tomoe could not bear to think of this any longer, and turned back to Toshima with equal anger, affecting a superior knowledge not much different from the Lady's haughtiness. She said, "Already, once, someone tried to trick me into divulging information about the priestess…" Tomoe said nothing else of the rokubu, who was ultimately responsible for the samurai coming in Toshima's time of need. "This is not ninja-house we have come to, no farmhouse, certainly not a jono temple. It is something *else*, and I would have away! Stay if you will; I will not."

Livid with the rage she had invented to cover guilt, but which she now embraced as genuine, Tomoe left by the only door she trusted. Toshima ran to the door ostensibly to call the samurai back, but pride bit her tongue as well, and she watched the strong woman march away—both of them hiding tears.

Depression descended upon the samurai thicker than the night's sudden, heavy rain. She forced her every step up the mountain side, although in her present mood she would rather sit in the torrent and succumb to pity and exposure.

In the distance, the smaller of the two peaks glowed with activity, though Tomoe had earlier assumed both peaks equally dead. High against the face of the taller peak was a cavern's mouth, lit by a fire within. That was Tomoe's goal: the lair of mad Keiko.

What drew her to the madwoman, Tomoe was not yet certain. The spry hag was attractive in her pleasantly maniacal fashion; but, too, something of insanity *per se* appealed to Tomoe. There was a kind of wisdom in madness, and Tomoe had some faint notion that it was the sort of wisdom which might provide resolution to her varying sorrows, guilts, and confusions. Keiko was never confused! What she believed to be true became true for her, and contradictory information could be applied without ruining the original theory. Tomoe remembered a strolling nun named Izutsu, who had affected an evangelizing tone to say that, "All human reality is a vast lie. There is only one great truth, and that embraces even lies." If this were so, then the reality of mad Keiko was no less valid than any other—and it was a far less painful reality than the one which Tomoe understood.

"Keiko!" she called, clinging to the slick, wet mountain trail. Pebbly ground gave way beneath her fingers. Streams of water furrowed the earth between her knees and legs. She could not continue further, the unhelpful weather holding her back. "Keiko!"

A torch blazed suddenly at the mouth of the cave, and the old woman stood with her head cocked left and her good right eye peering down. "Tada!" she cried gleefully. That toothless smile cut through her shriveled features, her silky tufts of white mustache moving with the smile.

Keiko reached behind herself where Tomoe could not see, then came back around with a coil of rope. She threw the rope out into the rain— the whole rope—and it uncoiled in the air, wrapped one end of itself around a solidly placed stone, landed its further end near Tomoe's hands. It was not done by magic, or Tomoe might have scurried back down the mount. It was done by rope-throwing skill, and Tomoe was more impressed by Keiko's mad talents.

"You are dirty, Tada!" scolded Keiko, and would not let the muddied visitor into her clean, warm cave. Tomoe saw the lit interior, saw that the old woman had piled good-sized stones between her living quarter and the place where Toshima twice and Tomoe once had entered without invitation through an invisible door. "Take off your clothes, Tada! Then you may come in."

Tomoe stripped, hung her clothing on sharp rocks outside the cave, where the rain would clean them as it cleaned Tomoe now. Rivulets snaked down the flesh of her back, her buttocks, her legs. Dripping, she entered the cavern, placed her sword against a wall, then squatted near the fire and held her hands out. She felt colder as the heat raised evaporative steam from her naked shoulders and glistening wet hair, gorgeous hair which had been allowed to grow long and thick and unruly.

"Wear this." Keiko handed Tomoe a dry, scratchy garment, heavy and warm. "So," said Keiko. "Why does the dangerous samurai's feet bring her to my retreat during weather ill as this?"

A dour reply: "I disliked the farmhouse."

The madwoman jerked back at the very mention, but composed herself instantly, smiled more broadly so that Tomoe saw the old woman did indeed have a few teeth left in the back.

"Wise of you," said Keiko. "Do you know who built the house?"

Tomoe shook her head, hunched inside the overlarge garment.

"I did," said Keiko.

Tomoe looked shocked.

"It is true!" The woman skipped around the fire with delight of her confession, laughing madly, and then stopped suddenly. She stooped down so that her face was a finger's length away from the nose of Tomoe, and she said, "I had a husband then. Lazy man. Fat! Filthy! But I loved him. Too much I loved him. Do not ask why! *Love has no reason.* I built the house alone; I built it for him and me. He was too lazy to help, but I did not mind, for we would live together and be happy.

"But when I was done, he ruined it. Ruined it! Wrecked it!" She looked woebegone, or angry, or both, and stood up again, paced her cavern quarters with nervous agitation. "You found the doors he added? Useless things! Pah! But I lived with him in the place; I lived there anyway, I loved him so much, despite his stench, despite how he had ruined the house I made with these hands."

Keiko looked at her hands as though they were not her own. Old, mapped with veins, crooked at the joints of every finger, the thumbs drawn back by some crippling disease. She whispered more to herself than Tomoe, "They were stronger hands in those days, smooth, without a blemish, without a line. I seem to remember…I seem to remember…" Her back was to Tomoe, Tomoe who still crouched near the fire, wrapped in a scratchy robe, listening. There was a long silence, during which Keiko stood motionless seeming to contemplate the nature of her own mortality. Age had crept upon her like a specter; she had not seen it come.

Then she reeled about, and continued her story as though she had never left off:

"All the while, my husband investigated the depths of his doors, for he did not understand them entirely himself. I forget who taught him the magic—priests, priestesses—but they discovered some corruption in his soul, and cast him out, his lessons half learned. I think he wandered through the doors in search of those who rejected him, or to converse with monsters who would aid him in his vengeance. And how I understand the hot emotions of one rejected! How I know it now! For, you see, he did not age when he walked those paths, and sometimes walked them years before returning to me, to my bed. I grew older than he, and soon he came to my bed no more. 'Hag!' he called me, grabbing my silken mustaches. 'Hag! I would not sleep with you!' And I said,

'Why not? All these years I have slept with someone fat and filthy! You can sleep with someone old!' But he laughed at me, and went through one of his doors, and never came out again.

"Was I sad? I was not! I was! Not! Was! At least, I had thought I would be sadder. Something…something I have forgotten…I think…I think…I might never have grown old but for him; I might always have been young. It is mad to blame him for that? I remember a palace, in which I lived like an immortal goddess, until I met the filthy man, and chose of my own will to shed eternal vigor, to grow old with this man I grossly loved. He took me for his wife, loving me for my beauty—but after all I sacrificed, vengeance yet gripped him more than love, and he let me age without him. My sacrifice was for nothing!"

"Keiko," whispered Tomoe. "Keiko. How much of what you say is true? How much of what you say is madness?"

"All true!" She moved about the cavern tensely, looking pensive, looking sad. "All mad!" Tomoe wished the woman would stop pacing; the nervousness was catching. "Once, I was a queen! (Or perhaps a princess, I forget.) You believe that? It is so! I gave up my country for the filthy man—saving only this one island, which I kept for him and me, a paradise it seemed, though soon to be my hell.

"All that I retained of my country can be seen from this mountain peak; and I could have asked no more beyond the arms of my lover. But he went away. For all I know, he wanders the paths to this day." She stood taut and all the more nervous, though less flighty, looked across the chamber and out into the rainy night to the far glow of the smaller mountain.

"I was glad, in the end, to be rid of his flabby laziness," she said. "I have more peace than loneliness. My one fear is that he will return, and claim me his wife again. I would not like that. I would not like it because I would welcome it! Do you understand me, Tada, my only friend?" The one sharp eye focused on the samurai, expecting and receiving no reply. "I would melt into his flabby arms as I always did," she said, and stooped in front of Tomoe as she had before. "I would gaze into his still-young face, as I gaze into your eyes; and once more he would only cast me aside and say, 'Keiko, you are too old for me!' And that is why I hate the farmhouse, Tada. It has cruel memories as well as the hellish magic which stole the years of happiness I planned."

Keiko held her crouch and began to rock on the balls of her feet. Tears rolled down her face like the torrent outside, dripping from the ends of her downy, long mustache. Tomoe said,

"I thought you happy, old woman. I came to learn happiness from you, to learn madness. But you are more wretched than I, lamenting a husband who was fat and useless and who you are better left without. Whereas I have lost good friends, and a good master, all because of sorcery; and therefore I have grown so afraid of magic that I shrink from the magic of life itself!

"I pitied myself, but you are more pitiful, Keiko, dreaming you were once immortal, because you grew too old to keep a lover; dreaming that a dead city was your nation, because you have nothing; dreaming the same city populous, because you are alone. I came here to seek your help, but what help have you for me?"

The madwoman stood abruptly, eyes dry, looking happy once again; for she was after all a madwoman, whose emotions ran extremes. She pushed on Tomoe's head with minor mischief, and unbalanced her from the crouch. Tomoe sat on her bottom, somewhat perturbed, looking up at the old woman who said, "You offered me help once. It proved your foolishness, but you meant well, so I will help you. You seek forgetfulness? I have plenty! I have used it on myself! You may join the citizens of my capital. Go down into the city. Ask for the man named Ya Hanada. He will give you saké, and grant you a single wish."

Tomoe crossed her legs, remained upon the floor. She covered her face to hide despair, and replied, "There is no one living in the city, old Keiko, crazy Keiko."

"Go down and see, samurai!" She scurried to the mouth of the cave, peered down through sheets of hard-driven rain. "The city is lit! Come see!"

Tomoe would not move. She sat before the fire, her back to Keiko, stubbornly silent, refusing to share the madwoman's vision.

"If you want an end to worldly strife, my friend Tada, you will find oblivion in the city. If you wish badly enough to find the people of my country, you will."

Still Tomoe sat rigidly. She had given up the idea that the madwoman could be of help. She put aside the notion that there was genius in madness. She heard Keiko behind her, rummaging around for something or another, but did not look back to see. Keiko said, "You want me to help you find the way, Tada? Very well. I will do it!"

Tomoe looked halfway around, in time to see the rock coming down upon her head, held between Keiko's bony, wrinkled hands. The samurai made an averting motion to no avail, for Keiko was swift, and Tomoe was struck unconscious.

The madwoman had killed her; she knew it. Tomoe's head throbbed. She was fevered. Perhaps, she feared, her skull had been broken—(had it been necessary for Keiko to strike so hard?); at least, her brain was so rattled she might never think better or see more clearly than now. *The woe of all! Once I was so wise, and now my brain's destroyed!*

Her own ruminations made her feel as though she ought to laugh, for not only was she in immeasurable agony, she was also immeasurably silly. Death was, quite possibly, more whimsical than anyone had ever guessed.

For a long while she did not move, for it hurt to try. She tried instead to remember how she came to the stone-cobbled street. Had Keiko dressed her, carried her down the mountain? The madwoman was strong, certainly, but this was too much to assume. Either someone had helped her, or else Tomoe had stumbled down off the mountain even with her head bashed in, and come here on her own. There *was* a dream-like memory of staggering through the gates of the city, tripping over the legs of dirty beggars who ought not have existed, slipping in the vomit of drunkards, passing stone buildings from which wafted the perfumes of "entertainers," the angry shouts of offended gamblers, the stink of saké; and once she had rested, an arm against a wall, and heard beyond a doorway the pretensions of a would-be philosopher qualifying the nature of reality to who-knows-who. It was indeed a decadent city, and in the dream (for dream she thought it until this very moment, and even presently was uncertain) Tomoe had wondered how she had not seen it all before.

Eventually she tottered and swooned, and lay, face-up, in a puddle wherein some man had previously pissed. When she awakened, it still seemed she might be imagining all this, for the lump had changed her reason.

"Dead!" a far-away voice declared, and Tomoe agreed, yes, dead.

"Dead!" another voice confirmed, as high and sweet as the first, so similar to the first, in fact, that it might have been the same voice but it came from another place.

There was further confirmation:

"Dead! Dead!"

Three voices there were, for three voices became hysterical with laughter.

Tomoe groaned. She said vulgar words. Then she wept tears because it hurt to do either. Then she opened her eyes, expecting to see laughing devils, but she saw three happy painted harlots tittering over her. Harlot-angels they were, and one of them bowed close and parted her red lips to place a query:

"Are you dead?"

The samurai turned her head too far to one side, and tasted the foul water in which she was strewn (for strewn she felt, like pieces of armor cast about). She felt the warmth of the women's bodies, radiating so near, and the sweetness of their odor mixed horrendously with the stink of the wet pave. It was daylight, but a haze of cloud diffused the light, giving the atmosphere an underwater approximation, a certain lack of clarity, affording no visible sun. Yet, for all the bluntness of her perceptions, all her senses were operable, and Tomoe made a grave decision with graver uncertainty: "I am alive."

The harlots tittered more.

"You are a fierce warrior! We can tell," said one girl, and the other two went hysterical again, covering their faces with small hands. "To have been injured so badly, you must have fought a giant!"

"Two giants," said Tomoe. Then confessed, "Or one old woman who is insane."

The girls did not laugh at all when Tomoe said this. They looked to one another as startled animals.

"I cannot move," said Tomoe. "My head hurts too much. If you would help me, I would be grateful."

They were delighted to do so, although their combined strength could not offer Tomoe a gentle transport. They raised her awkwardly from the street, from the dampness of the recent rain and other resources, and all of them together went tramping down the misty street. The sound of their passage echoed off grey, grim walls. The young harlots sang a childish song to aid their labor, and Tomoe tried to keep her head from jiggling.

They bore her to a disreputable teahouse and laid her on a straw mat, carefully putting her head on a wooden pillow wrapped in cloth. They fed her soup, which she vomited, and they fed her some more before she went to sleep. She woke periodically, hearing entertainment in other paneled areas: songs, instruments, lovemaking, laughing women and drunken men. After a long while—more than a day, she suspected—she woke more fully. It was no sound which woke her, but rather an unexpected silence.

The teahouse seemed to have held its breath, and all within were still. After so long a continual racket of one kind or another, this sudden change made Tomoe stir. She was alone, but saw the silhouette of a young woman on the other side of a rice-paper wall. There was a second silhouette, of a huge, broad-shouldered man. He was the one who wrought this silence, and he was the one who broke it, his voice guttural and threatening. "It will be you!"

The girl fell before him, weeping, begging. But the big man was unkind. He placed a foot upon the back of the effaced harlot, and drew his sword, prepared to slay.

Defying the agony of her skull, Tomoe rolled off the mat and onto her feet, and thrust her sword through the thin wall, into the heart of the man she knew only by his shadow. The shadow lurched backward, fell, and Tomoe brought her sword out of the wall, stained crimson.

The house erupted with commotion. Tomoe was suddenly surrounded by a dozen prostitutes hysterical with fear and joy, and a few men, half-in or half-out of their clothing. They all bowed to her the slightest bit, in deference and curiosity. One of the girls spoke, and Tomoe felt vaguely that it was the very one whose life she had just saved. "Now you have made enemies!"

Tomoe moved the pierced panel aside, and saw what lay upon the floor. She had murdered a hairy monster in a priest's saffron robes.

"What is he?" said Tomoe.

"His kind serve Smaller Mountain!" said a harlot. In Tomoe's continuingly dazed state, they all looked alike to her, their faces blurs; they sounded the same, their voices as elusive as their gaze. It may have been that only one harlot had ever said a word to her, from the moment she was found in the street; or it may have been that they all took turns. In whichever case, one of them said, "They take a single sacrifice each day, so that the mountain will not overflow."

Shinto deities accepted no sacrifices, neither human nor beast, but Tomoe had already surmised that crueler gods ruled here. A city of stone would not satisfy kindlier deities. The thought did not give her untoward trepidations, however, for everything still seemed part of a delirium wrought by her concussion. She assumed she would either awake from this daze, or she would not; but meanwhile nothing was quite real enough to bother.

"Well," said Tomoe blandly, "you need not fear the mountain's erup-
tion today. The hairy priest is this morning's sacrifice."

"His order will seek vengeance!" the same harlot said, or perhaps
another. "You are not safe here anymore. We are not safe with you among
us."

"Then I will leave. Can someone show me the way to the saké house
of Ya Hanada? I was told to seek him for a boon."

"I will take you," said a blurry, heavy-set figure. It was one of the
few men in the room. He finished tying his obi, bowing as he added,
"But you must know that Ya Hanada grants only sinister boons."

Ya Hanada was a plump, kindly-seeming fellow who saw Tomoe
and her escort to a private quarter of the saké house. Like all the buildings, it was of stone, and like the teahouse, it was partitioned with walls
of paper. Hanada smiled and bowed and scurried about the partitions,
seeing to all his visitors' needs. He vanished briefly, having much to
attend, but returned with his servants who might have been (for all Tomoe
could perceive) the same women she had met at the teahouse. The two
men—Hanada, and her recent compatriot—were also difficult to distinguish, except that Hanada was more ingratiating.

The two servants sat on their knees amidst the two men and one
woman, and made such pests of themselves with their efforts to please
that it was difficult to gain the opportunity to converse with their lingering host.

"How is it that you come to my house?" asked Hanada, holding a
little saké cup between the fingers of both hands.

Tomoe sipped the warmed drink, then sipped it again, and one of
the geishas was quick to keep it full. The saké burned differently than
she thought ordinary, but soothed better, and in fact her head ceased
throbbing for the first time in too long. But the world's lack of clarity
was not resolved, indeed, was made worse, and Tomoe felt light-headed
already.

"Keiko sent me, with a bump upon the head," answered Tomoe, and
for the first time, she found the humor which waited with quiet reti-
cence all this while. She laughed, considering Keiko's blow, and sipped
more of the incredibly relaxing liquor; and the others laughed too, even
though the mention of the madwoman gave them no comfort.

Hanada replied, "If she sends you, then I must serve you to the best of my capacity. For she is our queen, though she seems to have forgotten, and visits us only to ridicule. How did she say I must serve you?"

It was difficult to discover what was so funny, but something certainly was. Tomoe spat some of the saké on herself, trying to hold in the laughter, but she doubled over nonetheless and forced out the foolish words thus: "One wish!" she said. " I have one wish!" Tears of mirth squeezed from shut eyes, as she pounded the floor from her collapsed position.

Hanada bowed most courteously. "And what wish is that?"

Tomoe's nameless friend, who had shown her the way to Ya Hanada's establishment, was sharing her humor. They struck each others' backs, and laughed uproariously. But Tomoe had the problem the worse and ended up with her arm over her face, lying on her back as though defeated in a terrible battle, chortling ridiculously, barely able to catch a breath.

"I forget!" she said, and sat up sharply, her shoulders quivering while she screamed laughter and appeared the perfect idiot. She took her refilled cup from a grinning geisha.

"Then dwell upon the question carefully," suggested Ya Hanada, "for you have but one wish."

"I wish...I wish..." She hooted laughter, gasped for air, and finally said, "I wish I could hold my liquor better!"

And then she was able to catch her breath and control her laughter. Ya Hanada stood up and, bowing many times, backed out of the room to attend others, while the servants remained to give Tomoe more to drink. Tomoe's friend had stopped laughing also, and he leaned close, and said, "You wasted your wish, my friend. You should have wished to return to the world from which you came."

"But I like this one better!" said Tomoe, emptying her cup, and holding it forth for more. There was only one bottle for saké, but it spilled an endless supply for the guests. "But you are right! I wasted the wish! I should have wished for wealth! For position! Oh, but shall I complain? Is it not good to hold one's liquor?" She belched. "A useful skill!"

And Tomoe Gozen laughed some more, with the distinction of being able to control it.

ⓢ ⓢ ⓢ

And as it was her wish, Tomoe held her liquor well, and continuously. She was a sort of town drunk, but not like the sick and ruined beggars who clung to the edges of the city as if in fear of being shoved further out, back into reality. She was a merry, dignified drunk, and liked by all, indeed, she invigorated their lackluster dream-lives so that they sought her company.

There was no need to drink from little cups, she early decided. Carried with her, everywhere she went, was the magic saké bottle, which was never dry. She took it with her even to the public bathhouse, where men and women shed clothing and waded into a pool kept warm with heated rocks. Slaves (they looked like Shirakians, although Tomoe's continual daze—of drunkenness perhaps—made her uncertain) would remove the cooled rocks and replace them with hot ones, then hurry off to reheat the rocks again. Young girls moved about the waist-deep bath with sponges, cleansing and massaging the men and women who waded forth and played.

Certain of the bathers coupled, but Tomoe hardly noticed, at least was not appalled. She approved of communal joy! She stood off to herself, then found a submerged rock to sit upon, the water coming up to her shoulders when she did. She continued to pour saké into her willing mouth, now and then gazing about her with a broad grin even more foolish than that of Keiko. The bath was an event! She had many friends here, though she could not tell them apart and knew very few with names. Soon she was surrounded by these friends, and she gazed lovingly at their indistinguishable faces as they shared conversations which were always the same.

"And what is *your* goal in life, my dearest friend?" asked Tomoe, looking earnestly at the man who stood nearby.

"I have told you many times!" he said, but of course she did not remember. She said, "But I never tire of hearing it! Such a noble intent!"

This pleased him, and he began to tell her, becoming more dreamy than usual, "Someday I will breed horses. I will breed them for fierceness and intelligence. They will be impossible to ride, unless they love their master, and their master must be strong. Then and only then! Horse and rider will be as one, horse responding to every slight wish. The greatest warriors of Naipon would kill to own such horses, and bring me riches in order to ride them into battle."

Tomoe dropped her bottle and it sank, but she fetched it up again, and the drink had not been diluted at all. She said, "Noble, indeed! If my own beloved Raski had not been slain in a battle, I would give him to you as a present to start your supreme line, for he was of the finest stock, and used all his legs at once to kill. You have been such a good friend to me! Would that I could repay you. I regret the loss of my stallion the more, for he might have helped you found a dynasty of unequaled breed."

Another man interrupted, and Tomoe turned her attention to him with equal admiration and intense interest as he said, "Someday I will own a saké house which will make the house of Ya Hanada look like the sore thing it is. His is small and dingy. Mine will be vast! It will be of wood, not stone, and intricately carved inside and out, with tile-inlaid floors and cotton mats, not straw, and screens of silk instead of paper partitions, all painted by the finest artists. Only the most beautiful geishas may serve my customers, and the clients themselves will be of the highest nobility."

"Oh, my friend," said Tomoe, in the voice of someone overawed. "When you open your saloon, I pray you invite me in."

"Indeed I will! Indeed! It would honor my establishment to serve you!"

"And make you wealthy as well!" she said, laughing. "Unless you give out magic bottles like this one!" She took a huge swallow. For a split second she held back, and looked at the bottle closely, and her expression became horrified as she thought: *magic. Magic!* She nearly threw the bottle away, to run screaming from the hot pool and these friends she could not even recognize; for she loathed magic, feared it, knew it only as an unchallengeable foe. But these thoughts were instantly displaced by the haze that had begun well before her drunkenness. She continued to listen to the dreams of her compatriots, the geishas who would be authors and painters, the flabby gentlemen who would be warriors. *Someday* they would all do this. *Tomorrow* they would do that. *Eventually* they would discover. *Soon* they would invest. She encouraged them in all things, while a young girl sponged her back and the fresh, hot stones kept wraith-like steam between her and the faces she could never fully witness.

"What of you samurai? What do you dream? What goal will *you* never seek but always promise?"

Who asked this in so rude a manner, she did not know, for voices were mostly alike, and lips hidden by the vapors of the bath. But she took the cue in kind spirit, and replied in a tone which implied utter commitment.

"I will be pleased to tell you," she said. "You see, I have a nemesis, whose name is Ugo Mohri, whom I will fight and kill. He is like a rainbow! He is beautiful! He fights so well, I cannot describe. But I will fight better, I promise that; and then I will have regained the right to dwell in Naipon again."

"Better you should invite him here," said someone who was sincere.

"Perhaps I shall!" said Tomoe. "But I must practice my skills, or I will grow rusty. Yes, that is my most immediate intention. To improve further my already considerable abilities! I will do that tomorrow. I will do it very soon."

She took a deep swallow from the bottle, and shared smiles all around.

But their joyous sharings were interrupted by the sound of a harsh, gravel voice which said, "Practice now, samurai!"

At the pool's edge stood two hairy priests in yellow, each with longswords drawn. The pool immediately erupted, naked bodies flinging themselves to the opposite side, everyone vanishing in the mist until even the sounds of their footfalls had faded away. Tomoe alone had stayed behind, and she was without weapon, without clothes. She stood up, the water falling to her waist. She said,

"I will fight you with my bottle!"

And this she did. She rushed out of the pool in a headstrong manner with a great splash and commotion which took the unusual priests by surprise. She swiped through the air with her saké bottle so that it spilled its fluids in a shining arc and caught the nearer priest in the eyes. Then she flipped the bottle over in her hands to use as a little club, taking advantage of his temporary blindness to smash the bottle against the hairy man's temple. If he saw the world in a daze like her own, surely she had made it worse!

The stricken priest swung blindly and the other leapt to join. To avoid the two slashes, Tomoe fell backward, vanishing momentarily below the water her landing had made turbulent.

The second priest waded forth, and slashed into the froth where the samurai had vanished. But she came up behind with a still-warm rock in her hand. Using a trick of mad Keiko, she caved in the priest's skull, and he fell forward like a tree into a river. Tomoe took up the fallen priest's sword and turned to face the other, who had used his yellow robe to cleanse his eyes of the burning fluid. He backed away from Tomoe's armed approach, and said, "My brother is today's sacrifice, but we will meet again tomorrow."

Tomoe laughed, one leg out of the pool. "So! You will sacrifice yourselves against me, to keep the volcano quiet! But when I have slain you all? Then what will the mountain do?"

"You need not fear it," said the priest. "For there is an endless supply of us, though only one of you. You may best us for a long time, though we will borrow the swordskills of time's most mighty warriors to come against you, for we know few have ever had your skill. But eventually, life in this city will weary you, and you will become bored, for you are less dead than these others and less liable to be satisfied by empty intentions. Then, we shall defeat you. You will wish it on yourself."

When the hairy priest was gone, Tomoe waded about the crimsoned bath, questing for her dropped bottle. She grumbled and complained, having been several moments without a swig, and needing it to ease the priest's prognosis. Her bleary eyes could not see to the bottom of the shallows, yet it was not much more distorting than the air around. For a moment, she stood motionless in a bent posture, blinking her eyes and trying to clear them, a look of serious consternation upon her face. When she looked up, there in the endlessly misty atmosphere stood a figure clear to her vision.

"I am angry at you, Tada," said Keiko, standing where the hairy priest had been. The priest Tomoe had killed still drifted in the water, and Tomoe pushed him aside, to see if her bottle was under him. It was not.

She looked up again, and replied, "It is I who should be angry. My vision has been very bad since you hit me on the head, although I see *you* clearly."

"Your lover weeps, Tada. I know what it is to pine! I am very sorry for her, and disappointed in you."

Guilt tugged at Tomoe, but not very hard. She asked, "Is Toshima well?"

"Do you care? You who play games with ghosts?" Keiko did not sport her usual foolish grin, but looked entirely severe.

"They are not ghosts! They are my friends!"

"And good friends they are, to someone afraid of losing real friends. You said you feared magic, but you have taken shelter in it."

Tomoe looked away, felt around the bottom of the pool some more, seeking her bottle of forgetfulness. "It is your fault, Keiko! Are you so mad you do not know you sent me here?"

"You asked to come! I saw to it that you would have a way of freeing yourself if you changed your mind. But you wasted your only wish, preferring to be a drunk. Now you will dwell in Fool City throughout eternity! Now I will despise you as all these fools! I will ridicule you as I have always ridiculed them. City of Death! It is ever yours."

The samurai shook her shoulders all around, found her bottle suddenly (by her toes). She fetched it up, took a large swallow, felt better. It helped her regain her humor, and she smiled at threatening Keiko. She came plodding out of the water toward a towel with which to dry her skin and hair, but halted before Keiko and looked hard into the old woman's face.

"You were blind in the right eye," said Tomoe, sounding upset. "Now it is your left!"

"I am not blind at all!" said Keiko. "You are blind!"

She turned and went away, vanishing into the sea-like haze of distortion. Tomoe shrugged exaggeratedly, drank some more, found her clothing, and staggered from the bathhouse in search of friends.

Each day, Tomoe Gozen killed another hairy priest, and it was true, there was no end to them. They sacrificed themselves to her sword, and Smaller Mountain surely burbled its delight, though she could not hear if it did, and the city's haze did not allow her to look and see. (There might be no world outside the city at all, for most of what she could tell.)

Where the suicidal fellows came from and went to, she could not surmise. She never saw them except when they came to offer themselves to death (and death angered more than frightened them, for in the ghostly city, death was more profound than final). They never ventured to the places other inhabitants used, unless in search of her, and nobody she asked could say where the furry cultists stayed.

Curiosity rose like a shining bubble to the surface of her hazy awareness, and she decided she must discover the lair of the priesthood.

Through the city Tomoe quested. They would need a large dwelling if their numbers were so vast. But the city's largest structure—she guessed it was a temple, though it contained no idol or artifact—was one of the few places unused. At length she decided they must be the only folk capable of coming and going from the city at will, for the city housed them nowhere.

Therefore she sat herself to guard the only gate, and catch them as they entered. But when it came time for a new sacrifice, three of the hairy priests snuck up behind, suggesting some secret entrance elsewhere, or else a hiding place inside the city after all—underground perhaps. Or there was another possibility, which notion she slowly came to prefer: there were fewer of them than they pretended, and she killed the same ones time and again.

Although they came upon her unaware, she turned instantly to face her three attackers. She staggered about from drunkenness, but they knew by now this was deceptive. Tomoe Gozen had wished to Ya Hanada to hold her liquor properly, and thus when danger was nearest, she drew up with all her fighting skill, and despite the greater number, she dispatched one of the three with fair ease. The remaining two withdrew, for they sought but one killing per day, whether hers or one among their own.

The samurai tried to follow, still curious of their residence; but the yellow-clad man-beasts knew Keiko's trick of vanishing down alleys.

Tomoe remembered there were such things as invisible paths, but she remembered also that Keiko did not like them. There must be, therefore, some other way out of the blind alley through which the priests disappeared. For, if she recollected, this *was* the same cul-de-sac into which Keiko had eluded her on their first meeting.

This minor mystery revitalized her a little, though she stopped now and then to sip from the bottle, and pursued her quest in a wholly bemused state. She put her ear to the pave, thinking to hear some echo of footsteps in a tunnel's hollow. There was no sound. And every seam and corner of the cobbled street was incontestably solid.

For a while, the drunken samurai sat in the corner of the alley and pondered stuporously on this, the first riddle to enthuse her in many a day.

It would help, she felt, if she could see better. If her vision were clearer, she might spy some subtle indication of a disguised doorway through one of the walls. In her travels, she had met many people who saw poorly, and some far worse than her, so she ought not grumble loudly. She could at least see beyond her nose, as some she had known could not. Yet in some ways, she thought it must be more frustrating to see poorly than to be completely blind; though on reconsideration, a distorted light was better than none at all.

The thought of light triggered some ache in her, which she could not immediately place. For the briefest moment, there was a woman standing before her in the mist, swaddled in darkness, a hood drawn around most of her features. She drew away this mask, revealing eyes like ice and face like fire, and Tomoe started to rise from her seated posture, a hand reaching forth, the hand which held the unemptiable bottle, and she cried, "Noyimo!"

But the fluid nature of the atmosphere engulfed the apparition. And Tomoe was uncertain what the name meant, the name of Noyimo; and it did not seem that she ached for a shining face, but for the shining sun, dear Amaterasu, whose light dispersed evenly over the city's omnipresent roof of white. Amaterasu's face never smiled upon the city, thus Tomoe Gozen would seek Her out.

"I will climb above the mists!" said Tomoe to herself, and looked about the walls for some method of climbing to the highest roofs. It was then that she saw the manner of the hairy priests' disappearance, and of Keiko long before them: minimal hand-holds had been carved into one of the buildings' walls in a very subtle fashion. Tomoe doffed clogs, placed toes and fingers into these indentations, and went up the wall like a squirrel up a tree.

At the top, she was ready with her sword, but the hairy priests were gone for another day. As Tomoe had hoped, the area above the city was not misted, and she broke through the mists as a dolphin breaks the surface of the sea, but cannot fly further.

The bright sun warmed her face, and Tomoe was gripped with such melancholia. She could not contain it without weeping. She gasped like a fish out of water, and held her arms up to a sun which no longer knew her. She sobbed the longest while. She sobbed so hard she could barely speak the words: "Help me, Amaterasu! Forgive my passing cowardice! I will never fear the magic of blessed life again, if you will bring me home!"

But the sun only hurt her skin, hurt her eyes, and she crawled to the edge of the roof and looked back down into her adopted world, which Keiko said she might never leave again. Below, walking through the streets, she saw Toshima, Toshima like a ghost though it was Tomoe who was the specter. The vision rent Tomoe's heart. The double scar on her brow drew together with her expression of all-consuming grief.

"To...mo...ehh!" cried Toshima, her voice from another world. *"To...mo...ehh!"*

And Tomoe wept the more, as the Lady walked away.

Ya Hanada turned her away, for he had given her the single wish, and, claiming Keiko to be the entire fountain of his power, he could provide nothing additional without the madwoman's direction. "I have given you a magic saké bottle," he said with a cloying, fraudulent solicitude. "What more could my good friend desire?" He had given her the bottle, she realized at the last, so that he would never need to serve her within his house.

When Hanada shut her out, she went off and tried to break the bottle, sitting it on one stone and striking it with another. But it was as impervious as it was unemptiable, as indestructible as fate.

Valiantly she attempted to flee the city, but could go only a little ways before she gasped and choked and ran back through the gates to regain breath.

Spectral friends abandoned her, for she refused to be their darling, and they did not like her recent melancholy. She had never coupled with them, and finally ceased even to bathe with them (and soon she stank). She would not reinforce their frail promises of deeds and dreams of successes, always on the morrow. She never gambled; never waxed philosophic; would not stumble with them through the streets arm in arm in song and laughter. She would only dry their spirits, and few of them would have it. Those few who persisted in their attempts to cheer her she would kick in the groins and send them hopping. She would rail against them and call them worse names than Keiko ever did, Keiko whose visits became rare, as though the madwoman no longer found reward in what her ghost-observing eye revealed. Tomoe came to understand exactly what the old woman despised; but unlike Keiko, the samurai was part of the despicable package.

Eventually Tomoe neither smote nor belittled those few who hung about. Rather, she pretended they did not exist, as she suspected was more nearly true, if truth there was at all. She went to sit near the city's edge amongst the most damaged denizens, her unbreakable bottle held near her breast and at intervals to her lips.

On one of Keiko's rare visits, she lingered at the gate to malign Tomoe more than the attending company of derelict ghosts. "You smell like my husband, Tada! Phew! Do you like it in Drunkards' Town? Is life not grand in Yedo?"

"Kyoto," Tomoe corrected, her voice a feeble growl.

The others begged Keiko for the mercy of oblivion; and when she stamped away in disgust, they crawled in pursuit of her, though she ignored them. There was something changed about Keiko, for not only did she come less often, she took less joy at what she saw—as though she too felt guilty, for her part in Tomoe's ruin.

Unlike the others, Tomoe never begged for oblivion. She rarely moved at all, except in moments of peril or to sip from her bottle of solace. Thereby she created a sense of non-existence curiously her own.

The liquor sustained her somehow, or some other magic, for she drank nothing else and ate not at all, and exercised only when the hairy priests forced her. When they came, she would feel perturbed as she forced herself to stand. And she would do them battle, facing sometimes one, sometimes two, or three. Her sword, her unkempt clothes, her bottle—she owned nothing more, not even her own mind, but these few things she defended with excessive vigor. She would not even share the content of her bottle with ghosts (who owned even less and thought Tomoe wealthy) for she had become selfish despite the endlessness of her supply. And besides, she loathed the miserable beggars, who were like mirrors.

She seldom blinked her eyes either, for the air was so humid she did not have to; and, too, she fancied if she stared hard and long, eventually she would see more clearly.

The furred attackers in their yellow garb became monotonous annoyances interrupting her exercitation of smallness, although that is not to say they were predictable. It was no longer possible to foretell their coming, for night and day became as indistinguishable as the faces of her company, and she would forget whether it was this day, or the day before, that they had already come. Moreover, they each fought a different style, as though no two of them learned the sword from the same school. She could never anticipate them. Nonetheless, they were dull, for they looked alike, and their rough voices were alike, and they died similarly. They might have been replicas of one another, or there might only be three in all, for she never saw more than that at one time. And the daily corpse would always vanish, though she never saw how it happened or who took it away. Perhaps they were resurrected, to die again, to entertain and appease Smaller Mountain time and time again.

But if there were only three, rather than the great number they would have her believe, it would be difficult to explain their continual change of fighting style.

Careful reason was beyond Tomoe's recent capacity, yet arduous days of mental straining resolved the riddle of their ever-changing mode of attack. They had no skill of their own (if she could accept their own word on the matter); but, instead, they borrowed talents of great samurai who slept, or who had died. Now and then, a style was so unique and famous that she knew instantly what hero's skill she was pitted against. She might therefore have become awed or egotistical in regard to her own ability to counter, except there was no awe in her anymore, not for herself or others, and her ego had shriveled into a nutshell.

In spite of this, the daily assaults were good for honing her considerable skills; indeed, she obtained the best instruction she had known since the days of her formal training.

And Tomoe Gozen knew she might well be match for Ugo Mohri. Yet they would never duel, unless someday he, too, was cast into fools' paradise; or, unless, dreaming, his skill came to face her in a monster's hairy body. Even in the latter case, he would not know that he had been defeated, would know only the dream. By default, her nemesis would prevail, and this wore upon her greatly.

When she came to this understanding, regarding the uselessness of her talent, she thought never to fight again; for to what avail? How many days, or weeks, or months had already passed, she did not know, had no way of counting, could hardly distinguish one moment from another. But the occasion came when over her stood three familiar, hairy men in saffron robes. Without so much as a glance at them, she remained seated against the inner wall of the city, and said, "You were right. I choose to let you win."

They took her sword, the sword made by Okio and blessed by the Mikado, and she did not care; swords were of no value to the dead, she thought, and thought surely she was dead. How could the hairy men kill her, if she were already dead? How had she killed *them* so often, when they were her kindred spirits?

They took away her bottle next, and this she minded more.

Two of them lifted her, one to an arm, and the third one said, "Look into our eyes, Tomoe Gozen! See you madness here? You have slain us each a dozen times! Sanity cannot prevail against a multitude of bloody deaths. We have chosen to defy Smaller Mountain, though it means doom to all. Our choice is not to sacrifice you, or any other, but instead, we will keep you living as many days as we can, dismembering you a piece each day. We will attend to nothing else; you will be our new obsession. First we will take the fingers one by one, eventually a hand; some other day, a foot; and later on, the other hand, or the arm up to the elbow, the leg up to the knee. How long can it go?" He looked at her malevolently, and answered his own query: "As long as we can make it!"

They dragged her off, and Tomoe Gozen did not struggle, but continued to glower and stare. They bore her to the center of the city, and took her into the huge stone temple where she had searched for them before but not found them. They hauled her upward to a hidden place above the rafters, and bound her arms flat together behind her back, elbow to elbow, and wrist to wrist, until she thought her shoulders would unhinge; then they bound her ankles together and attached her feet to hands. They left her thus, in considerable agony, sitting upon her knees to consider her unimaginably gruesome fate.

In another room, she heard the sound of sharpening knives.

Briefly, she struggled, but only to ascertain whether she had allowed herself into a hopeless situation. She had. The furred men had tied her in an excruciating posture, so that any movement whatsoever resulted in worse matters. Despite this, Tomoe smiled grimly. At least she had the consolation of knowing that the hairy priests in their exceeding anger, and possible madness, were destroying themselves as well as her, and the whole of the miserable city and island upon which it stood. Smaller Mountain demanded sacrifice, not torture; and unless the sacrifices of days past had always been made to a myth, the volcano would erupt when refused its due.

All upon the island would perish, ghosts or not, including mad Keiko, including Tomoe, including…innocent Toshima…

It had been long since she sipped the sorcerous rice wine. Without it clouding her judgment, Tomoe's thinking altered. She began to breathe heavily with the dawning of her failure to defend Toshima, as was her samurai's duty. What really had driven Tomoe from that duty? She had fled in fear of magic, it had seemed, but as Keiko once pointed out, refuge had been taken *in* magic. Tomoe had escaped nothing of her presumed fear. In the end, she had escaped only Toshima.

Tomoe was not the first samurai ever seduced by a Lady; but there was a specific awareness that she could never fulfill that which her mistress commanded. Lady Toshima had altered the nature of the relationship: a samurai owed greater fealty to a master than a wife, and Toshima had preferred to be a wife.

All deserved to perish but Toshima. No one else had proven their lives meritable, and Tomoe least exempted herself. Yet she was forced to struggle to save herself, despite a preference not to do so, for the sake of Toshima. But the bonds were far too tight, too well made, immune to the samurai's efforts.

In another room, the sound of knives sharpening had ceased.

"Keiko!" Tomoe cried out in desperation. "Keiko! Mad mother of wickedness, save me from this!"

She began to bounce on her knees, irrespective of the pain it communicated through her bound feet, hands, elbows. The sockets of her shoulders would have liked to give up her arms. Falling on her side, she squirmed as best she could, which was not much squirming really. She clenched teeth and grimaced and pulled every muscle near to tearing. She slammed her head on the floor trying to regain her knees. All she gained was reiteration of the knowledge that she was helpless.

The doorway of the adjoining rafters-room slid aside, and there stood three torturers, armed with knives-cum-scalpels, something worse than murder in their expressions. Tomoe spat in their directions; they did not care. They started forward...

...but she did not see them enter the room.

In her ears, a ringing began, which became the chattering of a thousand minuscule creatures. Coldness enveloped her. The loft in which the priests had placed her had disappeared, so that she felt as though she were adrift in chilly limbo.

"Keiko?" she hazarded, but knew Keiko would never manipulate the invisible paths. Keiko's mystic husband? "Who?"

In the distance a figure was walking, slender shadow against shadow. It approached with nonchalance, and Tomoe was not certain if it were wiser to urge the person to hasten and untie her bonds, or to lie silent as a stone under the delusion that she might go unnoticed.

As the figure neared, she knew it for a magician-ninja, the face mostly covered, the dark robes like midnight darker than the darkness in which Tomoe found herself. The magician-ninja was still far away, and still approaching slowly, as though nothing in the empty universe was urgent. Tomoe cried loudly for assistance, her voice echoing through eternity, but the jono moved no faster.

"Noyimo!" cried Tomoe. "Noyimo, help me!"

And then the figure was at her side instantly, and cast off a shadowy disguise to reveal someone not tall and slender but squat and rotund. She recognized the rokubu, the filthy man she had met twice in Naipon, with whom she had exchanged a mon on each meeting, like beggars sharing alms.

"I am not jono," said the rokubu, looking down on her helplessness with sadistic glee. "But I thank you for the name of Noyimo! I dared not fight any jono, without their master's name, and Noyimo rules them all."

"Free me!" she rasped, breathing heavily through teeth still clenched. "Free me and I will kill you!"

"An unconvincing argument," he said, and reached into a fold of her obi to withdraw the mon she had kept since their second meeting. "With this, I have followed you. I bound us this while, for I had worked a year of charms upon the coin before returning it to you. Your larger destiny was manipulated through the coin, and through the aid of my unsuspecting wife. She made this ghostly habitat, not I; but I have used it better! I used it as a trap!"

"You trapped me well," said Tomoe.

"Not for you. For jono! You are the bait!"

"Because they cast you from their order?" Her tone was contemptuous of an obsession borne of trivialities.

He laughed. "That is what Keiko thought! But I am larger than that! There are other cults than jono. They serve Shinto; my clan has served Buddhism, but that is not why we are less famous. Long ago, when certain ninja spies discovered and guarded methods of controlling various magicks, it could not help but create revolution and many factions among the ninja clans. Over all these, the jono prevailed. My clan was all but destroyed, though some of us linger, and seek vengeance. Once, I infiltrated their very order! When I was found out, they thought to kill me, to drown me in the sea. They could not have guessed the Dragon Queen would take a fancy to me, raise an island beneath me, saving my life. She even made herself mortal for me!"

"Keiko?" Tomoe's head spun—from these revelations, from the

blood clamped by her bonds.

"She was the Dragon Queen, but now she is a weak old woman—the price of mortality!" The rokubu preened and puffed himself larger, his ego tickled by the cost of loving him. He said, "I wish that I could claim it was only my suave nature, but it was her curiosity more than anything—her curiosity to know what it was like to love a mortal. She had previously longed to try a man unmurdered by the sea, still warm as it were. I was the lucky villain she came upon, to touch with experimental ardor. A matter of sheer fortune, perhaps, being in a given place at a given time; or a well-deserved destiny, if I may be so vain. I do not know. At the time, I knew only that she had filched me from death for a little while, but would tire of me in a single night, no matter how well I performed. When done with her sport, she would draw the island, and me, back into her country—and I would reside among the slaves of the sea-folk."

"But something changed her plan?" said Tomoe, buying time, urging him to tell her everything, boastful as he was; for she hoped to learn some small thing which would improve her situation.

"I wove a spell around her," the rokubu continued. "I thought it would fail, for how could a mortal wizard place a glamour on a god? Nonetheless, I tried, for I had nothing to lose but my life, which I would lose anyway. And the spell worked! Possibly the Dragon Queen was so infatuated with her experiment she chose to allow my success as part of *her* scheme; I hope not. Perhaps the cause is that I am mightier than I knew! In whatever case, none could have been more surprised than was I.

"The spell was one which should have faded quickly, at least it would have if set upon a mortal woman. But on the immortal Dragon Queen, it took a different measure. The spell endured, and she has ever loved me with vengeance."

"A goddess who makes herself mortal," said Tomoe, "is only playing for a while. Death is an interlude to their everlasting lives. And divine love, whether gift or booty, is not to be spurned. Such fools are men! You might have lived with a goddess, and you took the road to revenge instead."

"And you? What kind of fool are you?"

"As vast a fool as you. For I have betrayed a friend."

"You have indeed! So now it is time that I return you to the hairy men of my Buddhist sect. They are the only ones among the sea-dead I could convince to serve me before Keiko; they think me, in fact, the personification of Smaller Mountain, for I have more disguises than you have seen today." He laughed again. "They think they have defied me, defied the spirit of Smaller Mountain. But they serve me better by torturing you. The jono priestess will surely come when she hears you screaming. And I will have her name!"

"I regret it," said Tomoe. "I regret all that I have done."

The coldness passed from her numb limbs, and she was again in the rafters, three hairy men brandishing knives around her.

In the corner of the room stood the magician-ninja, and Tomoe was sorry to see her. She did not wear her mask at all, as though she knew it would be to no avail to hide herself from the rokubu, who thanks to Tomoe knew her only too well.

Tomoe could barely see the figure standing there, but still she would recognize that shining face, even in the misty world to which the rokubu had returned her, even with the agony of tight bonds blurring her vision more.

The magician-ninja raised a hand, and the saffron robes of the menacing, hairy beasts turned crimson with fire! They fell upon one another screaming, trying to put each other out. Their hair quickly caught fire as well, the whole of their bodies aglow. They hurled themselves like meteors through the opening in the floor, plunging to the large temple chamber below. The smell of burning fur and flesh lingered. The sound of their wails and writhings faded into moans, then ended altogether. The magician-ninja said,

"Only fire can permanently put the enslaved sea-dead to rest."

The voice was deeper than Tomoe had expected, and relief engulfed her aching body when she realized it was Noyimo's brother and not Noyimo who had come to the aid. He walked forward, knelt beside Tomoe, but made no effort to unbind her. He looked upon her with a kind of sorrow but not a hint of anger at her inadvertent treachery. She was attracted to him, she realized, because he looked like his sister.

"You must flee!" she said. "The rokubu is somewhere near, upon the invisible path."

"I am not afraid," he said. His voice was at once serene and mighty, wise with years but very young; and it sounded far away. Tomoe wondered if the jono priest were truly standing over her, or was a kind of projection as had visited her behind a waterfall long ago. Then, Tomoe had struck out with her swords, and found a jono priestess as intangible as air.

In the distance, Smaller Mountain rumbled with an angry sound, the first noise Tomoe had heard from outside the city's walls since Keiko sent her here. Tomoe said,

"Your manner of killing the hairy one does not please the volcano."

A throaty growl rose again, vibrating the stone building.

"The one you call a rokubu invented the story of necessitated sacrifice, to encourage the hairy Buddhists to serve him in lieu of Keiko. They were of a race which came originally from a mountainous land called Llusa, further than the Celestial Kingdoms, and they preferred to worship mountains. Because they hailed from far inland, the Dragon Queen's hold on them was less than on other peoples she has managed to drown through time; and the rokubu was able to sway them from her with ancient Naiponese magicks, and his lies."

The magician-ninja pulled his mask up around his face, a face too much like another's for Tomoe to bear not seeing. He finished, "If the mountain erupts, it will be because Keiko wills it, not because of the hairy priests or the story the rokubu made them believe."

"He told me something similar," said Tomoe; "but not all his power is a lie. You will fight him? I would make myself useful in that battle!"

"I will fight him if I have to."

"Cut my bonds for me! I will fight him for you, to redeem myself."

"You cannot fight him, any more than you were able to fight me in Shigeno Valley." He raised his palm to remind her how he had once pushed her away though she had not been close enough to touch. "If the fight must be, it is for me to do; but for the moment we are safe. He will not know that I am here until the moment you are free—then a battle will begin, if he cannot be wavered."

"Then leave me tied!" she said. "I am very sorry to be the cause of all this trouble, and deserve to die in this place."

"Your blame, too, the rokubu invented. He is master of lies! You are one of many tools, and not necessarily his. Do not think yourself blameworthy. But you will stay bound a while longer, until you and I have said all that we must say to one another. When you are free, it could be that we will not meet again."

"You doomsay!" said Tomoe, trying not to show the pain of her arms and whole body, so that he would not unbind her suddenly, bringing the inevitable upon himself.

"I urge you against worry," he said, soothing. "The felon lies even to himself, if he thinks to defeat the jono. Even with our leader's name, we do not fear his kind. Our clan defeated his many generations ago, and the few who straggle have gained only one new sorcery against our many advances: the one who poses as a rokubu has discovered a method of conversing with the vague creatures upon the invisible path. We cannot do that, and are uncertain of its import. But it will not be enough for him! Even if I am slain, others will defeat him in time."

These words did not much encourage Tomoe, for the magician-ninja spoke still of his possible demise. She said, "He does have further aid. He has Keiko."

"That remains to be proven," he said. "A dangerous game he entered, to cast a spell upon a goddess. The greatest mages are careful of simple demons. But deities! Only idiots compel them."

"Still, he has the name I gave him."

"That is an annoyance, but will serve him very little. He might use it to call Noyimo upon himself, then contend with both of us at once."

"If it is of slight circumstance that I betrayed her name, why is it that your sister stays away?"

"Not for fear of him," said the magician-ninja, and looked at Tomoe with sorrow richer in his eyes. The eyes were all that showed of his face. "She will not see *you*."

Tomoe was stricken, and gasped.

"It may be that I should not tell you," he said, "but I will. My sister came to you one time, to a place behind a waterfall, intent on saving you from jigai. Toshima Shigeno had asked her aid especial, but in truth, Noyimo later said, she would have helped you anyway. But when she came, twice you swung with swords, slashing through her image. It was not possible to hurt her bodily, but your attempt injured her love for you."

"She thinks I would wish her dead? Tell her for me—tell her that I knew that I would fail. I had already faced you on the battlefield, and you pushed me back with one raised hand. I did not know my swords would pass through her as through smoke, but I knew by some means I would be unable to hurt her. I slashed to show contempt! Not to kill. But I have no contempt for her anymore, and even then, it was contempt for myself, who slew the lord Shojiro Shigeno."

"I will tell her," said the magician-ninja, "if I survive to do so. She will be glad to understand you."

"Then it is imperative you survive! Will you cut my bonds now, that I might return to my life among the ghosts?"

"I cannot unbind you. You are not bound."

"I am! It hurts!"

"The objects of the sea-dead are no more real than are themselves. You must escape this misty place altogether, not merely the ropes you think bind you."

"Keiko says I can never leave."

"The Dragon Queen is mad. The one called a rokubu saw to that many years ago."

"She was mistaken?"

"What she said to you is true only for those who come to her by drowning. You may return to the living world as you did once before, when you were cast onto the road to hell."

The remembrance of Ushii Yakushiji brought pain to match that in her rope-constricted body. She asked, "Have I ever truly left the road to hell?"

"Take heart, Tomoe. Do not imagine defeat. You can succeed again."

Tomoe was encouraged. She said, "I fought my way from hell with swords! Give me my weapon, and tell me whom to slay!"

"Slay only your fears, Tomoe." The jono priest moved away, to take up Tomoe's sword where the hairy men had put it with the magic saké bottle. That he could lift objects bodily made her wonder if he were a projection or not. Jono magic was beyond her understanding! He told her, "Yet you may in every case require a soul." So saying, he thrust the sheathed sword into her obi, but still made no effort to unbind her.

Tomoe struggled against the ropes, but it remained of no avail. She nearly swooned from the agony of every pulled muscle. She had been bound so long; pain was cumulative, save in parts of her gone numb. It was difficult to believe she was caught within illusion. The hairy men had tied her cleverly. It could not be denied.

"That is not the way to struggle," said the magician-ninja.

She stopped pulling at her bonds, looked up at him pitifully, like a wretched captured wolf. He reached forth and touched the double-scar on the samurai's forehead, and said, "Focus on this. Place all your will near the center of your brow. You must relax your body, as you would before a battle. You have been trained to find your center in your belly? Move it up your spine. Move it up until your center finds the scar."

"You are a Shinto warrior," said Tomoe, reminding him of things he knew quite well. "You would teach me Zen?"

"Another taught you Zen, not I. I help you use what capacities you have already gained without knowing. Shinto magic alone cannot free you, for it is magic of Naipon alone, and we are far from Naipon. The Dragon Queen is as much a deity of the Celestial Kingdoms as of the Eternal Isles; indeed, her domain encompasses the whole of the ocean, touching the shores of many Buddhist nations, extending to lands of which we know nothing. From certain of these countries Naipon inherited the forerunners of Zen; thus Buddhist magic is useful to preserve against the Dragon Queen. I will aid you with Shinto magic; you must aid yourself with Zen. Think of it as *ryobo-shinto,* the Two Ways of the Gods, the Mikado's own faith. Together, with your strength and mine, the two magicks may return you to the unmisted world."

He held her with his eyes, eyes remarkably like Noyimo's. She could not look away, could not help but listen as he intoned, "Focus. Focus."

Saiminjutsu, the art of hypnosis, was among the jono repertoire. He pointed with two fingers at her double-scar. "Focus. Focus."

At first she was sinking deeper into the sea, captivated by the magician-ninja's mesmeric intonation. Then she was rising, moving upward through the central axis of her being, toward the top of her spine. From the middle of her brain, her attention moved forward to a point, until it seemed she was peering outward through an eye she had not known she possessed.

Light shone from her forehead, brighter than the face of the jono priest who looked so much like someone else that Tomoe wished to touch him, trusted him entirely, allowed his spells to weave around her and help her with what she must do within. The light began to grow, the light which was a part of her, and she imagined that the scar of her forehead came unattached and floated before her face, shining like a shuriken from a burning kiln. The scar—her family crest—two waves of the sea—the sea which held her captive on an isle—two waves like a vagina, growing large. She could no longer see the jono priest beyond the expanding, whirling circle of light.

The haze which had for so long surrounded her dispersed, burned away by the waves of light. The ropes which bound her legs to her arms behind her back also disappeared, like mist. She moved slowly to hands and knees, crawled to the yoni-light, the vaginal portal, the glowing funnel—and when she had passed through it, she found herself surrounded by the all too familiar coldness of the invisible path. In nothingness she drifted—freed from the deathly city at last, but arriving in something by no measure more pleasant.

The light which had sprung from her forehead winked out the instant she entered the path. Utter darkness enclosed her, and the sensation of weightlessness—no up, no down—was worse than it had been before. Before, it had been possible to find one's feet, and to walk. This time she kicked her feet and could in no manner place them on anything. She made swimming motions, and thought she might be propelling herself through the frightful limbo, but was not certain.

Another thing was different from other visits here: the half-seen winged things which chattered and the shambling beasts who groaned a soundless dirge were not in evidence. The eeriness of those inhabitants had lent substance to the nowhere-place, and their absence made Tomoe feel completely deprived of sensory input. She tried to cry out, but no sound burst from her lungs. A horrific thought crossed her mind: she might only *think* she was moving like a swimmer. Since she could not feel her own body, it was possible she only imagined she still had one and that it moved.

Had it gone on longer, madness might have gripped her. But it became evident that she was moving through the emptiness, for at length she sensed the chattering and the dirge far off through the ether.

She realized her bodilessness was a kind of defense, wrought by jono magic, not by danger. Below her was a single figure in the darkness, the fat dirty rokubu. He held his arms out from his side in a dramatic pose of entreaty, as he addressed his half-visible audience of large shamblers and minute fliers. They did not perceive the witness adrift above the rokubu's pretended theater, for she was less tangible than they.

She could not hear the rokubu speak, but the fliers and shamblers did hear, for they grew excited. They closed in around him, the shamblers swaying to their dirge, the fliers a cloud of anxious swallows. The rokubu was laughing soundlessly, joyously, so that Tomoe Gozen guessed the beasts were convinced of his reason, won to his intent.

The rokubu would free the monsters from their limbo-world, to defeat all among the jono cult, beginning with Noyimo's brother. For this end he had wandered, unaging, upon the invisible path, resolving one of its riddles which the jono only suspected.

As if this knowledge were the only thing she had come to witness,

Tomoe Gozen was drawn out into reality, swam out of the cold, black pit. She escaped from the invisible path on the moment of her realization, and lay upon wood, not the city's stone.

Her hand went instinctively to the double-scar which had glowed and grown and provided the initial escape from Keiko's deathly city. But the scar was gone, and Tomoe somehow missed its smooth presence upon her brow. She had used it like an eye, and now she felt by some means partly blinded because it had left her.

She lay in a place of rafters much smaller than the temple's loft had been. She heard a prayer-drum beaten in a rhythm, and a woman's voice chanting below. Around her was a cache of weaponry, and she remembered that Toshima had mentioned a gymnasium and armory hidden between the ceiling and the roof of the false farmhouse.

The invisible path had led her back to Toshima.

Looking about for a trapdoor, she found it, and slid it noiselessly aside. Below, Toshima sat on her knees before a little shrine, beating on the tiny drum and chanting a prayer against destruction of a friend or lover, with no mind for herself. For a moment Tomoe thought she could still hear the dirge of the shamblers on the invisible path, but realized quickly enough that she heard the rumble of a volcano, the source of Toshima's concern.

Yet Tomoe was more disconcerted by the sight of the Lady than by the sound of the mountain. It was Toshima whom the samurai had fled, though the workings of her mind caused Tomoe to believe she fled for fear of magic.

The Lady was more beautiful than Tomoe had ever realized, although always Tomoe saw the surface beauty. Lady Toshima had changed miraculously while her samurai lover was away (and how long had Tomoe been gone? The hairy priests said she had slain each of three a dozen times, but only one per day. Forty days, therefore, had Tomoe dwelt among ghosts). It would be difficult to imagine this new Toshima hiding a more impressive nature behind coy allusions and childlike mannerisms ever again.

Among the courts of Naipon, the changes in Toshima would not be appreciated. The lady was a little weathered, her hair long and straight and bound back with a scarf. Her burns were long healed, but the pallor which was so highly regarded among the feminine nobility would never be Toshima's again. The woman had become strong, independent in her retainer's absence, and unselfish. These things the samurai saw, or heard within the prayer. Before that little shrine knelt a woman Tomoe could well imagine returning to Naipon and rebuilding the wealth of Shigeno Valley's rich farmlands.

The samurai whispered, "Toshima. I have returned."

Toshima fell from her knees in surprise, peered backward at the ceiling. Tomoe smiled sheepishly, then said, "Come up here with me and choose weapons. Two sorcerers will do battle in the ruins, one jono, one seemingly a rokubu but powerful. We must aid the jono priest. He does not know that the things on the invisible path will aid his foe."

Toshima stood, with many questions forming, but less need of careful explanation than of action. She had changed indeed, and welcomed the necessity of mystery and danger. She reached up to Tomoe's down-reaching arms, was pulled into the rafters. Tomoe said, "I was right to suspect ghosts, for ghosts abound, and monsters too. But the enemy is a man, who manipulated our very fates to bring us here, all to trap the jono. If you can throw knives as well as I once saw you throw a hairpin, then we might be of aid in the battle which is promised. I am told we cannot prevail against the rokubu, but I know from experience that monsters can be felled."

Already Toshima was selecting daggers at random and slipping them in her obi or inside her kimono. The kimono's large sleeves she tied back in preparation for the battle. There was a fine, long *naginata* halberd which she took up and swung around her head twice with expert speed and precision. It was a traditional weapon among women; even court ladies were instructed in its uses, expected as they were to protect their castles and their virtue. Tomoe would not be surprised to learn that Toshima had always been, though secretly, more skilled than most.

Tomoe strung a bow, and strapped a quiver of iron arrows to her back, beside the bow. The sword of Okio was thrust in her obi where the magician-ninja had kindly placed it there for her. Next to it, she wedged a good dagger. To each hand, she took a yari spear, testing the balance and nodding approval.

Together, Lady and samurai descended the rafters, and left the house in favor of ruins beyond a hill.

🕉 🕉 🕉

From the ruined city's gate, Tomoe and Toshima saw this:

In the air whirled what seemed a cloud of bats, which on more careful observance were tiny flying monkeys, nocturnal eyes dominating their narrow faces. They swirled about the head of the magician-ninja, who stood frozen with his arms held outward from his sides, one palm facing toward the rokubu, the other facing up. The fanged fliers were held at bay by some unseen barrier, and were angry to be so thwarted.

About him a ring of larger beasts had formed. They had extremely broad shoulders, much narrower hips, relatively stubby legs, and fatty tails which draped to the ground and dragged like those of lizards. Their heads were so short and wide it seemed they had no heads at all, only humps upon their shoulders with reddened slits for eyes. From these eyes there flowed a continuance of tears.

The fliers chittered angrily, unable to break the barrier by aerial assault. The shamblers stood shoulder to shoulder, hemming the magician-ninja within. They swayed from side to side and hummed their mournful, eerie dirge.

This, too, the women beheld before they stepped through the arched gateway: a fat and dirty rokubu with arms above his head and fingers spread, frozen as firmly as the jono priest by the exchange of spells. His face was a twisted mask of glee; he appeared a happy Buddha. Neither rokubu nor magician-ninja revealed awareness of the women in the archway.

Ruined stone buildings provided the backdrop for the two men facing one another at far ends of the courtyard. Doubtless theirs was a mortal combat, though the women could see no movement, could not fathom the manner of battle.

The circle of shamblers appeared to be slowly penetrating the barrier made by the magician-ninja. The fliers were managing by equally slow stages to lower themselves closer and closer from above, teeth and talons anxious.

Toshima began the activity. She tossed three daggers in rapid succession. Three fliers fell against the barrier, and slid to the ground as down the curve of a bell-shaped glass. They flapped awkwardly with knives through their little bodies. The cloud of fliers above the magician-ninja immediately burst in all directions, at first seeming to flee, but circling to investigate the woman who had killed three among their

numbers. Above Toshima's head, they began to reform their obnoxious conglomeration.

The rokubu's gaze did not waver. His attention was riveted to the magician-ninja, who also was oblivious to Tomoe and Toshima. The intensity between the two sorcerers caused the women to stand unnoticed; that, or the sorcerers were so ensnared by each others' powers that the rokubu could not stop the interference, and the magician-ninja could not encourage it.

Tomoe heaved one of the two yari. The long, straight weapon tore into the back of one of the dirge-sounding shamblers, so that their circle was disheveled and their progress toward the magician-ninja halted. Half the dirge-sounders turned upon Tomoe, revealing those hideous faces squashed upon their shoulders, deformed countenances of parodic sorrow, the eyes draining a constant stream of sad, thick, yellow tears.

Toshima's naginata carved wide arcs around herself, providing a barrier as clever as that of the magician-ninja. Her style incorporated both one- and two-handed maneuvers. The fliers strove to break this excellent defense. When they tried, she clipped their wings, or sliced them through the middle.

One of them had fallen, wing completely severed, but ran upon small feet, upright like a human, straight toward Toshima. One of her daggers came quickly to hand, was thrown with deadly aim, pinning the minuscule monster to the ground. It continued to watch her with large, malevolent eyes and scratched the air with tiny razored talons as it died.

The shamblers did not immediately attack Tomoe. They had divided into two groups, the first group continuing the effort to penetrate the magician-ninja's barrier, the others lining themselves shoulder to shoulder between Tomoe and the rokubu.

Her second spear preceded her assault, chucked into a shambler's belly. The line-up was broken. Then, sword to hand, she cut through their rank, thinking to fight them minimally, and take the rokubu instead. As she came nearer him, she saw that like the magician-ninja, he was not breathing. The sorcerers might each be dead!

Since the shamblers were unarmed, they provided poor defense against a sword. Tomoe was soon near enough the rokubu to slash his unmoving body.

The sword of Okio met resistance, and more, something of the barrier stung Tomoe and tossed her back. She was flung through the air and landed stunned upon her quiver of arrows, bruising her spine. Quickly, she looked about, but could not see where her sword had fallen. Regaining her feet, she fought with sheath and dagger, but could not kill the tough shamblers with these minimal weapons. They knew a primitive form of jujitsu, these broad-shouldered creatures from the invisible path, and used their mean skill in a stubborn effort to bring Tomoe down.

Still fighting near the gate, Toshima had expended all her daggers, so that tiny corpses lay around her feet. Yet there remained a fair sized swarm intent upon breaking the guard of the naginata.

One of the tiny beasts managed to grab the handle of the long weapon with its feet, clinging as a bird to a perch. Lady Toshima continued to swing her weapon around and around, carving through the swarm. The single clinging flier began to climb down the shaft of the weapon, toward Toshima's hands. She could not shake it off. Huge eyes glared from the narrow, simian face. When it showed its pointed teeth, she could have sworn the beast had smiled...and still, she could only slash the sky, to guard against others.

An unexpected knife took the fiend's life, but Toshima dared not stop long enough to thank Tomoe, or even to look around and notice from what predicament the samurai had thrown salvation.

The trick which saved Toshima had left Tomoe with only her empty sheath as weapon, having neither dagger nor sword. A shambler's tail lashed as would a whip, scoring her fingers—but she did not drop the sheath. She engaged the whipper arm to arm, and it threw her over its shoulder; but Tomoe had left a dizzying knot upon the shambler's flattened head, then landed on her feet.

By now she had seen where the violent force of the rokubu's barrier had tossed her sword. But too many shamblers stood between her and the finer weapon.

She managed instead to fight her way to a certain shambler's corpse, from which to reclaim a yari. Sheath thrown aside, she struck with both the sharp and blunt ends of the yari, beat the surrounding shambler's back, slaying them to either side. When it became evident she would kill them all, the second group of them turned from harrying the frozen magician-ninja to battle Tomoe instead.

One of the shamblers paused, bent to the ground, claimed Tomoe's sword. Its thick tail twitched excitedly, and it hurried its shambling steps, swinging the sword with contemptible form.

Lady Toshima was wearying. There were far more fliers than shamblers, and of them she took large toll; yet they were still thick as gnats above her swinging naginata. The Lady panted and strained, and fought well, but lacked the endurance of tested samurai. The impish flying felons chittered and thrilled, detecting their adversary's weakening.

Tomoe climbed the rubble of a collapsed building, and stood on a huge block of stone, parrying against her own sword with the yari, and stabbing at the shamblers who tried to climb up and grab her. She had wounded or slain most of them, most having withdrawn so that they might die to the sound of their own dirge. When she saw Toshima's danger, Tomoe made a magnificent leap which stole her from the midst of the few remaining and largely dying shamblers; stole her from the thrust of the sword of Okio.

She landed on the city's mainwall, where the shamblers could not reach her. Instantly, she brought her bow to bear. One after another, she let the iron arrows fly, and each one found the heart or face of a flier. Lady Toshima made a happy cry, and fought the better when the fliers were unsettled. The ground was strewn with their tiny corpses, some of them twitching in pain or throes of death. Their numbers dwindled quickly from the sky, to the effort of bow and naginata.

Then the shamblers made an unexpected score. The first yari Tomoe had thrown had been retrieved from the monster it slew—retrieved by another shambler. The monster threw the yari from an angle Tomoe could not see. With the chittering of the fliers and the dirge of the last two shamblers, she could not hear the weapon hurtling toward her back. The first she knew of it was when the spear-point burst out between her ribs having entered midway down her back.

She did not flinch. She continued to loose arrows until she had no more, and only then did she totter. Below her stood the two remaining shamblers: the one who had thrown the spear, and the one who bore her sword. They waited for her to fall, but they did not appear glad of victory. Yellow tears flowed from red eyes, eyes which peered from the hump of their shoulders. They swayed to and fro, as if mourning Tomoe Gozen.

Tomoe experienced surprisingly little pain with the yari through her body, its haft at her back, the bloody point sticking out beneath her heart. Miraculously it had missed vital organ, but it seemed fate's whimsy rather than fortune, for it would only prolong her death from loss of blood. She still had the other yari, and raised it with a shaking, vengeful hand—tossed it into the flat, peering face of the shambler who had wounded her severely. It fell to its knees, then tumbled backward, so that finally only one of the beasts lived and hummed.

Blood flowed down her front and back. Soon she was too weak to maintain her perch. When she fell, her only weapon was the bow, for which she had no more arrows. She landed awkwardly on her feet, and the landing wrought great pain as the handle through her body was jarred. The shambler swung the sword; Tomoe guarded with the bow. The bow's string was sliced through, with a loud snap and vibration. Tomoe continued to guard, and tried to poke at eyes with the bow's tip; but she was much weakened.

All around lay strange corpses. Near the gate, Toshima leapt and shouted and killed the fliers, not yet aware of the samurai's terrible injury. In the courtyard, the two sorcerers had still not moved, faced each other dearly. But something new was occurring:

The jono priest blinked in and out of existence like a flickering candle, perhaps trying to escape, but held by the unflickering rokubu. Tomoe barely had the awareness to notice this development. She had fallen to her knees, kept her guard against the sword with a wood and metal bow. The bow was being hacked in twain. Had Toshima not killed the final flier then, and turned with quickly vanquished joy of victory to see Tomoe Gozen, the samurai might well have died by the hand of the shambler.

Lady Toshima ran forward without a sound, without a cry, and the naginata carved along the shambler's spine. It dropped Tomoe's sword, fell forward on the samurai, pinned itself to her by the point of the yari which protruded from her body. She pushed the beast away, and continued to sit there on her knees with as little motion as possible.

Suddenly, all around her stood ghosts. The mists of Keiko's City of Death returned to harm her vision. One ghost in particular bowed and scraped in an excessively solicitous manner. It was Ya Hanada, who said, "You have returned! We missed you, and wished to thank you for dispatching the hairy sacrificers. Ah, life is better now! You will like our city more!"

There was a smile upon his blurry face, and he held out a saké bottle which Tomoe recognized only too well. She knew that she could rise, and be free of the spear and attendant injury. Instead, she remained on knees, panting, glowering, and said, "I will not die. I am too stubborn."

Hanada moved back into the mists, disappointed. The mists, and the ghosts, dispersed. The only person before Tomoe anymore was Lady Toshima, horrified to see the yari sticking out from the samurai's body.

"Toshima."

The Lady knelt quickly to her retainer's side. All around them, strange corpses were fading from the courtyard, drawn back onto the invisible path.

"Toshima."

Toshima refused tears. She asked, "What can I do?"

"Take hold of the spear," said Tomoe. "Draw it out."

Lady Toshima cupped hand to mouth, and would have liked to take refuge in childlike incapacity. But she had grown too much. Shaking, she stood; she stood behind Tomoe. She gripped the yari's haft in both hands.

"Draw it straight," Tomoe instructed, "or it will yet damage me inside."

The samurai refused to shout, as she refused to die. The thick shaft pulled free as Tomoe's jowls shook and her eyes peeled back into her head. It made appalling sucking sounds as Toshima applied all her strength to the task. The samurai grunted, took long heavy breaths, but did not lose consciousness.

"I must stop the bleeding," said Toshima, throwing aside the reddened yari. She unwrapped her obi, then opened Tomoe's kimono, fought an urge to look away from the awful wound in front and back. Tomoe moved as little as possible, while her torso was tightly wrapped in the Lady's sash. When it was done, Toshima pulled the samurai's kimono up around the shoulders, and whispered to Tomoe, "The sorcerers are moving."

The magician-ninja began to bend, his body twisting backward. He still blinked in and out of existence, almost frantically. The face of the rokubu was intense with fury, no longer simple glee. Hatred strengthened him. Tomoe and Toshima realized the rokubu was winning. The magician-ninja's face was hidden behind the cloth wrapped about his head, although the eyes were visible, and still unafraid. Tomoe said hoarsely, "His spine will be broken."

She was too weak to move, in too much pain to try, and could not encourage Toshima to make any effort to intervene where sorcery was concerned. She said, "There is nothing we can do."

It was a gruesome thing to watch, the uncomplaining jono priest folded in half, until his head touched his buttocks and his spine made a loudly audible snap. When the deed was finished, the rokubu sprung back to life, and shouted at the heavens, "Noyimo! I have slain your twin!"

Dark clouds of smoke billowed from Smaller Mountain, shadowing the sky with maleficent shapes and visages. Smaller Mountain rumbled at its roots, as a lion growls at the bottom of its throat, prepared to roar, to leap, to rend.

No one saw her come, but Noyimo had appeared unexpectedly above her brother. She crouched, and if she was sorrowed by what she beheld, it was hidden behind her mask. Looking toward the rokubu, she formed a strange design by intertwining her fingers, and aimed this mystic weave upon her foe.

Around Noyimo and her murdered brother, the barrier was reconstructed, stronger than before, glowing, translucent, bronze and pink. The barrier had a definite shape: a temple bell.

The rokubu spread his fingers, struck violently before himself, flinging some spell at Noyimo. The half-visible bell rang insidiously, and it was plain that the noise was terrible for Noyimo to endure. Yet she held her knit fingers, and crouched by her brother like a protective cat.

What might have transpired then, no one would ever know, for in the arched gateway appeared an old blind woman, both her eyes white as bone.

"He has returned," growled Keiko, cocking her head left and right, her face an unbearable twisted mask of hatred. In the distance, the smaller peak belched smoke and spilled liquid stone.

Gone was the maniacal pleasantness of the mischievous woman Tomoe had met before. Gone was the child in an oldster's body. She spoke with the voice of spite and anger, and commanded, "Tell me it is true! He returns!"

"She cannot see!" Toshima whispered. Keiko turned her blind face to where the two women knelt, one wounded near to death, the other near to sorrow.

"Love blinded me before," said Keiko. "But now I see too well."

Tomoe answered, though it took a toll to speak. "Then see your husband standing there, old Keiko."

Her head turned slowly, ears scanning the courtyard. It did not take much effort to hear him, for the rokubu began to laugh.

"Old woman!" said the rokubu contemptuously. "I thank you for your sundry efforts on my behalf! Today I prove myself this earth's most mighty wizard. Even the tides of the ocean—even the Dragon Queen—bow to my will!"

He flung a fiery shuriken at the blind woman. The metal star shone and sparked and struck Keiko in the throat. It was a killing wound. When Toshima turned away, sickened, Tomoe eased the Lady by telling her in a raspy voice, "The rokubu is madder than the madwoman. A mortal goddess slain becomes immortal once again."

Keiko began to change. Her eyes cleared. The wrinkles of her face and hands began to smooth. Her wild grey hair and gossamer white whiskers became glistening black. Her young, strong hands reached to her neck so that slender finger could dig out the shuriken and toss it on the ground.

The goddess began to grow, until she towered over all within the courtyard. Her clothing had changed from rags into something shimmering and glorious, half akin to a wedding kimono, half similar to the court robes of women in the Celestial Kingdoms. She might have been a famous beauty, this giantess above them, except that her eyes were flat and lidless like those of a fish. She gazed down at the little people: dead jono priest and mourning jono priestess within a translucent bell, wounded samurai and strengthened courtly lady—but especially she gazed upon the rokubu who now effaced himself before the towering woman. He quivered with fright, and begged mercy more vehemently than he had boasted power.

"Foolish husband," said the incredible goddess, and the island quaked beneath her voice. Smaller Mountain spat ash.

Tomoe was less interested in this drama than in Noyimo, whom the samurai watched with unreadable expression. Noyimo let the pink glowing barrier fade, and with it went her brother; for magician-ninja had no funeral rites and their bodies were always destroyed by magic. It was part of their cult and custom, to keep their identities even beyond one life. When the barrier had vanished, Noyimo ran across the courtyard, behind the feet of the giant goddess, and came to the side of Tomoe. For a moment, the eyes of a Lady and those of the masked magician-ninja met across a samurai, and a host of conflicting feelings flashed between them: jealousy faded into understanding, ignobility into truce, envy into admiration, anger to concern.

"She needs help," said Noyimo, and Toshima nodded. Noyimo said, "Tomoe, I think I can make you strong for a while, until we can get you to the *onna-no-miko*…in time, we pray, to heal you."

Tomoe gazed between the two women, not at either of them directly. Her forehead was drenched with sweat, though her body shook with chill. She said, "I am too good to die." Noyimo placed one hand below Tomoe's breasts, the other on her back, and made a spell to halt the worst of Tomoe's pain, bleeding, loss of strength and progress of deterioration. Noyimo said, "We must hurry. Keiko is taking her island back into the sea."

The samurai crawled upright on her knees, and took up her sword where the last shambler had dropped it. Toshima darted away and back, giving the samurai the sword's sheath. Aided to left and right by the two women, Tomoe stood uncertainly, her legs oddly fluid. They hurried toward the gate of the mainwall, not taking time to look where the rokubu continued to cower and grovel at the feet of a goddess.

The three women came to the top of a rise, beneath the smoke-shrouded heaven. Beyond, they saw the would-be farmhouse already taken by the sea. Noyimo was disturbed, and said, "That was our route of escape. I could leave on my own, but the two of you must use a door to obtain the invisible path."

The house collapsed as huge waves clutched at it, dragged it beneath white, frothy waters. The women looked back at the city, saw its ruins in the lower lands, saw the inrushing sea filling the valley, saw even the tiny figure of the rokubu before the gigantic Dragon Queen.

Keiko was changing again. She turned into a dragon, reared upon her haunches. Fire shot from her nostrils, and burned the rokubu to ash in a single breath. Then the dragon swung her fierce head and wailed a kind of regret. She flung her tail about, destroying what buildings had not already fallen into rubble.

Smaller Mountain grumbled displeasure, and Toshima shouted above the din, "There is another entry to the invisible path. In Keiko's cave." She pointed at Taller Mountain, where the maw of a cavern could be seen far up the side.

"Can you make it?" Noyimo asked of Tomoe, who nodded vaguely, still not looking at either woman.

They took to the higher peak of the island. Behind them, the Dragon Queen had knocked over the walls of her city, as the sea rushed in. She dragged her tail after herself and took to the forested land between the two peaks. There, the flames of her breath lit the trees. Lava poured from Smaller Mountain's crown, and the ground was split asunder by the quakes. The Dragon Queen writhed as though defeating an invisible foe, and the waves of the sea came higher, into the forest, dousing the fires and raising steam. The sea lapped with loving devotion at the oily, rainbow scales of the Dragon Queen.

Swiftly, the island was going down.

Upward they struggled, clinging to rock and bush. Toshima gave no complaint, though at climbing she had little skill, and the mountain dealt her numerous minor wounds. Noyimo progressed with the least effort, drawing the other two upward with her dark, tangible power. Tomoe went with a lumbering lack of speed, slowing the steep procession.

The samurai spoke no more. Noyimo's spell had erased pain, and had halted the progress of physical deterioration. But it did not heal, did not strengthen except by illusion; and Tomoe's flesh, if not her mind, knew it had been abused. Therefore the samurai was forced to focus all attention to the task of staying above the rising waterline. Little else existed for her, beyond this simple quest, and she forced her way on.

Keiko had left a rope hanging from her cave's entrance. It hung over the steepest access. This rope helped the three women gain entry, barely before the water had gained the same height. Already, Smaller Mountain had fallen below sea level, continuing to erupt beneath the steaming, boiling waves. Taller Mountain was the barest isle, itself inevitably to be drawn under. Of Keiko the Dragon Queen, there was no longer evidence. She, too, had returned to the land called Neinya, her home upon the ocean floor.

Rocks cluttered the back of the cavern, where Keiko in her mortal guise had blocked the invisible path. Lady Toshima and the jono priestess heaved and dragged the rocks from the way, but Tomoe Gozen stood uselessly and teetered on weak legs. She was scarcely aware of the other two.

A thin trickle of water seeped into the recesses of the cave, while outside the sea bubbled and churned and made an awful, threatening racket. Tomoe felt herself snatched by well-meaning hands, drawn by her shoulders into a cold, dark, uncomfortable place. There was silence.

Noyimo alone could guide them. It was a timeless place, so that

Wendy Adrian Shultz

none of them could be sure how long they walked the invisible path. Noyimo's dark robes seemed to shine like some sort of impossible black ice. Toshima followed this blue-tinged, darkling lightedness. She pulled Tomoe along.

As the rokubu had never aged while upon the path, so was Tomoe Gozen preserved against her terrific wound, more fully than by Noyimo's transient spell. If it were true, as it later seemed, that they spent many days on the path, none were the worse for it, having had no need of food or drink, and having wearied no further. But Tomoe, at least, was no better for it either.

It was a tedious venturing, the sameness of the empty universe broken only twice. First was near the place where the rokubu had put secret doors in the house Keiko made. The house had been destroyed by the sea, but the rokubu's strange door had not yet come undone. The ocean bulged onto the invisible path at these spots, shedding greenish light, but could not fully enter. Within these trespassing bulges there swam curious, loathly fish with smiling lips and lanterns on their noses. The second thing that provided an interlude to the tedium was a space littered with a vast number of corpses: the slaughtered shamblers and fliers which had returned after death to their nowhere-place, and the burnt, twisted body of the rokubu. Noyimo led a careful trail between these drifting, weightless corpses, leery of brushing against the foulness they encompassed.

Beyond those two observances, they saw nothing, felt only the cold. Yet, Noyimo at least seemed certain of the route. An unguessable amount of time elapsed when Noyimo finally stopped, turned to reveal her shining face, and said to the other two, "Through here is a jono temple on Nogoshi Hill overlooking Kamakura."

She indicated a spot, and though there was nothing there to see, her voice held certainty. Tomoe's vague awareness surfaced at the promise of passage to Naipon. Toshima led Tomoe to the spot Noyimo had indicated, and directly, all three women vanished from the invisible path.

Somewhere in Tomoe's lowered consciousness, a promise was made: a promise never to enter the invisible path again, whether she lived a long life or one more day. Yet, much as she despised the path, she was pleased it had brought her home.

From Nogoshi Hill, she could see the city of Kamakura stretched below, reaching from Hochiman Shrine in the north to Yuigahama Beach. Along the beach, warjunks were harbored; yet none would have guessed

Kamakura's flowered streets provided comfort to a military regime. It was too beautiful. The long, narrow city filled the shallow valley with its widely spaced castles and its more closely built mansions along uncrowded boulevards. Even the hovels were works of artisans, as the poorest of Kamakura were famed for their pomp and glamour and lordly gait. The Shogun placed great store in an appearance of beauty, peace, and comfort. Strength alone was understated.

"Follow," said Noyimo.

Nearby was a black temple. Noyimo said, "None but I could authorize your sanctuary in the jono temple; generally, none leave such a place until they are fully trained to the cult. Or they never leave at all. Even I must abide by certain restrictions, to take you within. You must trust me. I will take you blindfolded to a place inside that is comfortable, and you will not wander from it without my assistance, or it will mean your lives. Whatever you hear, whatever you smell, whatever you feel or fear—make no sound. Do not raise the cloth from your eyes. Our secrets protect more than ourselves—so you must never question these directions."

Serious though the warnings were, Tomoe required no blindfold after all. Noyimo's spell had worn away, and the samurai collapsed from loss of blood.

She dreamed of safety.

EPILOG:
Duel At Heiji Castle

For three days, Tomoe Gozen was nursed by onna-no-miko, women healers. They chewed medicinal plants and spat the stinging substances in her wounds. They placed the skins of mudfish on the rents at her front and back. They forced her to eat a soupy concentrate which birds had partly digested. They manipulated muscles, organs, circulation, and the eight senses by applying the tips of their fingers to learned points of the body. These measures, and others, were handed down from mother to daughter since antiquity; much of their craft was guarded secret, not because it defended their station, but because their craft could be mis-used.

After those three days, the samurai's health was stable, and the wounds had closed properly. Yet, Tomoe Gozen did not awaken in all this time, and the onna-no-miko wished to discover why.

It became necessary for one of the healers to enter Tomoe's mind, to walk with her through paradisiacal dreams. If a dreamwalker could prove to the dreamer what was false and what was objective, Tomoe would eventually recognize the velvet darkness of the chamber as real-ity, and the sunlit valley of her unconsciousness as fictive.

🝔 🝔 🝔

Because the land of her dream was pleasant, it was difficult for the dreamer to let go. Tomoe favored the sunny hill and meadows over the gloomy chamber in the jono temple. In the temple, there were eerie sounds, and black-cloaked novices of excessively serious mien; whereas in the valley, which she had built with her own intellect, there were chirruping insects and singing birds and a peacefulness which inspired.

Tomoe sat alone on the green hill's side, grinning foolishly at Amaterasu who, on this land, never set.

Unexpectedly, one of the onna-no-miko joined her, sat beside her, said, "I am told you once lived in the illusions of a ghostly stone city."

"I did that," said Tomoe.

"I am told you once fought your way from hell."

"Or to it, if I believe a Buddhist nun."

"I am told you battled oni devils in the dream of Izanami."

"That, too, is true."

"Then you must help me understand how it is you have not yet learned to discern, and overcome, illusions." The onna-no-miko indicated the green country with a sweep of her hand.

Tomoe looked at this intense woman, who was barely more than a child; too young, thought Tomoe, to be a skillful healer and dreamwalker.

"It is a pretty dream," said Tomoe. "And unlike those others you mention, this one is of my own creation. Why should I destroy it? Should the gods destroy Naipon?"

"It will all come undone in any case, when your flesh returns to death. Your body lies hot and dying. Your organs are bruised and traumatized, but it is nothing courage cannot cure."

Tomoe was unmoved.

"If not of yourself, samurai, think of others," the young healer continued. "Think of a jono priestess who believes your life is worthwhile. Think how you have sworn service to Lady Toshima, Lord Shigeno's heir. Think of the Shogun's samurai who pines for his equal in battle. Think of a very young onna-no-miko, who will punish herself if she fails."

The samurai looked away, into the distance where hills rose and fell like gentle waves. She said, "I would like to know what lies beyond each rise."

She gazed happily over the dreamland.

The onna-no-miko hid her disgust poorly, then stood, then walked away. Tomoe did not watch her go.

Toshima was in the dream. No. She was not. She was in the black velvet room. There was warmth. Comfort. But there was an uninviting strangeness as well: the weird chanting of jono novices in adjoining chambers, some of whom might never see the light outside the temple should they fail to master the jono arts acquired—the comings and goings of various folk by entries and exits unfathomable—the noisy static of formalized magicks, or sorcerous kata sets practiced by diligent yet unproficient wizardlings just as samurai children practiced with bamboo swords—the shuffling of beasts and the rattling of chains in the haunted spaces behind every wall—but most disconcerting to Tomoe Gozen was the sound of Toshima's crying. Tomoe tried to flee back into the sweetness of the dream, because her body ached, and because it hurt to hear Toshima weep. A sick samurai felt tears drop upon her pale, knotted fingers; and she flinched imperceptibly.

An older healer was nearby, not the youth who had previously invaded Tomoe's dream. The mature, nurturant voice counseled a distraught Toshima. "Life is delicate," she said. "A silkworm's slender thread is all that holds us to one life and from another. Strong as silk can be, a good knife will always cut it."

Toshima found no comfort in this. She argued, "Tomoe Gozen is stronger than you suggest."

There was a weight of sorrow in the healer's voice when she said, "Few are the lives to equal in fragility the lives of samurai."

Toshima relented, and confessed, "I suspected she was frail."

"It is properly so," said the healer. "Things which are frail survive. They bend as the willow bends. They bow. They serve. If Tomoe Gozen is afraid to live, it is because she cannot serve. A samurai requires a master, or to no one will she bow."

A cloaked jono novice came into the velvet room by secret means and blindfolded the healer who was saying, "There is nothing more the onna-no-miko can do. We will come no more." She allowed herself to be led away quietly. Toshima was left to sit beside Tomoe upon the floor, pondering the healer's advice. After a while, she leaned forward, whispered to the samurai, "The healers say courage can heal your injuries. I know you are courageous. Why do you not waken?" Eyes moved beneath closed lids. Toshima spoke softly, "We took liberties with each other, on the Dragon Queen's island, when our destinies were torn from beneath us by a sorcerous rokubu. Now, we must recall our stations. I am master of a samurai. I will be mistress to none but Shigeno Valley. It will be difficult to rebuild and hold my land; but I have a strong retainer, who is a hero, and others will join us. Is this not so? You cannot die without my leave to do so. You can only die for your master."

Tomoe's tightly knotted fists relaxed, but her eyes still would not open.

Tomoe gazed once more upon the verdant valley, which was changing to something less refined. The fields were turning to mire, with the blood of a peasant population, of eight thousand samurai, of the thick fluids of ghouls. Amidst torn woods stood the skeletal remains of a burnt, charred mansion.

The ideal country had become ruined Shigeno Valley. Had she lost control of her previously pleasant dream, or had this always been the place of her most introspective quest?

It was a terrible valley, but it had not always been so. It need not remain so. A castle could be built where the mansion had been. A moat could be dug around it, wider than an arrow's range. Bridges could be made across the moat, and across the rivers which fed it. If peace would not come to Naipon, then overlords must fortify their holdings. Shigeno Valley needed a fortification of obvious merit, a castle whose peaks rivaled the distant peaks of mountains, to stand against the thousand treacheries which befall a "weak" lord.

Lady Toshima was not weak, but that would need to be proven. Given her fine perversity, she would never strengthen her holdings by gainful marriage. The cleverness of the Lady was doubtless sufficient to the task set before her. But without many strong samurai, the best decisions would be difficult to enforce. Tomoe Gozen had been selected as chief among those samurai.

Thinking this, darkness fell absolute upon the once-sunny, once-green country. Amaterasu had finally set.

The samurai's eyes tried to penetrate the starless night. First she saw the face of Toshima Shigeno, and then the darkness became a velvet room. Toshima smiled, and spoke sardonically, "You have decided to live, samurai?"

Tomoe struggled to sit up. The wound through her body ached, but had healed a good deal after nearly four days. She coughed, spat a little blood into a rag, and said hoarsely, "One dream is as good as another. I have sworn fealty to this one."

Behind Toshima stood the jono priestess, gloomier than Tomoe had ever seen. This was the first time she had visited since helping to bring an unconscious Tomoe to the velvet room. It was as though the sorceress had waited for Tomoe's choice between comatose dreams and reality; but she revealed no joy over Tomoe's decision.

"A few days ago," said Noyimo, "one of the onna-no-miko was taken by an assassin. By torture—we shall not discuss its nature—enemies learned that a Lady and her samurai had returned from exile. The Shogun would have urged the jono cult not to harbor criminals; therefore, I had one acceptable choice. An announcement was placed in the city square: Tomoe Gozen and Ugo Mohri will do battle at Heiji Castle. It will happen in two more days."

Toshima gasped. "She is not yet strong!"

Tomoe had climbed onto her knees, taking deep breaths. She said, "Doubtless the choices were few, unless we move slower than the Shogun." It was strange to speak words so close to treason! Indeed, the only escape from a treasonous act—and a hopeless one—was to fight the Shogun's champion.

"Ugo Mohri desires the match," Tomoe said with certainty. "And do I."

"It is too soon!" said Toshima, clenching her hands together.

The samurai disagreed. She said, "I require food. I require my sword. I require two days to practice and regain my tone. Strength will not defeat Ugo Mohri. Speed and skill alone can test him."

"I could aid you," said the jono priestess, her bright face shadowed by evil thoughts.

Tomoe looked at her sharply, replied, "You could do so only against my wish. What honor would be left me if Ugo Mohri died by sorcerous aid? I will send him gifts of wild garlic to keep you away. Otherwise, if you interfered, I would be bound to slay you, or attempt it, even against my will, and then to kill myself, unless we died together."

Lady Toshima stood. She stood beside Noyimo who hid all concern too well. The Lady touched the magician-ninja so that she would say no more, and cause no anger. What passed between these two surprised Tomoe, and she was not certain she lacked jealousy. For a short time, the eyes of sorceress and Lady held one another, and then Toshima said, "If you wish to help, acquire fine garments for Tomoe Gozen. She must not look tawdry against the beauty of Ugo Mohri."

"Two days," said Tomoe to herself, finding her unsteady legs. Blood rushed through her head. She nearly swooned. "Blindfold me," she commanded, for only blindfolded could she leave this room. "Take me to the yards to play!"

"Willful samurai!" scolded Toshima, affecting the childlike voice Tomoe had not heard since a day long past, a day in a tea garden, when Toshima professed love as a prelude to many adventures for herself, and for Tomoe. She said, almost with humor,

"Anxiously, you play with death."

"Anxiously," agreed Tomoe.

The announcement posted in the city read, in vertical columns of brushed characters:

> Ugo Mohri
> the Shogun's Champion
> and Tomoe Gozen
> the Mikado's own Samurai
> will meet in mortal combat
> at Heiji Castle
> noon
> on Yellow Bamboo day
>
> ---
>
> Heimin are invited.

The invitation to farmers was a longstanding tradition, yet many were surprised that tradition was not, in this case, circumvented. The placard, in fact, was not one which the Shogun would have commanded to the post. He would have preferred Tomoe Gozen mentioned in the same breath as treason, rather than in association with the Mikado. There were many who could not understand or appreciate the need to place the Mikado in exile; they would easily make of the coming duel an allegorical meeting of larger powers.

Spies instantly informed the Shogun of the sign. Samurai retainers—four of them in all, as though it was expected to be a difficult task—arrived quickly, with the intention of replacing the placard with one preferable. How they failed was a curious thing:

They pulled the wooden placard down, complaining and wondering about who could have erected it. Immediately after, the retainers were accidentally jostled by a troupe of exceptionally untalented jugglers. These street entertainers instantaneously effaced themselves in front of the four tough samurai, begging pardons. They were booted away. When this unmomentous confusion had passed, the retainers proceeded to destroy the one placard and put up the other, discovering too late that they had broken the Shogun's message and reattached the original.

By then, the jugglers had scurried off; and in any event, it did not occur to the four retainers that the inept jugglers were the reason for the mistake. Rather, the retainers doubted they made a mistake at all; but, they suspected, the finely brushed characters of the Shogun's official calligrapher had actually rearranged themselves, had moved like insects, had been made to recreate the original, unacceptable message by sorcerous means.

When they tried to take the wooden placard down once more, tiny white sparks of fire bit their fingers. Therefore, they left the placard after all, and if there were repercussions from an angry Shogun, no one ever heard about it. It was preordained (the Shogun was advised) that Ugo Mohri win all duels against disenfranchised samurai; what matter then (the Shogun may have decided) if heimin associated Tomoe Gozen with the Mikado in exile. Indeed, when Tomoe Gozen fell, it would indicate to superstitious farmers the august son of Amaterasu was rightly kept away.

The duel was arranged by a presumedly neutral Lord, whose castle was an impressive fortification, albeit less remarkable than the Shogun's, as all castles (by decree) must be. On Yellow Bamboo day, Lord Hidemi Horota allowed farmers leeway through the gates of Heiji Castle. They were confined to the northern edge of a huge, enclosed yard devised specifically for exhibition. There, the heimin pressed against an imaginary (but respected) barrier, anxious and excited.

Lord Hidemi Horota sat among pomp and dignity and colorful raiment atop a raised platform to the east of the ground, before a large, squared gateway. On either side of him stood personal samurai, and one more sat upon the steps leading to the platform's seat. In the event of treachery, this forward samurai would stand from the stair and take whatever arrow or blow was meant for his Lord.

Along the southern edge of the yard were many comfortable chairs, arranged in groups by class of the sitters, and behind them were the palanquins which had delivered the various nobles. The *bakufu,* or office of the military, was well represented. Although the Shogun did not personally appear (which would have lent too fearful an importance to the event), several of the highest aristocrats of Kamakura, indeed of Naipon, along with many of their honored guests and privileged servants, were in attendance.

On the remaining end of the field were the combatants. West was the direction associated with death. There, painted cloths had been erected to form a double-enclosure, separating the opponents. The cloth structure was open in front, partitioned in the middle. In one side of the open enclosure sat Tomoe Gozen on a backless seat, fists on her thighs, her small retinue lined up behind her. On the other side of the partition sat Ugo Mohri, with a considerably larger retinue. His arms were folded inside his colorfully embroidered kimono. His face portrayed easy tranquillity. He sat upon a little seat identical to the one that held Tomoe, and his knees were far apart.

They were visible to all, but could not see each other.

The sun was fierce and high, the sky sparsely clouded, the yard mossy green; and in the center was a huge two-sided drum mounted horizontally. There was a drummer to each side of this instrument, bearing sets of wooden mallets. They beat slow, rhythmic tattoos whose sound filled the area between the further walls of the yard. By stages, their beat became more complex, and more rapid. They had been doing this for a long while, during which time the variegated audience arrived and took their proper places. Several uncouth heimin removed wooden sandals and clapped them as cymbals, adding to the frantic din of introduction.

At length, the racket was caused to end, and the drum was carried away. The yard became as silent as it had been noisy.

Ugo Mohri stood from the seat and walked forward, without looking back, until he stood before the platform holding Lord Horota. Mohri bowed with grace, and though Horota did not personally acknowledge the Shogun's champion, all the Lord's retainers returned the bow with the utmost respect. When Mohri turned around, his eyes glistened to see Tomoe Gozen, who sat still in the cloth chamber, waiting for her turn. When their eyes met, they told each other nothing.

He could not escape admiring her appearance, less colorful than his own fancifully colored kimono, yet grand in simplicity. She wore a full-sleeved *kosode* blouse and hakama trousers, the kosode gleaming white silk, the hakama black cotton. Her scabbard was fastened loose from a blue and black obi, rather than through it as was more customary. She had tied a black scarf about her head, and knotted it around her hair, leaving the ponytail to hang far down her spine.

The scarf was symbolic as well as functional. It meant: I am ready to try.

Her face lacked the serenity for which Ugo Mohri was famous; but there was a calmness about her nonetheless: a silent, unboasting kind of calm which might have veiled secret compassion.

Ugo Mohri walked to the yard's center, bowed to the other three sides of the field. It was expected that each opponent would first provide a brief display of skill. Thus, all eyes were upon Ugo Mohri, which pleased him.

From a compartment on the side of his sword's sheath, Ugo withdrew a length of cord called *sage-o*. He threw an end over each shoulder, pulled the ends under his arms, and tied them in front. He pulled the *sage-o* in a certain manner so that the bow he had tied moved to the center of his back. This tie held the long sleeves of his kimono away from the forearms. This done, he sat upon his knees, in the classic pose of *iaijutsu*, the art of the rapid draw.

Four of his aides came from the cloth enclosure, each carrying a large piece of heavy paper, each paper a different color: red, blue, yellow, white. The four men surrounded Ugo Mohri, armed only with these papers.

Heimin to one side, aristocrats to the other, Tomoe at his back, and an important Lord before—Ugo Mohri's pleasure was highly visible. Everyone watched him attentively, wondering what sort of display he had in mind to impress them. Thus far, they were more curious than impressed, for sword defeating paper would scarcely entail amazing feats.

The four men raised their respective colored papers. They tossed these sheets toward Ugo Mohri, then leapt backward.

The *iai* draw required total concentration and intense determination focused toward a particular action, performed with acute rapidity and exceeding accuracy. As the papers came toward him, Ugo raised one knee. His sword came from its sheath, slashed in four directions as he twirled halfway around. The sword re-entered its scabbard as he returned to both knees, now facing Tomoe rather than Lord Horota.

Eight pieces of paper, not four, fell to the ground.

The four men stepped forward and reclaimed the eight pieces of paper, and held these pieces in upraised hands. They threw them once more, and Ugo Mohri's sword moved forth with even more blinding speed, singing through the air as he turned to face the castle's Lord as before, and fell back into the sitting posture. Every piece of paper had been cut in half again, so that sixteen pieces fell to the ground. What few spectators had blinked their eyes saw nothing more than Ugo Mohri's mystifying ability to face west then east without having apparently flinched a muscle or altered a pose.

The four aides hurried forward one last time, and gathered up the sixteen bits of paper. They came together in a group and began to fold the colored pieces into a whole. They made a patterned paper lantern and presented it to Lord Hidemi Horota's forward samurai, who took it to the Lord himself.

Ugo Mohri had not merely cut the papers, but had cut them into specific shapes and sizes so that the lantern could be made. Heimin stood with mouths agape. Aristocratic warriors nodded to one another appreciatively. Ugo Mohri stood, bowed once more to the Lord of Heiji Castle, then returned to his seat in the partitioned enclosure, arms folded over his chest.

He had looked slightly disappointed that Tomoe Gozen's expression never altered.

Tomoe stood. She walked toward the castle's Lord, looking bow-legged and strong in her crisp hakama trousers. There was something terrible in her walk, and it was not like Ugo's swagger; it was more offensive than conceited. It said: *I will participate in your circus. But it is still a circus.* She bowed curtly, and the samurai to either side of the Lord returned her bow uncomfortably. The one seated on the step raised himself up a little, as though he had seen something dangerous in her manner, as though he feared she might rush the platform and kill his master.

She turned. Already, a target had been wheeled to the center of the yard and propped up, facing her and Lord Horota. She bowed north, then south, lastly to Ugo Mohri. Their eyes met as before, without message. She drew her sword, confronting the target.

Again, the onlookers were puzzled. The target was for archery, but Tomoe Gozen bore a daito blade. It was more confusing than Ugo's paper.

The young boy who had wheeled the target forward ducked behind it, rather than leaving the field. Tomoe glowered at the target somewhat inappropriately, as though it were a hated enemy several paces away from her. She held her sword outward to one side, and crossed one leg over the other to approach this presumed foe. She was not near enough to strike, and it seemed pointless to do so anyway. Her audience, however, was only the more attentive due to the apparent valuelessness of her maneuver.

Atop roofs, there appeared three cloaked figures: ninja! Lord Hidemi Horota's samurai moved in front of him immediately, concerned that ninja should appear on the castle's roofs. Half the audience looked to where the ninja stood, darkly clad, only their eyes visible. Those eyes glared into the yard at Tomoe Gozen.

Tomoe continued to focus on the target, oblivious to the ninja.

Ugo Mohri leaned forward from the three-sided tent, his expression tense and intense, trying to gain a view of the three ninja and Tomoe.

The ninja crouched, flung three overlarge shurikens at Tomoe Gozen, one after the other.

There were three melodic chimes: *Brring. Chring. Clant*, followed by three dull sounds: *Tunt-tunt-tunt*. The large shurikens were deflected by her sword, and into the target.

The ninja slunk away, vanished.

The boy hiding behind the target stood, and turned it to the four sides of the yard so all would see how the shurikens formed a careful triangle in the center of the target.

Upon Tomoe's face, no hint of pride. She sheathed the sword of Okio. She faced the Lord once more, bowed, then returned to her section of the fabric enclosure.

Whispered commentary rose about the periphery of the yard, but quieted when the Lord of Heiji Castle stood. He scanned the crowd he hosted. A servant brought a scroll, and from it Lord Horota read a series of partially subjective and overly elaborated crimes accredited to Tomoe Gozen, none of them quite invented, but only one of them important by most measures: the death of eight thousand samurai, slaughtered by a ghoulish legion under Tomoe's auspices, and she in the auspices of a foreign sorcerer. It was this collusion which caused her to become a disfavored hero in the first place, and the criminality of that association would be decided by the outcome of today's confrontation.

Lord Horota ended the statements of accusation with a formalized phrase: "To these items, are any opposed?"

There followed a moment of silence, in which the charges, or even Tomoe's right to "vindication by combat," could be challenged.

In that moment, Lady Toshima stepped through the squared gateway behind the platform. Though once courtly in her appearance, she was presently without cosmetics, without costly garments. There had been much talk in Kamakura about the famous author, who was once a famous beauty as well, but made herself look so plain. If challenges to her beauty ever tempted her to return to her previous nature, she overcame the temptation. Doubtlessly, there were some who considered the notorious Lady more beautiful than before, but if the majority shared this opinion, they were reluctant to suggest it.

Toshima ascended to Lord Horota's side from the rear. It was unprecedented. The Lord himself was clearly surprised. But his samurai made way for the woman who was kin to the Mikado, master of Tomoe Gozen and, a few maintained, heir to Shojiro Shigeno.

She carried a scroll similar to that read by Lord Horota, but sealed with the Mikado's emblem: a chrysanthemum. She broke the seal, stretched out the scroll, and did not merely reply to the charges against Tomoe Gozen, but leveled charges of her own at Ugo Mohri.

"Once," she began, "Ugo Mohri served the august son of Amaterasu. Today he serves the Shogun. Is it possible the Shogun's champion was fonder of his glamorous wealth than of fealty to the Mikado? That is what is tested here today. But there is another matter, too. We are told by high officials that the Mikado is held from his beloved Naipon to his own benefit, and ours; and we may believe this is true, because the Shogun never lies, and serves the Mikado in all things." She looked up from the scroll a moment, smiling feigned innocence, old innocence. She unrolled the scroll a little further, continued, "Yet it is also true that circumstances are ever changing, and that we have always known the Mortal Flesh of the Eternal Isles must one day return to us. Today we test not only the faith or treason of a disfavored hero against the fealty or criminality of a champion, but also the readiness of the Mikado's return from exile."

Upon hearing these statements, Tomoe Gozen's expression finally changed. She was proud of Toshima's wording—an author's genius. Whatever the outcome, the Shogun would retain face. But any questioning of the proposal or the match at this stage would have an adverse effect on the Shogun and his position. Effectively, Toshima had insured this: If the Mikado's own samurai defeated the unfaithful executioner, the emperor would return to Kyoto, and Tomoe Gozen would be favored. If Ugo Mohri bested Tomoe, she would be ill-mentioned on the Tablets of the Samurai, and the people of Naipon would await the Shogun's next arrangement (for all believed this day *was* arranged by him) to discover the time of the Mikado's homecoming.

Lady Toshima ended formally: "To these items, are any opposed?"

Since opposition would compromise the Shogun, there was none. Toshima had gambled everything on the fact that the Shogun legitimized his regency through the Mikado, and could reveal no lack of faith in Amaterasu's godchild. A Shogun could be disfavored too, though it usually meant revolution; therefore no shogunate official would indicate any weakness of fealty where the Mikado was concerned, despite the hypocrisy of their methods of faith.

As her father's only heir, Toshima would secure Shigeno Valley by her bold maneuver. And she would have gained the base of support on which to rebuild the valley's wealth.

Unless Tomoe fell.

If Toshima's samurai fell to Ugo Mohri's blade, Lady Toshima might well vanish into some dungeon, and none would send queries after her.

Lady Toshima handed her scroll to one of Lord Horota's servants. Then she stepped down the front steps of the platform and crossed the yard, taking not her rightful position among the nobility, but joining Tomoe Gozen's retinue.

Lord Hidemi Horota waited an appropriate space of time, but knew there could be no opposing voice. His own "neutral" role had become neutral after all, and he was visibly shaken by it, since his personal wealth in huge measure required the Shogun's favor.

Horota stepped to the front of the platform, and held a yellow scarf at arm's length over the edge. It was a signal to begin.

Tomoe Gozen and Ugo Mohri stood, walked to the center of the yard, bowed as one to the Lord, to the aristocracy, to the heimin, and lastly to Death, in the west. They sat upon their knees facing one another two paces apart. Their swords were scabbarded. Ugo's sleeves were already tied back; Tomoe withdrew her own *sage-o* and tied the fullness of her kosode's sleeves. She pulled the *sage-o* so that the fine bow moved to the center of her back, beneath her flowing ponytail. While she did this, Ugo tied a cloth around his head to indicate, as had Tomoe, his willingness to strive. His queue of hair was not touched by the cloth.

They bowed to each other, hands flat upon the ground, foreheads resting before their knees. When they looked up again, their eyes bore into one another and did not waver.

The two samurai were positioned for a mutual iai draw. Iaijutsu commanded an unequivocal level of coordinated, instantaneous action or reaction. Swords would be bared and, without any alteration of the sudden, deadly, sweeping motion, the swordfighters would return swords to scabbards. When warriors of equal skill fought in this manner, there was rarely cause for more than a single mutual draw, and simultaneous death was common. Tomoe's skill at iai was an unknown factor in the match. Although Ugo Mohri had proven by his exhibition that he excelled in iaijutsu, Tomoe had shown something more clever and less revealing.

The eyes of the opponents did not veer from one another. At the periphery of their vision, they waited for the yellow cloth to drop from Lord Horota's hand.

The cloth fell.

Tomoe raised one knee, as did Ugo Mohri, and each took one step forward as they stood. Before the cloth had fallen a third of the distance to the ground, two swords had been drawn, two duelists had come to their feet, one clangor had resounded. The two swords carved similar figure-eights in different directions, then returned smoothly to their sheaths. It had been so swift, the most carefully trained eye among the attendant witnesses could not guess whose performance was better.

Tomoe and Ugo faced away from each other. Upon his face: that indefatigable serenity. On Tomoe's face: pain.

Blood oozed down her front and back. Her body shook. She rocked from the stress of the single draw. The effort of the iai draw had ripped the half-healed wound acquired on Keiko's island, and it was that piercing wound which brought the rush of blood to stain her white kosode.

Behind her (she did not turn to see) Ugo Mohri fell to his knees, his visage yet unchanged. Slowly, he leaned backward, and moved his arm enough to reveal the terrible rent in his side. Blood and organs spilled. Tomoe turned, her look of pain meeting his of serenity.

She knelt at his side, and whispered something no one else would hear: "I am sorry to have killed you, and with the sword you gave to me."

Ugo Mohri replied happily, "It is a samurai's death."

Wendy Adrian Shultz

She had thought she would be pleased. She had thought she would
tell him he earned death by his unfaith with the Mikado; that if he had
served better, this duel would never have come to pass, and he would
live. But now she felt no antipathy, and could not believe, despite all,
that the remarkable Ugo Mohri had been as unfaithful as circumstance
made him appear.

It was natural that she would be glad to have won, and she *was* in
many senses pleased, but not for the sake of her present life, and not for
the pride in her prowess. She was glad because it benefited the Mikado
and Toshima. She was glad because she had adhered to the way of the
warrior, and it had vindicated her charges of treachery.

But having slain a hero—in that, she held no pleasure.

Ugo leaned further back until he lay upon his shoulders, his legs
still under him. His blood crimsoned the yard.

The audience had ceased to exist for either of these great warriors,
who gave each other final words. Ugo was already blinded by the loss
of vitality, but his unseeing eyes held no trace of agony. He could barely
speak, so Tomoe Gozen bent close to hear him say, "Now, you are a
favored hero."

"As you will remain," she promised. "I will weave the kodan tales
myself, without Toshima's charges."

"You are kind; but leave nothing from the tale. So that you will
know it all, and tell it completely, I must say to you quickly: this is the
fate of my choosing. In all of Naipon, only you were my match. I knew
it on the day I bid you cast off forbidden style, and train for our final
meeting. I had to know which of us was better. That is why I left the
Mikado. To test myself against your sword, which would never have
been possible while both of us served the same master. I am not sorry I
tried, for in the end, I have still served the Mikado, and myself as well."

She looked at him, surprised, but believing. Ugo's arm relaxed on
the ground, and Tomoe knew in a moment the legended man would be
dead, and the legend would grow larger.

She said to him, "Good-bye, Ugo Mohri, noble samurai."

He closed his eyes. His last words were hardly so loud as one breath,
"Fare you well, Tomoe Gozen."

And he opened his eyes once more, agony rising from the depths of
him. Tomoe could not bear that he should die without the serenity she
had once sought to conquer. Instantly, she was upon her feet. Her sword
was drawn. She thrust the weapon between the ribs of Ugo Mohri, and

into his heart. With that swift plunge, she had preserved his serenity, and Ugo Mohri was as beautiful in death as he had been in life.

Tomoe Gozen was victorious.